At that moment there was a knock at the door and a faint gleam of light crept toward them. A shrill voice speaking in French said, "The electricity will be off for a while."

Apparently it was the owner of the hotel making her rounds distributing candles. Daigo's companion raised her rich, melancholy voice in French and said, "It's all right. We won't need a candle."

Daigo waited in silence. He felt his companion wanted to preserve the intimate darkness in order to tell him something, and he decided to give the woman an opening. "You were telling me that everything is fine."

The woman paused, took a deep breath, and said, "The simple truth is that there is a certain woman I would like to kill. . . ."

Also by Shizuko Natsuki
*Published by Ballantine Books:*


MURDER AT MT. FUJI

# THE
# THIRD LADY

## Shizuko Natsuki

BALLANTINE BOOKS • NEW YORK

Library of Congress Catalog Card Number: 86-91663

ISBN 0-345-33765-4

Manufactured in the United States of America

First American Edition: June 1987

# 1

# Autumn Tempest

THE CATHEDRAL BELLS TOLLED MATINS, AND THE MOURN-
ful sound reverberated across the rolling, wooded hills. The
sound reechoed, making it difficult to tell when one toll
ended and the next began. When at last the sound of the
bells died away completely, Daigo noticed that the wind
had begun to rise. The French doors with their thick pillars
and beams glowed with a deep brown luster and began to
creak as the wind began to gust. Daigo watched as the
heavy Gobelin curtains that framed the. windows began to
sway nervously.

Daigo had a glass of Calvados on a low round table, but
even as he sat relaxing, he could sense that the wind was
building in strength, and again he heard the force of it rattle
the windows. From those windows in this Louis XIV salon
he could look out on the hotel's courtyard to the holly
hedge and beyond to the cobbled streets of the village, the

1

fields of wheat and grapes, and he could even see a part of the forest of Fontainebleau off to one side.

It was nearly dark outside, but he could still make out the outlines of the distant forest and the pointed roofs of the village houses.

The forest of Fontainebleau, southeast of Paris, is widely known for the beauty of its autumn leaves. Now, however, most of the trees were barren of leaves, and even the evergreens looked cold and bleak. The chestnuts and lindens were a faded brown. The firs, the yew trees, and the cedars clustered together in dark bands. The fields spreading out over the broad, gentle slope were only dry stubble. The melancholy scene was typical of winter in Western Europe.

This old hotel had three or four chestnut trees in the courtyard, and although it seemed as though they still had most of their leaves, the trees would surely be bare by morning if the wind continued to blow tonight. Even now, each time the windows rattled, countless leaves danced in the sky. In the deserted front courtyard Daigo could see the white cast-iron tables and chairs on the brick veranda. In summer it was used for outdoor dining, but there were no guests there now. Even as he watched, the swirling leaves scattered across the bricks.

"If you had come here two or three days earlier, you could have enjoyed the lovely autumn scenery of the Ile de France, but since the day before yesterday the weather has been very strange. It has suddenly gotten quite chilly, and every night the wind has come blowing down out of the northeast. We are just witnessing the changing of the seasons." This remark had been made to Daigo by a young instructor from the University of Paris at a recent colloquium. Daigo recalled that remark as he watched the approaching storm. "It's always this way," the young scholar had continued. "Suddenly, in the course of one or two days, autumn is gone and winter is upon us." He had gone on to say that the weather this year had been particularly unpredictable and changed often.

In fact, it was only the middle of October, but the cold in Paris was like mid-winter in Japan, and Daigo had been reluctant even to go outside, but today he had felt the perspiration forming under his sweater as the day became almost sultry. Perhaps it was the weather, but in the afternoon he had suddenly decided to come here to Barbizon, and had left Paris. Millet, Corot, Courbet, and others who were Naturalist painters of the nineteenth century were called the Barbizon School. They had all moved here to this small village of Barbizon on the edge of the magnificent Fontainebleau forest. Daigo had been here briefly some ten years ago, just about the time when he accepted his post at the university, and ever since then the memory of this landscape had stayed with him and haunted him like a melancholy shadow. It was like a portrait, *Memories of the Mortfontaine*, that had been painted on the canvas of his heart.

He had wanted to stay at the same old place where he had stayed before. It was a farmhouse just like all the other farmhouses around, and he had had his lunches served on the terrace. But this time he could not find that hostel, so he had decided to stay at this old country manor that had been made into a hotel.

Someone had mentioned the name of this place, which was called the Château Chantal. It had thick white walls, and heavy wooden beams could be seen imbedded in them. Adjoining the hotel was an ivy-covered building used as a restaurant, although one got the impression that the hotel was attached to the restaurant. The ancient hotel and its surroundings created a very gothic impression, and it was this that had attracted Daigo to it in the first place: the dark, gloomy atmosphere, the stone and brick construction, the round slate roofs, and the wine cellars. Surely deep in those

wine cellars slept some good Burgundy. Everything about
the hotel's old-fashioned atmosphere made it seem just right
for the late autumn landscape. It was like something out of
a painting by Rousseau or Courbet. It especially reminded
him of Courbet's painting of Sillon Castle, and Daigo wondered if he might be able to see the spires of the castle
from this salon. But when he craned his neck around to
look, he found that it had grown dark outside, and the thick
gray darkness obscured his view.

As he gazed at the color of the darkness outside, he
realized that it was not so much that it had gotten dark, but
rather that the storm clouds had come over. Usually by this
hour one would see the stars glittering in the sky, but tonight none were visible. The thick gray-black clouds were
swirling and turbulent. At that moment several large drops
of rain began to hit the window. The wind began to howl.
It seemed they were in for a regular autumn storm.

Daigo had planned to go out for a walk after dinner, but
now abandoned that plan in the face of this storm. He
brought the glass of Calvados to his lips as he reflected on
this.

Well, I guess there's nothing I can do about it, he
thought. Besides, it seems to have gotten rather chilly.

He stretched out his legs and leaned back in the chair.
He greatly enjoyed the strong, aromatic liquor and felt its
warmth spread to every part of his body.

Daigo's conference had ended the previous day, and he
had nothing to do until his plane left late the following day
to take him back to Japan, so he had been somewhat at
loose ends. By shutting himself away in this melancholy
old hotel, it seemed as though he could slow down the flow
of time and thereby put off the imminence of his return
home. Once he returned to Japan he would be thrust back
into his ordinary, everyday routines, and suddenly he would
be aware once again of the various small wounds and dis-

appointments of professional life, and this thought filled him with melancholy. In his present surroundings, it seemed he was able to forget those mundane things—at least for the time being.

In fact, however, there were important issues which he would have to think over and decide while he was here. Perhaps it was the wine that made his thoughts wander a bit.

Gradually the rain and the wind became even more violent, and the windows rattled continuously. By now it was pitch dark outside. The sound of the storm actually seemed slightly exaggerated, like the sound effects of a storm on the old-fashioned radio dramas. Such was the storm that howled with fury outside the hotel.

It suddenly felt chilly in the salon. Daigo slightly raised himself from the chair and looked around with eyes that were becoming blurred with drink. The room was illuminated by light that was tastefully refracted through the glittering crystals of a chandelier, and everything seemed peaceful and snug here in contrast to what was happening outside. The walls were covered with velvet wallpaper, and the mantelpiece had a mosaic design. On the mantel was a medieval helmet of iron, there was an antique French doll with white hair and a steady gaze, there were candlesticks and other decorative objects; they all seemed old and dusty.

The salon was not really very large, and although it was filled with a musty odor, Daigo seemed to notice also a faint fragrance of an expensive perfume.

Probably this building had first been built with the intention of using it for a hunting lodge. Daigo imagined what it must have been like then, with a fire burning in the fireplace and the evening darkness filled with the murmuring voices of women bedecked with layers of necklaces. The fragrance of the perfume was more definite now, and it was that that had brought to mind the image of necklaced women.

This salon was located on the second floor and marked the boundary between the hotel and the adjoining restaurant. It was freely accessible to all guests of either the restaurant or the hotel. When the restaurant was crowded, it was used as a place for patrons to wait until their table was ready. Since it was located just off the lobby, it was a place where patrons often came to relax after their meal. But tonight, since it was not a weekend and since the weather was bad, there did not appear to be any other guests staying at the hotel. Apparently the few who had dined at the restaurant had promptly gotten into their cars and returned home.

There was a bright flash of light outside followed by a crash of thunder. At that moment Daigo distinctly heard the sound of someone in the room sucking in his breath in surprise. The thunder had startled Daigo, of course, but what really startled him was the realization that he was not alone in the salon. Ever since he had come into the room some time ago, he had believed that he was its sole occupant. When he looked about, however, he saw an espresso coffee cup on a table near the window. Up till now he had supposed it was just another of the knickknacks that cluttered the room.

Between Daigo and the table stood a large wingback armchair. On the floor just in front of the chair he could see just the tips of a pair of gray high-heeled shoes. Apparently there was a woman sitting in the chair, and she seemed to be alone, because there was only one coffee cup on the table and he had not heard the sound of voices conversing.

Stretching his neck out to peer in that direction, he caught a glimpse of the legs that wore the shoes—legs clothed in dark stockings. They were beautiful, long, slim legs with no hint of flabbiness about them. These legs were beautiful in a way that was quite different from the legs of the typical Japanese woman. Nevertheless, Daigo suddenly had a feeling that the woman was Japanese. This feeling came partly because he could also see a glimpse of her arm on the armrest of the chair. The sleeve of her dark blouse was decorated with a red see-through pattern that seemed appropriate to the Japanese sense of taste.

It was not surprising, of course, to run into other Japanese in Paris and its surrounding area, but Daigo, inspired by a mild curiosity, shifted in his chair. Now he could see her long, straight, coffee-brown hair and a bit of her pale forehead.

At that moment there was another flash of lightning and a peal of thunder that seemed to be very close. This time the woman's moan was clear. Daigo resumed his seat and smiled to himself. When he had first become aware of the woman's presence he had felt surprised and chagrined, but now he sensed that she was a quiet, friendly woman who was afraid of the thunder. At this point he noticed a paperback book with a Japanese title on the cover lying on the coffee table in front of her.

His first thought was to say a few reassuring words to her in Japanese, but then he thought better of it and asked tentatively, *"Vous êtes Japonais?"*

After a moment's hesitation the woman's husky voice replied, "Oh, are you Japanese too?"

"Yes, I am," said Daigo with a forced laugh. His French was far from fluent, and apparently it had given away the fact that he too was Japanese. "Please forgive me," he continued. "I was completely unaware that you were present when I came in. Have you been here the whole time?" Even as Daigo asked the question he still could not see the woman's face. Suddenly, he had an overpowering urge to see this woman face to face. He had intended only to say a word or two of polite conversation, but somehow the woman's presence had rattled him, and he felt mildly confused.

The woman did not reply to Daigo's question, but he sensed an affirmative response.

"Have you eaten dinner already?" he asked.

"Yes."

"Are you traveling alone?"

The woman did not reply, but she did not deny it.

"This restaurant is well known for its escargots and for its chicken. Their coq au vin is especially good." Chicken cooked in red wine is one of the classics of Burgundy cuisine, and the Restaurant Chantal was proud of its menu.

"I enjoyed their ham," replied the woman.

"Ah yes, that's a specialty here, with a rime of green mold on the outside. And then there are the cheeses."

Daigo recalled his own dinner earlier in the evening. When the salad course was completed, they had brought a large selection of cheeses. There had been many soft cheeses, such as Camembert, but there were also some hard cheeses, such as a goat cheese covered with black mold, and an orange cheese called *rivalo*. Altogether there had been more than ten cheeses, and although Daigo was already full, they looked very inviting, and he had sampled several of them. By the time he had finished with the cheeses, he was too full to eat more than a bite of the apple tart that was served for dessert.

"They say that you can tell the quality and style of a French restaurant by the cheeses it serves." The woman's voice took on a gentle tone as she spoke.

With food as the topic of conversation, the atmosphere seemed to become more intimate. It was clear that the woman was alone and there was no one else in the salon except themselves. Daigo felt as though he were expelling a long and painfully held breath of air. He leaned forward.

"I must say, you really startled me. I had no idea you were here, you were so quiet."

"I hadn't realized that you had come in. I was busy reading my book. You seemed to be making an effort to keep very still." There seemed to be a teasing note in her husky voice as she spoke this time.

"I wasn't especially trying to keep quiet. I was just engrossed in my thoughts," he said somewhat self-rightously. The woman made no reply, so he continued. "I was trying to remember where I had heard the name Château Chantal. Can you help me out on that?"

"You probably read about it in Maupassant."

"Oh yes, that's it. Mademoiselle Pearl."

"Pearl was an orphan who was taken in and raised by the Chantal family as one of their own."

"Yes, that's right. I remember it now."

Pearl had been abandoned on the Chantal family's doorstep on a snowy night. Although she was in love with the Chantal's third son, she kept her true feelings to herself and allowed them to arrange a different marriage for him. Then one night, years and years later, her true feelings were revealed by a mutual friend. She had declared, "I feel drunk, giddy, suddenly I know what it is to be holy." Daigo had often remembered these lines during his drinking bouts as a student.

He recalled that he had earlier been thinking about pearl necklaces and wondered if it was an unconscious association between this place and Maupassant's story. Taking another sip of his Calvados, he felt exhilarated by the woman's presence. He felt a certain close intimacy with this woman even though he had not yet even seen her face.

"Are you also here at Barbizon alone for sightseeing?"

"Yes. But when I arrived in Paris yesterday, I had a sore throat and felt I was coming down with a cold, so I have just been staying at the hotel and have not been around to see anything.''

''I take it then that your hotel is in Paris?''

''Yes.''

''It looks like you may have some difficulty in getting back to Paris tonight.''

''I have a car here. But with all this rain I suppose I will wait a while before I try to go back.'' The woman did not seem displeased to carry on the conversation with Daigo, and the mood was quite relaxed.

Picking up his glass, Daigo stood up. It was only natural at this point that he would be interested in seeing what the woman looked like, and he was about to move closer to her. Yet just as he stepped forward there was another, deafening crash of thunder. At the same instant, all the lights in the room went out and they were plunged into darkness. The echoes of the thunder reverberated through the pitch-dark salon.

Daigo paused for a moment in confusion, then moved forward across the carpet. Apparently the whole neighborhood had experienced a power failure, because no trace of light came from the windows. It was so dark Daigo could not even make out the shapes of the furniture in the room.

Groping his way forward, Daigo managed to seat himself in a chair diagonally in front of the woman. He quickly sensed, however, that he was much closer to her than he had imagined. Before he had been only faintly aware of the woman's perfume, but now it seemed nearly overpowering. Daigo sensed the woman's warm breath on his cheek. She seemed to exude an aura of bittersweet melancholy that struck him as being strangely elegant. Finding a table on which to place his glass, he reached out to gently caress the woman's arm. He felt her slim arm tremble beneath the thin fabric of her blouse.

''I was startled,'' he mumbled, but there was a new

urgency in his voice. "Maybe it was having the lights go out suddenly. No, I sensed it even earlier while I was talking to you—a woman I have never seen or met before—it seemed somehow that there was something uncanny about our meeting. It seemed that something strange was about to happen."

"In one of his books, Maupassant wrote that the things he liked best to describe were water, accidental meetings, and pessimism."

"Pessimism?" Somehow the word seemed to trigger an uneasy feeling in the bottom of Daigo's heart. He had always had three goals in life. One was to maintain his name, his integrity, and his family's tranquility. At the same time he felt a desire to accomplish something heroic. And finally, he sometimes felt a vague, poetic urge that led him to seek some vision of something that was pure and infinite. All these urges were a part of him. Up to this time, however, he had always managed to maintain some equilibrium or balance among these three urges. And yet at the same time it seemed that whichever of these dominated his spirit at any given time, there was always present a deeper urge toward pessimism that was fundamental to his nature.

"I wonder why optimists always consider pessimism a negative virtue?"

"You're right. I suppose it is because a pessimist generally has the feeling that one day everything around him will explode, and he feels surrounded by threats of disaster. Somehow, suddenly, one day he loses the ability to believe that things will ever get better. Once he has that feeling, he is like a mouse that is always afraid he will be pounced on by the cat; he can never relax."

"Ah . . ." Daigo felt that the woman had perfectly expressed his own feelings on the matter. Perhaps he himself had already fallen into that pessimistic condition. And yet he felt that especially when he was in one of his gloomy moods. He would never dream of taking another person into his confidence and sharing his feelings with that other person. He had not one close friend with whom he could share his thoughts and feelings in times of adversity and ill luck. There was his wife, of course, and she was a good woman, but he did not consider her a friend. And yet now, for some reason, despite his efforts to restrain them, his innermost thoughts and feelings seemed to come welling up, and he felt a need to tell someone how he felt. Perhaps it just came from being here in complete darkness with a woman he did not know, a woman whose fragrance seemed to have a pleasant narcotic effect on him.

Somehow in the presence of this woman he seemed to be someone other than himself. Or perhaps just the opposite was true—perhaps now for the first time his real and true self could find expression.

Apparently the power would not be restored for some time. On the contrary, outdoors as well as in the room everything was in total darkness, and the only sounds were the roaring of the wind and the thundering of the rain. Occasionally they would hear a muffled sound from downstairs, but there did not seem to be any disturbance or unease on the part of other patrons of the restaurant. The tranquility of rural Europe seemed quite different from what one would expect in Japan.

"I believe that if a person is able to identify the gloom and ill feeling he feels coiled in the very depths of his heart and is able to express that to someone, to get it off his chest, then the pessimist may become an optimist." It was with a sense of near intoxication that Daigo murmured this insight. But his mood now was quite different from anything he had ever experienced when he was intoxicated by alcohol.

"I suppose there is some degree of relief in that." The melancholy resonance of the woman's voice caused Daigo to catch his breath. He suddenly realized that this woman, too, had something on her mind that she felt she could confide to no one.

What sort of conversation is this he, wondered, smiling at his own lack of restraint. How could he be talking like this to a young, obviously well-educated, and probably beautiful woman who was staying in Paris on her own through the gloomy weeks of late autumn.

"Excuse me, but I wonder, where are you from in Japan?" he asked.

"I live in Tokyo."

"Alone?"

"Yes."

"Have you been traveling for long?"

"I have been away just a week today."

"When do you plan to return to Japan?"

"Well, I really haven't decided yet." The woman's quiet voice had a musical, almost negligent quality about it.

"You seem uncertain about your plans. Is there any difficulty?"

"No, everything is fine." The tone of the woman's voice as she said this made Daigo think she was teasing him, or perhaps even that she was ridiculing herself.

"Everything is fine, then?"

"Yes. If you would like to hear how fine everything is, perhaps I will tell you. It may amuse you."

"I'm not sure I understand what you mean."

At that moment there was a knock at the door and a faint gleam of light crept toward them. A shrill voice speaking in French said, "The electricity will be off for a while."

Daigo's French was not good enough to know precisely what she said, but he understood her meaning. Apparently it was the owner of the hotel making her rounds distributing candles. Daigo's companion raised her rich, melancholy voice in French and said, "It's all right. We won't need a candle."

The woman's remark surprised Daigo, but then he realized that he too did not wish to have the candle. This darkness that enfolded him and his unseen companion seemed to create a certain bond of intimacy and allowed them to speak freely to one another.

Before the dim circle of light approached any closer, Daigo waved the owner away. Without a word she nodded two or three times and departed, closing the door behind her.

Daigo waited in silence. He felt his companion wanted to preserve the intimate darkness in order to tell him something.

The silence continued for a time, but Daigo was sure she wanted to express something that was buried deep in her heart, and he decided to give the woman an opening. "You were telling me that everything is fine."

The woman paused, took a deep breath, and said, "The simple truth is that there is a certain woman I would like to kill." The woman's voice was strangled with tension, but she seemed well in control of herself. "For the past two years this one thought has constantly dominated my every waking moment. Perhaps I have not done it because I lacked the courage or the opportunity, but I will definitely kill that woman in the near future."

This statement left Daigo with a feeling of mystery and a burning sense of curiosity. "Why do you feel you have to kill this woman?"

"I cannot allow her to live. She is arrogant, and her heart is as cold as ice. It was because of that arrogance and pride that two years ago she killed a person. Ever since that day I have told myself that I would have to kill her."

The woman's voice was a barely audible whisper, but

Daigo could feel the intensity of her sadness and anger transmitted to his own heart.

"Was this person she killed someone you loved?"

In place of an answer, all he heard was the woman's deep sigh.

"But why haven't the police done something about this woman?"

"The police carried out a routine investigation, but they could not find any definite proof that it was murder. Yet I know it was."

"In that case, why didn't you go to the police and tell them what you know?"

"Well, you see, I had no evidence, and they would not simply accept my statement that I knew who did it. Maybe the woman put some sort of curse on me, but I swear to you that my heart will know no peace until she is dead."

This time it was Daigo's turn to take a deep breath. "It is just the same with me," he murmured as he sucked in a sigh.

"What?" asked the woman with a note of suspicion in her voice.

Could it be that the woman had just been making up the story she had told? This thought flashed through Daigo's mind, but he decided that even if he was being teased, he really did feel like telling the woman his own melancholy secret.

"It is just the same with me. I realized that as I was listening to your story. There is a certain man I want to kill; I have dreamed about it over and over. I have prayed from the bottom of my heart that he be killed. I feel that I can do nothing with my life unless that man is killed."

"Who is this man?" The woman's question was far more urgent than when she had been telling her own story.

"He is a university professor. He is in the same laboratory that I work in at the university."

"In other words, you are a university professor?"

"That's right, and the man I am referring to is my boss."

"Is he an evil person?"

"As far as I am concerned, he is an evangelist of evil. He's an inhuman monster. It is because of monsters like him that people say that academics are divorced from reality." Without his realizing it, Daigo's jaw was clenched and trembling.

"What did he do?" asked the woman bluntly.

"In simplest terms, he was involved in a business conspiracy. In the business enterprise he made a serious blunder and tried to cover it up. His company made a certain kind of confection that was popular for a time with children, and later nearly twenty of those children came down with cancer. For the most part the parents of the children were poor, and in their grief over what happened, they sought some compensation. But prior to that there is no telling how many children and their families suffered agony due to this. When all of this came out, the product was examined, of course, but the ones who conducted the examination were working hand in hand with the company, and they issued a false report so that the company could evade its responsibility and not have to pay any compensation."

"I see. But why didn't the victims have the analysis done by a different university research team?"

"Our university is the national university in that part of the country and is by far the most prestigious. All of the professors of hygiene at the other universities in the area are intimidated by our research teams. Besides, the victims do not have the resources to have the lab reports prepared in Tokyo or Osaka. It requires a certain amount of influence and connections to get this sort of study done. The victims might have accomplished something if they had been able to stir up the media over this issue, but the man who is responsible for the tragedy has strong political connections, and he was able to have the story squelched. Since the number of victims is not all that large, it has been very hard to get the truth out."

The woman said nothing.

"Of course I had any number of angry confrontations with the professor over this. I pointed out to him that some of the ingredients in those confections contained powerful carcinogenic substances. No sooner had I done that than he began to take steps to have me dismissed from the university. Even now he is trying to get me transferred to a position in a rural university in Alaska. He pointed out that since they are short of qualified researchers there, I would be able to move into a prominent position, but his offer only amounts to coercion by another name. Even though they say that we are at the university in tenured positions, the fact is that the future careers of junior faculty are controlled by the manipulations of the senior fellows, but a lot of people don't know that."

The storm appeared to be abating a bit. It seemed as though the lightning was satisfied at having knocked out the electrical power for the time being and was now ready to move on. Even the pounding of the rain on the windows seemed fainter now. The shrieking of the wind also became more distant in a way that seemed to emphasize the stillness of the room.

"It's horrible to think of all those little children with cancer," murmured the woman through her quiet weeping. "Five years ago I was giving French lessons to a lovely little girl who was stricken with cancer. Even now I can hear the sound of her voice as she cried out in pain." By now the woman was wracked with weeping.

"Then you understand how I feel when I say I want to kill that man. There is no crime more heinous than causing innocent little children to suffer. There is a passage in *The*

*Brothers Karamazov* where Ivan and Alyosha are discussing the problem of God where even the pious priest Alyosha declares that people who kill innocent children should be shot. Yes, the fact is that certain types of people ought not to be allowed to live in the world."

"I agree with you, but I expect that it takes a lot of courage to declare that someone ought not be allowed to live."

Courage. This was perhaps the word Daigo dreaded most of all.

"Let's try to forget about all this." As though in a trance Daigo reached toward the woman's chair and grasped her warm arm. "For now, at least, let's try to forget it."

Daigo felt the pressure of the woman's other hand as she pressed it against his. He bent his head forward and breathed deeply of the woman's fragrance. "Shall we . . ." he murmured quickly, and with both arms he reached out to embrace her.

As he grasped her and pulled her toward him, she twisted around and sat on his lap facing away from him.

He rubbed the side of his face along her shoulder, and as she twisted her neck around, their lips came together. The woman's mouth was delicate and elegant. With their lips still locked in a kiss, Daigo unzipped the back of her blouse and slipped his hand around to caress her breasts. Their taut, young firmness responded to his touch.

The blouse and brassiere were all in one and slid easily from her shoulders. Daigo noticed that the woman's earlobes were pierced, apparently for earrings. With his lips he explored the smooth, soft skin of her neck. Already he was becoming aroused. He believed that the woman felt the same way. This intoxicated frenzy was almost spiritual, and at that moment some lines from Maupassant came to him.

"Perhaps this short embrace may infuse in their veins a

little of this thrill, and will give the rapid and divine sensation of this intoxication.''

By the time their breathing had subsided, the sounds of the storm had also become more subdued, and the salon was filled with a mood of gentle melancholy. Daigo suddenly had a vision of himself and the woman as a single still statue.

Presently, still on his knee, the woman gracefully readjusted her clothing and at last returned to the other chair. After a moment of further silence, the woman spoke, and now a new intensity made her voice quiver. ''Tell me about this evil professor who has caused you such anguish. Who is he? Where is he from?''

''He is a professor of health at the J university in Fukuoka. His name is Akishige Yoshimi.'' Daigo spoke straightforwardly, for he felt that to be any other way is to promote self-deception. He continued and asked the woman, ''What is the name of the woman you hate so much you would like to kill her?''

''Her name is Midori Nagahara, and she is the eldest daughter of the owner of the Emerald View Hotel at Lake Hakone.''

''How about yourself? Why don't you tell me something about yourself?''

''Me? I'm Fumiko Samejima.'' The woman drew Daigo's hand to her and on his palm with her finger she traced the Chinese characters for Fumiko to indicate which of the possible Chinese characters she used. ''I live by myself in Tokyo, and for the most part I stay home and do translation work there, but on Tuesday and Friday afternoons I go to my office from noon to about six.''

There were many other things Daigo wanted to ask about this woman, but he felt that first he should tell her something about himself. ''I'm Kohei Daigo. I live in Fukuoka and teach at the college I mentioned earlier.'' He was about to go on, but the woman suddenly put a finger to his lips to silence him.

"That's enough, please don't tell me any more. These things are not important. I think I already understand you better than anyone else. The most important thing is that you have already shown me how you feel in the very depths of your heart. And I have shared my own deepest feelings with you. Compared to that, all these other details of our lives are insignificant. Why don't we leave each other now while we still have not seen each other's face."

The woman was speaking passionately now, like a mother admonishing her son.

"But what happens in the future? When will I ever—".

"Our meeting tonight has been a rare and fateful opportunity. I have a feeling that we may never have the good fortune to have another such meeting on a night like this, in a salon like this. It would be wonderful, of course, if we met again someday in Paris, perhaps, or Tokyo. But even if that happens, I doubt that any subsequent meeting would have the magic of this encounter here tonight."

Daigo was so surprised at these words that he did not know what to reply. The woman continued, "And yet, I already feel as though you are my other self, and I certainly hope you feel the same way about me."

"Of course I—"

"Thank you. The sharing we have had here this evening is not something we have to talk about, but it will be a wonderful thing if it helps us face our individual futures."

Before Daigo could think of anything to say in response, the woman stood up, brushed her finger gently against his cheek, and quietly left the room, her footsteps making little sound on the carpeted floor. Daigo was somewhat stunned by this sudden departure and stood rooted to the spot, unable to think of any words to call the woman back.

As the door closed behind her, Daigo suddenly felt emotionally drained and slumped back in his chair. Half his mind urged him to pursue the woman and tell her he wanted to get a look at her face, but this urge was not enough to get him to his feet. What held him back was the fact that the woman had not seen his face either. Suddenly he became aware of a faint trace of the woman's perfume in the chill air of the room.

He mulled over what the woman had said about their relationship being one of purity and courage. He wondered what she had meant by courage. Listening to the distant sound of the wind, Daigo lost himself in a reverie.

# 2

# Time for Decision

"You'll be home for dinner as usual, won't you?" asked Daigo's wife as she helped him into his coat. Her query was not so much a question as a ritual they went through every morning as he left for work. Teaching as he did at a public university, and since he had no outside interests or distractions, he had a very routine life. With the exception of an occasional research trip, his daily routine consisted of going to the university in the morning and returning home in the early evening.

"Yes, I'll probably be back around six," he replied.

"Shall we have oyster stew for dinner tonight? The oysters are quite good at this time of year." Shihoko knew what her husband liked and looked at him now, seeking his approval. When she smiled, crow's feet appeared at the corners of her eyes, and he noticed that the freckled skin of her round face was slightly dry and rough.

At thirty-six she was beginning to show her age, but as far as Daigo was concerned, he felt Shihoko had not changed at all since he had married her ten years ago. She was the daughter of a professor at a certain public university from which Daigo had gotten his degree. After graduating, Daigo had worked as his professor's research assistant and eventually was promoted to the rank of assistant professor. When he reached the age of thirty-two a position in health sciences had become vacant here at J university in Fukuoka, and he had received the appointment. Shihoko's father was a good friend of the man who had been the president of J university at the time, and he had strongly recommended Daigo. He was also helped by the fact that his articles on the regional incidence of cancer were recognized, and through this combination of events, he had come to hold the position of assistant professor at J university. It was in this context that he had mentioned the possibility of marrying the twenty-six-year-old daughter of his professor, and after a simple matchmaking ritual the marriage was agreed upon.

Daigo's married life with Shihoko had been ordinary and uneventful. Shihoko was not particularly concerned about having many possessions, and she was a cheerful, family-oriented woman. She was a good helpmate for Daigo. They had two daughters, one in the third grade, one in the first grade. Both girls appeared simple and ordinary, and seemed to take after their mother.

Daigo always reminded himself that he was fortunate to have such a good wife. She was a good woman who did not desire to have too much, and who ignored Daigo's worst faults and bad habits. Shihoko's stability was a blessing for Daigo in his present condition. She gave no sign that she noticed any change in her husband since he had returned from his conference in Paris.

Daigo said he would enjoy having oyster stew for din-

ner, and left the house. In the tiny garden between the
house and the front gate grew a profusion of crysanthe-
mums and late-blooming roses. Daigo's home was among
a group of tract houses in the northeastern section of Fukuoka near the sea. Three years ago he had managed to get
a mortgage loan and they were able to move here from
their government-run apartment. This housing project was
built in terraced levels and surrounded by fields and golf
courses. Although this was really a suburb away from the
center of the city , it was conveniently close to J university.

It was after nine o'clock, and rush-hour traffic was slack-
ening as Daigo drove his Toyota along the national highway. It was a heavy, overcast morning, quite unusual for
early November. According to the television report, this
was the first cold spell of the year. In fact, it was so cold
that he had had difficulty getting the car started.

As he drove, Daigo's thoughts returned as usual to the
same subject: that night, that stormy night at Barbizon, and
Fumiko Samejima, who had simply gotten in her car and
returned to her hotel in Paris. About fifteen minutes after
Fumiko left, Daigo had gone to the restaurant lobby and
looked out the front door, but by then the parking lot was
a rain-washed pool and there were no cars in sight. After
another fifteen minutes or so the electricity was restored,
and once again there was light.

It occurred to Daigo that Fumiko might not have been
telling the truth about staying at a hotel in Paris. Perhaps
she was staying right here in the Château Chantal. But
when he inquired at the front desk, he was assured that
there was no guest by that name registered. In fact, he was
informed that there were no Japanese women staying at the
hotel that night. In Paris foreigners staying at hotels are
required to show their passports, so it is not possible to use
a false name.

Early the following morning Daigo had left the hotel and

walked around Barbizon. Although the storm was past, the streets were littered with fallen leaves. The morning mist was rising, and the whole village seemed deserted. He wondered if Fumiko might suddenly appear somehow, somewhere along one of these deserted streets. When he stopped to think about it, though, he realized that he had no idea what she looked like since he had never seen her. And yet he felt certain that if he met her again, he would know immediately and instinctively that it was Fumiko.

"Why don't we leave each other now while we still have not seen each other's face" is what Fumiko had said. Daigo had agreed that she was probably right. Nevertheless, in one corner of his heart he felt he desperately wanted to have a good look at her face and at her figure. He definitely wanted to see her again.

In the end he did not see any sign of her that day. Perhaps he could find her, he thought, if he checked all the hotels in Paris. But the fact was that he was scheduled to take a return flight to Japan that night, so he had had no time to make a search. As far as that goes, he could not even be sure that the name Fumiko Samejima, which she had given him, was her real name. In the weeks that followed, his uncertainty grew.

After returning to Japan Daigo made no effort to dismiss the incident from his mind. He recalled it from time to time as some sort of poetic episode of the sort that might appear in the books of poetry he liked to read occasionally. Yes, the memory of Fumiko and the encounter with her frequently came to mind. It seemed that each time he remembered the event, it came to him more clearly and forcefully. Still, he was not able to reach any sort of clear decision about what to do in the matter.

Today, as he drove through the light traffic, he decided that when all was said and done, there was nothing he could do about Fumiko. Concerning the other business, however, if he just kept his mouth closed and refused to quarrel with his colleague, Professor Yoshimi—if he saw everything that was going on and pretended not to—he would probably never find a way out of his current dilemma. If he could just hold out for another seven or eight years, he would reach retirement age, and there was a good chance that he would be able to retire and find a good position as a consultant. Indeed, many of Daigo's colleagues had been alienated by the arrogant and high-handed ways of Yoshimi, and he had expected he would have their support in the struggle against the negligent food company. But it appeared that Yoshimi had stalemated the efforts to bring his misdeeds to light.

For the time being I will just have to be patient and careful, he thought. He called to mind the smiling faces of his wife and daughter as they would look when he faced them this evening over the oyster stew. The happy domestic scene was one that gave him a feeling of warmth and repose.

By now he was approaching the university, and realizing that he still had half an hour before his first class, he suddenly decided to stop by the university hospital. It was here in the children's ward of the hospital that last summer in quick succession three children had been admitted with liver cancer. They had all come from the region of S city in Fukuoka Prefecture and were the children of office workers and farm families. During the six-month period from March until August of this year, nearly twenty children from the region around S city were either diagnosed as having liver cancer or some other unknown ailment. In the cases of at least eight of these children, the diagnosis of cancer was definite. Since September the number of diagnoses had decreased, but they still continued to come in.

The children affected were between the ages of four and ten, and for the most part had been admitted to the university hospital or the public hospital in S city. So far, four of the young patients had died. Some of the children had been operated on and were now convalescing, but since they were suffering from the side effects of the cancer treatment as well as from liver damage, they would be in the hospital for a long time to come. Three of the most serious cases were being treated at J university medical center, and Daigo had been visiting them occasionally since August. At that time, the attending physicians already suspected that the source of the outbreak was a kind of cookie called Popico. Virtually all of the children affected had eaten the cookie, which was made with a mixture of peanuts and potato starch. The company that made the cookies had its main office in Fukuoka, but their manufacturing plant was in S city. To the extent that it was possible, they instituted a recall of the cookies, and the outbreak of illness was curbed.

The health center and the prefectural hygiene division had requested that the health department at J university analyze the content of the cookies in their laboratories. Professor Yoshimi had been responsible for producing the lab results, and in the beginning he had gone to visit the children patients along with Daigo. Since that time Yoshimi had not once bothered to look in on the children. But on his way to and from his own laboratory, Daigo found that his feet naturally took him from time to time to see the children.

It was not yet ten o'clock. In the corridor of the children's wing, carts distributing breakfast trays still cluttered the hall and nurses moved busily about among them. Somehow Daigo sensed an air of melancholy in the wing today that seemed to hang like a pall over the hospital's normal morning routine. This feeling of melancholy seemed to intensify when Daigo reached the rooms containing the cancer victims. Usually family members of the victims would be found standing in the corridor talking, but today there was not a soul to be seen. Presently a nurse appeared, head down and shoulders slumped.

"What's wrong?" asked Daigo, tapping the nurse's shoulder.

"Oh, Professor Daigo, late last night Tatsuo died." The young nurse could only say that much before she hurried away struggling to control her emotions.

Daigo felt a deep, dull pain in his chest.

Tatsuo was the son of a man in S city who owned a rental car company. He was in the second grade. The boy had loved science and was happiest when he had his books with their illustrations of local flora. Whenever Daigo dropped in for a visit, the boy would ask him to quiz him on the names of the new plants and trees he had memorized. Recently, however, he had suddenly stopped talking about plants and instead would gaze at night out the window near his bed and ask about the stars. Apparently Tatsuo's brave young soul was preparing itself to leave the earth and return to heaven.

The first thing Daigo noticed when he entered the room was Tatsuo's empty bed. Someone had placed a yellow and white tulip on the freshly starched sheets. In the adjacent bed little Yumiko was throwing her head wildly from side to side and crying incoherently. Through her tears she seemed to be saying, "It hurts, it hurts." Daigo could see that the six-year-old's face was already much more gaunt than when he had seen her a couple of weeks ago. It seemed to be no larger than the size of a clenched fist. It was clear to any observer that the dark shadows of death were already stealing over her pale flesh. The child's mother was busily massaging her stomach to help relieve her pain.

Yumiko's father worked for a bus company in S city,

and her mother would take the child with her when she went to her part-time job in one of the neighborhood stores. In this way the family of four, including her elder brother, had been able to make ends meet.

Since the onset of Yumiko's illness, her mother had stopped working in order to be with the child. In the case of children, parents are expected to pay 30 percent of the hospital expenses. In addition to that there were special medicines and treatments for cancer patients that are not covered by insurance, so the parents were faced with a monthly medical bill of 250,000 to 300,000 yen at a time when they could not afford to pay even as much as 200,000. As they were a family that had been having difficulty making ends meet in the first place, what were they to do now?

This difficult financial situation was not limited to Yumiko's family alone. The majority of children who had been hospitalized came from lower-middle-class and lower-class families. Since the children were young, so were their parents, who had not yet reached their peak earning years, and most of them were struggling financially. All the families involved were enduring unspeakable emotional and financial hardship.

Sensing Daigo's presence, Yumiko's distraught mother looked up. The mother realized that tears had come to Daigo's eyes, and her own bloodshot eyes gave way to weeping.

"Professor Daigo, she's been like this since last night. She's in great pain, and yet when little Tatsuo passed away last night, she knew what had happened. She cried out, asking that Tatsuo not go and leave her behind. I think she knows she is going to die." Having said this much the mother covered her face with her hands and gave herself up to crying. But a moment later she took her hands away and looked up at Daigo. "The real cause of this illness is the Popico cookies made by the Minami Food Company, isn't that right? Those cookies had poison in them, didn't they? Please tell me the truth."

The mother was probably not yet thirty, but she had aged to the point where she appeared to be fifty, and now as she looked questioningly at Daigo there was a glint of insanity in her eyes. She clutched his wrist and continued. "I have decided that we don't want compensation from the company. Right now all I want is for whoever is responsible for what has happened to Yumiko and Tatsuo to be identified and that justice be done. This is outrageous. Even if we know the facts, it won't bring Tatsuo back. But still, I want to know who is responsible. It is Minami Foods, isn't it?"

What the woman was saying was true, there was no question about it. Daigo could only stammer.

There was no room for doubt that powerful carcinogens had been included in the ingredients used to make Popico cookies, produced by the Minami Food Company over a six-month period from July to December of last year. The majority of the patients lived in areas where products from the S manufacturing plant were distributed, and the one thing they had in common was that they had all eaten large quantities of the Popico cookies. The cookies were inexpensive, and children loved them.

Daigo had even identified the cancer-causing agent. There is a bacteria called A toxin, a poison that grows in the oily starch of peanuts, potatoes, rice, and barley. The basic ingredient of Popico was a form of potato starch imported from Southeast Asia, and one batch of the potato starch was probably old and the mold had begun to grow. In any case, they must have known from the beginning that the potato starch was old but had gone ahead and used it anyway. Since the number of people who had come down with cancer was relatively few, the growth of the mold was probably confined to a small portion of their ingredients.

Daigo was certain of this because Yoshimi had assigned him to run the tests on Popico. When Daigo and his two assistants had completed 90 percent of their analysis and before they had written their formal report, however, Daigo had discussed the results of their findings with Yoshimi, who immediately relieved Daigo of the assignment. He had said that there were things in Daigo's explanation which he did not understand and that he would repeat the analysis himself and come up with a conclusive result. Consequently, two weeks later, at the beginning of November, when Yoshimi's formal report was made to the Prefectural Health Division, its content was considerably different from the results of Daigo's analysis.

According to Yoshimi's report, there was some suspicion that the potatoes used as ingredients might have been old, but there was no sign that any mold had been present. Consequently he concluded that the Popico cookies were not directly linked to the cancer in the children, but that the illness had resulted from some combination of factors. In order to identify this "combination of factors," each child's case would have to be studied individually, and therefore it would be some time before a definite conclusion could be reached.

By making this report, Yoshimi was conspiring with Minami Foods to completely evade their responsibility. Even before the formal report was issued, it was clear to Daigo that there was definite collusion between the company and Yoshimi. Daigo also knew that Yoshimi was very greedy about making money, and there was no question that he had received a substantial amount of money from Minami Foods.

On the other hand, as far as the patients and their families were concerned, even a settlement from the company could not bring back those who had died or bring those who were ill back to health. Yoshimi had sold the lives and the well-being of the young patients and their families for his own greedy profit.

Daigo naturally had made a vigorous protest, but Yoshimi had ignored him. Daigo had sought support from his assistants, but Yoshimi had already gotten them over to his side, and they merely scowled and refused to say anything. Both Yoshimi and the assistants were graduates of J university, while Daigo was an outsider; and since the president of the university, who had brought Daigo here, was by now retired, Daigo felt that he was all alone in his crusade to bring out the truth.

On numerous occasions since that time, Daigo had pressed Yoshimi to change his stand and present a true report. Yoshimi responded to these attempts by setting traps for Daigo. Suddenly there was an urgent attempt by an Alaskan university to recruit Daigo for their faculty. He tried to resist their attempts to lure him, but as he was only an assistant professor, they could offer some strong inducements. Nevertheless, Daigo felt this was a matter of fundamental principles, and no matter what favorable conditions the Alaskan university offered, he was determined to stay here and see this matter through, even though Yoshimi had arranged many traps of this sort to get rid of Daigo.

"Professor, you know the truth in this matter, don't you?" Thus Yumiko's mother persisted in demanding an answer. "Why don't you publish the truth and make it known? What's the matter? Are you afraid of your colleague, Professor Yoshimi? Is that it?"

He wasn't really afraid, but under the present unpleasant circumstances, if he went public with his own dissenting view, he would probably be crushed by Yoshimi's political pressure. There had to be some other method. He was groping to find some way to get the upper hand over that man. With these thoughts and arguments on Daigo's mind, he suddenly pulled free of the child's mother and escaped out of the hospital room.

When he reached the lobby of the hospital, he was just in time to see a long black Mercury glide to a stop in front of the building. Right away he saw that it was Yoshimi's car.

Indeed, Yoshimi himself alighted from the car, his well-built body clothed in a subdued gray suit. Akishige Yoshimi was fifty-two this year. He had a clean-cut jaw and some white mixed in his hair. At first glance he gave the impression of being a distinguished scholar, but if one looked closely at the intense eyes and thick lips, Daigo felt they clearly reflected the greed and brutishness of his personality.

For an instant their eyes locked and Daigo felt the hatred and contempt in the other man's gaze. He clearly realized that Daigo had been at the hospital once again to visit the young cancer victims. No doubt Yoshimi himself had come to the hospital for some entirely different reason.

Daigo gave the briefest possible nod of recognition and started to go on past when suddenly Yoshimi gave a brutal smile and stepped toward him. "Ah, Daigo, I need to talk to you about that job in Alaska. I got a call yesterday from the dean there. He said that I must by all means send him some promising young man. Alaska may be sort of rural, but as you know they have recently discovered oil there and they say their cities are really booming. Their university budgets are booming the same way, so they can spend all the money they want, and they say they can have all the money they need for their research. I think it would be a really fine opportunity for you."

Daigo did not bother to respond.

"He said I should make a recommendation to him before the end of the year, so you think it over, and if you want the job, just let me know. I'll be waiting to hear from you.'' Once more he grinned, showing his white teeth, then turned on his heel and walked away. Daigo noticed that even before he turned away, all trace of the smile had left his face.

Somewhere in his heart Daigo felt a faint surge of fear and tragedy and knew that he was being manipulated against his will.

# 3

# The Message

LATE ON THE AFTERNOON OF DECEMBER 2, KOHEI DAIGO found the letter lying on the desk in his office. He discovered it when he returned from his laboratory. It was in an ordinary long narrow envelope with the address in neat printing which indicated that it was for Daigo at J university. Above the address was a red special delivery stamp. No doubt it had arrived at the university's mail department and one of Daigo's assistants had brought it up and put it on his desk.

Up to this point there was nothing strange or suspicious about the letter.

As he sank down in his chair, Daigo turned the letter over. On the back was the return address written in the same printed letters saying "Emerald Estates, Inc." and giving an address in central Fukuoka. Emerald Estates was a land investment company capitalized by a large insurance

35

company. Daigo knew about this company because several years ago they had helped to provide the mortgage which enabled him to buy his present home. The office in Fukuoka was only a branch of the home office in Tokyo, but they had very modern offices in a new office building in the heart of town that seemed emblematic of all that is modern in life.

Daigo, however, was troubled, wondering why they would be sending him a special delivery letter. As he gazed momentarily at the return address on the back of the envelope, Daigo was gradually overcome by a distant memory. He slit the envelope and withdrew two sheets of ordinary postal stationery. The neatly printed words of the letter were in the same writing as those on envelope.

> Greetings. This is about the vacation villa we discussed the other day. The sale of this property is a matter of some urgency, so if it is convenient for you, I would like to have you take a look at it at 5:30 on Friday, December 3. I hope I will have the pleasure of showing you the property at that time.
>
> Since the chance to buy this property may never come again, I sincerely hope that I may count on seeing you there at that time.
>
> Yours truly,
> Hai Mizushima
> Manager

The entire letter was written on the first sheet of paper. The second sheet was blank.

After Daigo had read the letter over a second time, he sat gazing at it with a look of some amusement. He could not remember anyone in the office by the name of Mizushima, much less a manager. The person who had helped them buy their home three years ago had since been transferred to another part of the country. He had sent them a note when he had been made branch manager.

Indeed, Daigo could not imagine what the letter was all about when it included a sentence like "This is about the vacation villa we discussed the other day." There was certainly no reason why they should suppose that he was in the market for a vacation retreat. He still had another seventeen years to go on his present mortgage, so he was tied up for some time to come.

It was clear from the content of the letter that they expected him to buy a vacation home. And they also clearly indicated that the wish to buy such a vacation home had come from him. Daigo's first thought was that the letter had inadvertently been misaddressed. But that explanation did not really dispose of the matter, and he had an uneasy feeling about the nuance expressed in the last part of the letter.

For the most part, this was a standard business letter, but it seemed to have a strangely intimate message. He recalled the vague sense of positive feeling he had felt before he opened the envelope. That had not simply come from the fact that the letter was special delivery. In the past when he had received letters from Emerald Estates, they had been sent in plain, businesslike brown envelopes with the address written horizontally, and the name of the company had been written on the back of the envelope in Roman characters. Never had he received from them this sort of white envelope with the name of the company written in ink.

At the same time, the message was clearly intended for him. He did not recognize the handwriting. He could not even tell if it had been written by a man or a woman, but it was obvious that it had been written by a person with some considerable education.

He turned his gaze to the stamp on the envelope. It had been posted between 6:00 P.M. and midnight on the day before yesterday. In that case, if this letter had been dropped in the mail at one of the post boxes in the center of Fukuoka, it should not have taken such a long time to be delivered to J university, which is located in the same city. With this thought in mind, he looked at the postmark for when the letter had been received, but the ink was faint and he could not make out what it said. All he could be certain of was that it did not say Fukuoka.

For a time Daigo sat staring at the letter, unseeing and unthinking. It occurred to him that if this letter had intentionally been sent to him, then whoever sent it was expecting him to appear at the offices of the company at 5:30 on Friday afternoon. Friday, December 3 was tomorrow.

Presently Daigo thrust the letter into the pocket of his sportcoat and stood up. He took the opportunity to make sure that he also had a coin in that pocket. Ordinarily if he had to make a telephone call from his office he would use the telephone next to his desk, but if he did so, a large part of his conversation would be overheard by his assistants and students. For some reason Daigo felt that he did not want them to overhear this conversation. It was just a feeling he had.

The gray autumn twilight was falling as he walked across the campus to a public telephone booth. There he looked up the number of Emerald Estates and dialed it. A female receptionist answered his call and he asked for Mizushima.

After a short wait he was greeted by an overly cheery voice. "This is Mizushima, sorry to keep you waiting." It was not a voice Daigo recognized.

"Yes, I'm Professor Daigo of J university."

"Oh, yes, Professor Daigo. I'm pleased to make your acquaintance, thanks for calling. I was just thinking about calling you, but you beat me to it."

As soon as he heard Daigo's name, Mizushima began to speak enthusiastically. Since Mizushima seemed to know who Daigo was, there must have been some connection between them, but on the other hand, Mizushima had clearly stated, "I'm pleased to make your acquaintance."

"Well, then, if five-thirty tomorrow afternoon is convenient for you, I'll have a car ready and be waiting for you."

"Wait a moment, you mean we're going to go look at a vacation home?"

"Of course. I discussed the matter with your secretary the other day, and she told me all the features you are looking for. I have located two houses, one in the Dazaifu area and another in Meinohama that overlooks the sea. These are new vacation villas. They may have some drawbacks, but they are quiet neighborhoods, and you can drive to the center of the city in less than an hour. Now, about the price—"

"Hold on, wait a minute. You said something about a secretary?"

"Oh, so she's not really your secretary? Well, that was the impression I had. Please forgive me. Let me see now, she said her name was Tsukawa. She telephoned the day before yesterday. She gave the telephone number of your laboratory and everything."

He was talking in such a way that it seemed as though he was searching for a memo in his pocket or desk drawer to confirm what he was saying. Daigo had been stunned by references to a secretary and to someone named Tsukawa. For Mizushima to take an unknown woman's words at face value and to believe that an assistant professor at a national university had a personal secretary merely demonstrated how out of touch Mizushima was.

But Mizushima was still trying to explain the situation

saying, "In any case, she seemed like a very sensitive person. As you might expect."

When he said "As you might expect" his voice contained a hint of a smirk. It was clear that he now supposed that the woman named Tsukawa was Daigo's mistress and that he wanted the vacation home as a place in which to keep her.

"I know you are very busy, but you have taken the trouble to get in touch with me, so I will make every effort to show you a place you will like. So it's agreed then that we will meet tomorrow?"

Daigo wanted desperately to say, "Wait a minute. What sort of voice did this woman Tsukawa have? Do you have any way of getting in touch with her?" But he had no chance to ask. He decided that if he asked these questions, Mizushima would only take it to be some sort of pointless joke, and he would have surely responded with a joke of his own. It became clear to Daigo that he had no choice but to go to Mizushima's office at 5:30 tomorrow and be taken to see the vacation homes. Daigo hung up the telephone feeling there was something of a mystery at work here.

The black Mercury came gliding past the telephone booth where Daigo stood, following the street that was littered with the fallen golden ginkgo leaves. It was the car that belonged to Akishige Yoshimi. Apparently Yoshimi was returning to his office.

Yoshimi was sitting rigidly in the back seat with his usual intense look. Apparently he did not notice Daigo in the telephone booth as he went past. Unconsciously Daigo hid his face behind the telephone and watched the car. He reached out one hand to the glass door of the telephone booth. Daigo was prepared to do whatever he could to keep from coming face to face with Yoshimi. He knew that Yoshimi would once again begin to pressure him for an answer about whether or not he would accept the position at the Alaskan university.

It was a community college in a small town in the interior of Alaska, but oil had recently been discovered there and the town had been booming, and they would give him lavish amounts of money for his research. Yoshimi had been careful to outline all these positive aspects of the position in his pursuit of Daigo. But if he made the decision to move to Alaska, it was highly unlikely that he would ever be able to return to a position in Japan. It was clear that Yoshimi was trying to bury him in Alaska. His wife, Shihoko, had been aghast at the idea of going to Alaska. On the other hand, there was more than a little concern that if he did not take the Alaskan post, he would be hounded into an even worse position somewhere else.

The public scandal at the news that Minami Foods products had caused cancer was dying down, but to some extent the concern was still there and would be for a long time. Of the children who had been admitted to the medical hospital at J university, eight-year-old Tatsuo had died, and six-year-old Yumiko seemed destined to follow, and this brought back all of the old pains and recriminations. The tragedy of the young patients and their families was continuing. Nevertheless, Minami Foods was using Yoshimi's report as a shield, and although they had made a token payment to the bereaved families, they were denying any fundamental responsibility.

At the same time Daigo was being pressured into either accepting the Alaskan position or not. And yet he also had to wonder if there was not some other route he could follow. On the other hand, he supposed that the things each of us confronts in life is a matter of fate, and this was a feeling that continued to attack Daigo. He recalled the uneasiness he felt in his heart each time he met Yoshimi.

"So I'll see you at five-thirty, then," he heard himself

muttering under his breath without really realizing what he was saying.

There was a rumor to the effect that Yoshimi would be attending a wedding reception the following evening, and this thought came to Daigo's mind. One of Yoshimi's students was marrying a girl whose father held an important position in a bank, and Yoshimi had been asked to participate in the wedding. He would be attending the wedding and the reception with his trusted assistant Yamada, but Daigo had not been invited to the affair.

At 5:30 the following day Daigo kept his appointment and showed up at the Fukuoka branch office of Emerald Estates, where he met Mizushima. Mizushima was in his late twenties, a short man, and more mild-mannered than Daigo had expected from his voice over the telephone. But after they met, things turned out pretty much as Daigo had anticipated.

Mizushima began by showing him two slick pamphlets that featured the two modern vacation homes, one on the sea coast west of the city and the other to the southeast in Dazaifu. After explaining everything, from the settings of the houses to their facilities and the procedures for taking out a loan, Mizushima led Daigo to a small company car. Mizushima instructed to the driver to take them first to the house in Dazaifu.

From Mizushma's way of talking, Daigo gathered that his so-called private secretary, Ms. Tsukawa, had telephoned Emerald Estates three days ago on Tuesday afternoon and had given Mizushima Daigo's name and position and had told him that Daigo wanted to find a vacation home right away. She said he was looking for a quiet place within an hour's drive of the center of the city, that he was able to pay somewhere in the area of 15 million yen, and hinted that if he found exactly the right place, he would buy it right away. That, of course, was a prospect that made Mizushima enthusiastic. In recent years vacation homes had been springing up in Fukuoka and its suburbs like bamboo after the rainy season, but then a recession hit and the demand for such homes fell off, and there were many cases of investment companies going bankrupt. Even though Emerald Estates had a large amount of capital backing and was in no danger of going bankrupt, they were nevertheless eager to sell off these homes as quickly as they could.

From the sound of the girl's voice she seemed to be in her twenties or early thirties. She had a gentle, deep-pitched manner of speaking. The woman did not say where she was calling from, merely that Daigo would come to the Emerald Estates office on Friday at 5:30 and that he would like to be shown some homes. Daigo learned this much information indirectly from what Mizushima was saying.

"After you called yesterday, I got another telephone call from Ms. Tsukawa at about seven. I must say she is a very polite person."

It was clear at least that whoever this woman was, it was not Daigo's wife. At 7:00 last night she was preparing Daigo's dinner, and even when he had mentioned Emerald Estates, she had shown no particular interest.

So the question was, who was this woman?

Daigo could not help thinking of Fumiko Samejima, the woman he had met casually and quite by chance in the salon of the Château Chantal in the village of Barbizon on the outskirts of Paris in mid-October. It was probably an overstatement to call it an encounter. They had not even had the opportunity to look each other in the eye. On that dark and stormy autumn night they had come together in the darkness for an intoxicating moment that seemed hardly to belong to this world. Daigo thought of that meeting from time to time almost in an effort to verify to himself that it had really happened.

Nevertheless, the question remained, why would Fumiko have gone to the trouble to telephone a real estate agent in Fukuoka and make an appointment for him? Daigo was firmly convinced that the special delivery letter had come from Fumiko, or at any rate from this mysterious woman who was using the name Tsukawa. She had even gone to the trouble to call Mizushima again last night to make certain that Daigo would keep the appointment. Why? What was her purpose? No matter how he turned the matter over in his mind, he could find no answer.

Daigo decided that if this was some sort of message from Fumiko, he would go along with it and do what she wanted. He instinctively felt that this was the proper thing to do.

Dazaifu and Meinohama are on opposite promontories of land that flank the city of Fukuoka. It was six o'clock by the time they set out in the car, and because of the rush hour traffic, by the time they had seen the two vacation homes, discussed them, and returned to the office it was nine o'clock.

Mizushima was obviously expecting that Daigo would put down some earnest money on one of the houses either that day or the next, and Daigo said that both houses more or less corresponded to what he had in mind, but some problem had developed in his plans for financing the purchase, and once he had that straightened out he would make a decision on which house he wanted and would be back in touch. He parted from Mizushima in front of the Emerald Estates building, which was closed for the night, and went to the underground parking lot where his own car was waiting to take him home.

It was ten o'clock by the time he got to his own home in Washiro, where Shihoko was waiting without comment. This morning he had told her that a colleague from a university in Osaka was going to be in town briefly and that they would be spending the evening together. Shihoko seemed undisturbed and did not say anything, so he took this as evidence that no woman had called during his absence.

For some reason Daigo was assailed by a strong feeling of despair and frustration: once again he had been expecting some sort of message and had not found it. While he was being shown through the vacation homes, he had held his breath in anticipation, expecting that at any moment Fumiko might step out of an empty room. By the time he and his wife went to bed, he felt completely drained and exhausted.

The next day was Saturday, and Daigo slept late. He had no lectures to give, and though on some Saturdays he went in to his laboratory if he had an experiment in progress, most of the time he stayed home and read or prepared articles for scholarly journals.

At nine o'clock, Shihoko suddenly opened the bedroom door. Daigo was still in bed reading a magazine when she said, "Oh, aren't you up yet? There is a telephone call for you. I said you would only be a minute."

"Who is it?"

"A Ms. Tsukawa, who handles scientific affairs for the newspaper."

An electric thrill ran through Daigo. "She must be some sort of reporter," said Daigo, trying to keep his voice steady as he got out of bed.

"That's right. She wants to see you today to make arrangements for you to participate in a panel discussion for a special New Year's issue they will bring out."

"Today?"

"Yes, that's what she said. She had made an appointment to see you at two this afternoon at the local archives section of the Prefectural Library."

"I guess I'd better go talk to her."

"No, she hung up already. She said it would not do for you to forget the appointment, so she just called to remind you. She said to tell you that she hopes to complete all the arrangements today, and that the meeting will probably last about two hours.''

"You mean that's all she said, and then just hung up?'' Daigo could not conceal the tone of disappointment in his voice. Shihoko seemed puzzled by his response and frowned.

"She said not to bother getting you out of bed, that it would be too much trouble for you. She was very polite.''

"She is a woman reporter, and you are sure she said her name was Tsukawa?''

"Yes.''

"I had completely forgotten about that meeting today,'' he said hurriedly. Of course he had no recollection of any panel discussion being arranged by a local newspaper, but he hoped he would have a chance to see her today. Suddenly it seemed as though he could almost smell a faint trace of her perfume, and for a moment he longed desperately for this woman he did not know.

The Fukuoka Prefectural Library is a part of the Prefectural Cultural Complex, located near Senta Bay. The sky was a clear, deep blue for the first time in a long time, but the dry, cold wind announced that true winter was just around the corner.

Daigo parked his car in a corner of the front courtyard, which had a double row of poplar trees, reminiscent of the north country, and a fountain. Daigo entered the building and made his way to the second floor. At the entrance to the reading room he was greeted by the laughing faces of two young girls. Daigo ordinarily used the library at J university, but he came here perhaps two or three times a month. He would occasionally have professional articles copied and had a nodding acquaintance with the three people who worked here.

The reading room seemed unusually crowded for a Saturday afternoon. To the left of the general reading room was a tiny cubicle that housed the local archives. The check-out desk at the entrance was manned by a single young man. It was five past two when Daigo entered the reading room. He was hurried by the realization that he was a bit late.

Ordinarily he was accustomed to seeing four or five patrons in the reading room, but today there was a large group of what appeared to be high school students and three others sitting at the tables with open books or perusing the shelves. Oddly enough, they were all men; he could see no women in the room.

As usual, Daigo walked to the shelves containing books dealing with environmental protection. In this room were held the collections on local history, farming, forestry, sea products, and environmental protection. This library collection was better than the one at J university for topics dealing with the land.

Nervously keeping one eye on the entrance, Daigo tried to read a book of comparative studies on the state of water pollution in the prefecture, and finally took it to the librarian and asked to have ten pages copied.

By 3:30 the woman he was waiting for had not appeared. While he waited several young female patrons had come and gone. He had looked questioningly at each woman, but they had all ignored him. His wife had said that when Ms. Tsukawa had called that morning she had said that the meeting would begin at two and last for about two hours. Therefore he decided to wait until four. Most of the remaining time was wasted as he sat looking out the window at the tall poplars blowing in the wind rather than reading his book. At 4:10 he left the library.

He was disappointed, angry, and somewhat uneasy. He was so upset by this new failure to meet Fumiko that he found it difficult to control his breathing. He did not know what to do at this point. If he went straight home, he would probably just upset his wife and children.

In the end, Daigo did something that was quite out of character for him: he went alone to a cocktail lounge on the eleventh floor of a hotel in the heart of the city. There were many small bars and drinking places that were closer, but it was too early to go to one of them.

Daigo sat at the bar, which had a view of the harbor, and drank about half of his Scotch and water. He tried to analyze all the events that had happened from the time he had received the special delivery letter until now. He tried to make sense of the series of events that had been orchestrated by a woman calling herself Tsukawa. Presently, however, he found himself thinking about his quarrel with Yoshimi and his present condition: it seemed things were closing in on him and he was becoming increasingly isolated. In the end he was in a very depressed mood. Whenever he started thinking about these things he wound up vacillating, uncertain, and depressed.

As the sun began to set, the surface of the sea was a chilly blue-gray with whitecaps whipping up.

When Daigo arrived home, shortly before seven o'clock, a distraught Shihoko met him at the front door. "There you are. Mr. Yamada at the lab has been trying to reach you on the telephone. Apparently there has been a terrible accident at Professor Yoshimi's house."

"An accident?"

"He did not give me any of the details, but Yoshimi—"

Just at that moment the telephone in the front hall began to ring. Daigo picked up the receiver.

"Hello, Daigo? This is Yamada." Yamada's high-pitched voice seemed to whistle through his nose.

''My wife says something happened at Yoshimi's house.''

''Yes. Apparently Yoshimi is dead.''

''What?''

''I heard from his wife a short time ago. She had been out and returned home at six. Yoshimi had collapsed in the living room.''

''Collapsed?''

''Well, not exactly. Apparently it was not a natural death, because they called the police right away. I am planning to go to Yoshimi's house right now.''

For some reason the thought that occurred to Daigo was, So that's the message.

# 4

# The Visitor

WHILE THE TECHNICIANS WERE STILL BUSY TAKING FIN-
gerprints, Inspector Furukawa of the Fukuoka First Police
Division left the living room. He paused in the dark corridor near the spacious, stone-paved entry hall. Outside the
front door was a sandy open space for parking cars. Beyond were clumps of camellia and crape myrtle stretching
for perhaps ten yards to the ornamental hedge that shut out
the outside world. Nevertheless, the distance from the front
door of the house to the front gate was quite short. The
front gate was made of iron and was apparently left open
during the day.

The surrounding houses were not so large that one would
call them mansions. There were two or three small shops
across the street and a little farther on. Behind them Furukawa could see a ten-story apartment building. This was a

middle-class neighborhood, and Yoshimi's house was by far the largest in the area.

Furukawa noticed a group of onlookers beyond the rope that blocked the gate. It occurred to him that this was usually a rather busy street. It was the sort of street that during the day would see a steady stream of housewives and salesmen coming and going. He was pretty sure that sooner or later he would be able to turn up an eyewitness.

Furukawa recalled the expression on the face of one of his men who had been sent around the neighborhood to question the residents. He had been told to make every effort to locate an eyewitness because so far they had not found a single piece of physical evidence at the scene of the crime that might identify the murderer.

The living room, where the murder had occurred, was spacious. It was furnished with a thick Persian carpet, a standard sofa set, and large mahogany cabinets. When Furukawa and his men had first arrived, the room was dim and quiet, and it did not appear that anything was wrong. The only sound was the gentle purring of the radiator, but when he looked closely he saw the crumpled form of a middle-aged man lying on the floor beside the sofa. On the coffee table was a cup, more than half full of coffee, and a silver sugar-and-cream set. That was all they had to work with at the scene of the murder.

Investigators soon learned that Akishige Yoshimi had died as the result of ingesting cyanide poison that had been mixed in his coffee. The faint, lingering fragrance of almonds and the mottled coloring of the dead man's skin were the classic features of death by cyanide. When the coffee in the cup was tested, it proved to be the source of the cyanide.

So someone had come to visit Yoshimi, who was in the house alone, and Yoshimi had served coffee in the living room. Seeing an opportunity, the murderer had put cyanide in Yoshimi's coffee, then watched while he drank it and collapsed. The murderer had probably then fled, taking with him the other cup. To avoid raising Yoshimi's suspicions, the murderer would have had to drink coffee too—thereby leaving lip- and fingerprints on the cup. The murderer had taken the cup with him rather than washing it to make certain that no incriminating evidence remained.

Indeed, the murderer had left no evidence behind at all. After investigating the scene, police could not even be certain of the sex of the murderer. Furukawa was pretty sure that they would never find any fingerprints. That was why it was so important to find an eyewitness who saw the murderer either enter or leave the house.

Furukawa noticed several news reporters cutting across the front lawn and quickly hurried back inside the house. In the sitting room, which looked out on a Japanese-style garden studded with fine stone lanterns, Mrs. Kiyoe Yoshimi was talking to a man in a navy blue suit who appeared to be about thirty. Although the house was kept warm with a central heating system of radiators, Kiyoe's pinched, narrow face was pale, and she seemed to be shivering continually. She was an aristocratic woman of about fifty. She had regular features, but her eyes held a certain sharpness.

"Excuse me," said Furukawa, interrupting them.

Kiyoe indicated a seating cushion and introduced them. "This is Mr. Yamada, my husband's laboratory assistant."

Furukawa shook hands with the man and took a seat, then fixed his gaze on Kiyoe. "I would like to have you tell me in greater detail exactly how things were when you discovered your husband's body."

Kiyoe turned to Yamada and said, "Will you be kind enough to telephone once again to see if you can find out when Shoichi left Nagasaki?"

After Yamada had left the room, Furukawa once again expressed some brief condolences to the widow, then he continued. "In order to make sure that we have everything just right, I would like to hear you go over the matter again. Can you think of any reason why your husband might have wanted to commit suicide? Perhaps it was not the result of any problems he had at the university. Perhaps his health was failing, or something like that."

"No, there was nothing like that. He has chronic asthma, but this fall it was not bothering him much. In fact he was in good health. As I was leaving the house this morning he said he was going to the indoor pool we have here in the neighborhood for some swimming. It was the first time in a long time he had done that.

Kiyoe's bloodshot eyes stood out in her otherwise pale face, and she was evidently struggling to control her voice as she spoke. "I understand you left the house about nine this morning."

"Yes. As soon as I got the breakfast things cleared away, I called a taxi."

"After that your husband was here in the house alone?"

"Yes."

The Yoshimi home was a large Western-style house, but recently the old couple had been living here alone. Of their three children, the oldest son, Shoichi, had graduated from the psychology department of J university and was currently working in a hospital in Nagasaki; a close friend of Yoshimi was the director there. Both their daughters were married and had families, the elder one in Hiroshima, the younger one in Tokyo. Naturally all three had been informed of the tragedy, but none had arrived home yet. They had had a young maid who had quit working for them in September, and now, while they were searching for another one, they had their old housekeeper drop in from time to time. But for the most part, the old couple lived alone.

"So you took the taxi to Hakata Station. What then? Did you take the bullet train?"

"Yes. My daughter had planned to drive to Hiroshima Station to meet me when I arrived." Kiyoe had left this morning on a trip to Hiroshima, where her eldest daughter's husband worked for a large steel company. Kiyoe had gone to visit them because her eight-year-old granddaughter was having her debut performance as a classical Japanese dancer. Kiyoe had promised her granddaughter long ago that she would be there for the performance, so today she had gone, leaving her husband at home to mind the house.

"Now, as I understand it, you arrived back in Fukuoka shortly before six this evening, and I suppose you caught a taxi at Hakata Station and came home."

"Yes. I suppose it was about five forty-five when we got in. I know I was in a hurry to get home so I could get my husband's dinner on the table on time."

When Kiyoe arrived home she found that the front door was not locked, but this was not unusual when Yoshimi was at home alone. The house was completely dark, without a light showing anywhere. Only the radiators were functioning. At first she had imagined that her husband had misplaced his house key and had left the door unlocked and gone off to practice golf at the driving range. She did notice, however, that all his pairs of shoes were there by the front door. This made her feel a bit uneasy as she went into the house and looked around. It was about 6:15 when she had discovered her husband's body sprawled on the floor in the living room.

At that time Yoshimi's hands and feet were already cold, which were pretty definite symptoms of his condition. She said she knew at a glance that he had been the victim of foul play, so immediately after calling a doctor, she had also telephoned the police, and had been careful not to touch anything.

"I see. In that case, had he said anything about expecting visitors today?"

They had been over this same ground in an earlier interview with the widow, and as they got to the heart of the story, a sorrowful look appeared on Furukawa's face. Masao Furukawa was forty-one years old and wore dark-rimmed glasses on his round, ruddy face. He was the chief investigator in this case.

"I heard no mention of any guests. There was no suggestion of it."

"No telephone calls from anyone?"

"No, I don't remember anything like that. There were no calls at all this morning before I left the house."

From time to time the widow dabbed at the corners of her mouth with a spotless white handkerchief, but she continued to answer his questions with stout-hearted determination.

"In that case, then, all we can suppose is that either someone called to make an appointment after you left the house, or else that person just showed up here and committed the crime."

"I expect so." Kiyoe narrowed her eyes in concentration, but apparently no other alternative presented itself to her.

"Since the coffee service was out on the table, can we suppose that your husband prepared coffee for himself?"

"I expect that was very likely the case. We always kept the percolator on the stove in the kitchen, and my husband drank a lot of coffee, especially since last spring, when he gave up cigarettes. He would often serve coffee himself when he had guests. Of course, if I was at home at the time, I would serve it, but if not he could do it by himself. Oh my, now that I stop to think about it, all this would never have happened if I had stayed home today." For the first time Kiyoe seemed on the verge of losing her self-control. She dabbed furiously at both eyes with her handkerchief and choked back a sob.

"How long have you known that you would be going to Hiroshima alone today?"

"Well, let's see. The date of the performance was set back during the summer vacation, so I suppose I've known since then that I would be going alone."

"How much discussion of this was there among the members of your family?"

"Well, we talked about it among ourselves, but I don't think we talked about it to people outside the family."

"Do you think we can rule out the possibility of anyone outside the family knowing you would be making this trip alone?"

"I don't know about ruling out the possibility. We could have talked about it among ourselves at almost any time, and anyone could have overheard us. Last night at the wedding, for example, my husband could have mentioned it quite casually to anyone."

"Your husband attended a wedding reception last night?"

"Yes. One of my husband's former graduate students, who now works for a petrochemical company, is marrying the daughter of a man who has an important position in a bank. They had a reception at one of the hotels beginning at six last night. It was apparently a lavish party, including more than two hundred guests." Kiyoe herself had not attended the reception, but even the laboratory assistant Yamada, to whom Furukawa had been introduced earlier, had been invited. Furukawa decided that later he would have to ask a few questions about this wedding party.

"Let's get back to the matter of the coffee. Are you sure the other cup has not been found anywhere?"

"Yes. We've searched the entire house." Kiyoe's eyebrows formed a strict and angry line across her forehead.

A coffee cup with a persimmon motif that matched Yoshimi's cup, which was found on the table, was missing along with its saucer. Kiyoe had owned half a dozen of these, but now only four could be found on the shelves in the kitchen, along with the one on the coffee table. The other could not be located anywhere in the house.

Naturally the inference was that the murderer had left finger and lip prints on the cup and so had taken it with him. Did this imply that they could suppose that a single visitor had come?

"When you arrived back at the house at five forty-five did you notice any signs of any suspicious cars or people lurking about?"

Kiyoe hung her head and bit her lip. She seemed to be devoting all her effort to trying to remember. "I don't remember anything like that. The porch light was off, so the whole area around the house was dark. If there was anything suspicious lurking about, I would not have noticed it." Grief welled up in her eyes once again as she struggled to answer the question.

At this point in the interview, one of the detectives who had been asking questions around the neighborhood signaled to Furukawa from outside the sitting room. From the look on his face, it appeared that he had come up with something. Furukawa excused himself and stepped into the corridor.

"At two-twenty this afternoon there was a housewife who stopped in at the shop across the street to buy a spool of thread." As might be expected, the young detective's cheeks were flushed and his words came out in a rapid jumble as he tried to make his report.

At any rate, the gist of his report was that the housewife in question had seen the figure of what she took to be a young woman entering the gate of the Yoshimi house. At the time there had been no cars and no other pedestrians present in the area. The street was awash in the early winter sunlight, and it seemed to create a sort of lonely air pocket in which nothing was moving.

"The housewife was standing in a corner of the store at a counter trying to select a spool of thread. The store clerk had just gone into the back room to get the thread the woman had ordered, and while she was waiting, the woman looked out the window."

Intuitively she had realized that there was someone in the street outside the shop, and when she looked up, she saw a woman entering the front gate of the Yoshimi house and walk toward the front door. She was of medium build and medium height and wearing a black coat. From behind it appeared as though she had her hair up. The reason the housewife supposed the girl was not a salesperson was that she was carrying a cloth-wrapped bundle that appeared to hold a gift for the people she was visiting, or perhaps it was just the relaxed mood the girl conveyed when seen from behind. To put the matter strongly, the impression the housewife had received was that the girl was the young wife of a good family. At that point the housewife's attention was brought back to the selection of thread. In any case, the housewife's home was some distance away, and she had no connection with the Yoshimi family.

"Was she quite certain that this incident occured at two-twenty," asked Furukawa, consciously focusing on the heart of the matter.

"Yes. On that point she considered when she had left her house, and she was quite definite about the time. Nevertheless, just to verify the matter, I checked with the store and they assured me that the housewife had come in at about two-fifteen and had stayed in the store until about two-thirty." The young detective was very earnest and certain in his reply.

If they could make sure this fact was accurate—that a

young lady had visited Yoshimi at 2:20—it would be an important step in the investigation. It would give another clue to establish the time the murder had occurred.

At the time the crime was discovered, it was estimated that it had been committed between 2:30 and 3:30. Since they were able to do a post mortem on the body fairly soon after death had occurred, they were able to keep the estimated time of death within rather narrow limits. That and the fact that the lights of the house had not been turned on dovetailed nicely.

The sun sets approximately forty minutes later in Fukuoka than it does in Tokyo, and at this time of the year it is generally dark by 4:30. This was the time of the year when the days are at their very shortest.

In this regard, it is important to know that the living room of Yoshimi's house faced east and is shaded by the leaves of a large tree, so it lost the sunlight early in the day. Furthermore, Yoshimi had often cautioned his wife that it was dangerous with so few people living in the house, so they should keep lights on even during the day, and he was always going around the house turning on lights.

Thus, the fact that there were no lights on in the living room made it seem that either the murderer had turned the lights off or, more likely, since the gate light was not on nor was the light in the kitchen where the coffee had been made, he or she had visited the house before it was dark enough to need lights, meaning before 4:00 P.M. at the latest.

All of this circumstantial evidence did not mean that the girl who had visited the house was necessarily the murderer.

Furukawa's firm response to the impulsive young detective's report was intentional. When he returned to the sitting room the eyes he focused on Mrs. Yoshimi reflected his determination to solve the crime. He was determined to get from her the names of anyone who may have hated Akishige Yoshimi, or anyone who might have been his enemy.

"I quite often spend my Saturdays at home, but yesterday I had some research to do and went to the Prefectural Library." Daigo spoke rather louder and more forcefully than usual because he was trying to control a nervous tic near his eye. Inspector Furukawa was sitting directly in front of Daigo, and the light was reflecting off the inspector's glasses in a way that made Daigo nervous.

On Sunday morning, the day following Yoshimi's murder, Inspector Furukawa had unexpectedly shown up shortly after ten o'clock. It was a brilliantly clear day, just like the day before, and only the piercing cold of the wind was evidence of winter. The living room of Daigo's home faced south, and although it was much smaller and more cheaply furnished than Yoshimi's living room, since it did not have a large garden filled with tall trees it was blessed with plenty of sunlight on clear days. The sunlight seemed to radiate from the inspector's glasses and from his healthy, round face.

"Last night we established an investigative team to work on this case and held a conference to see what progress we had made toward solving it. The conference lasted until two this morning. After I leave here this morning I will go directly to the West Fukuoka Precinct Station, which is the investigation headquarters. My home is just on the other side of that hill behind your house, so I thought I would drop in and talk to you on my way to the station, since it is on the way." With this by way of introduction and explanation, Furukawa made his way into Daigo's living room.

That Furukawa was very interested in Daigo was evident

by the fact that this was the second time he had questioned Daigo about the murder. From the nature of the questions he asked, it was also clear that he had learned from Mrs. Yoshimi and the lab assistant Yamada about the antagonism between Yoshimi and Daigo. After receiving the news from Yamada the previous night, Daigo had gone straight to Yoshimi's house. By the time he got there, police officials and news reporters were already bustling in and out of the house. Eventually he had gotten a rough idea of what had happened from Yamada, and after brief questioning by one of the police officers, he had returned home.

No doubt the investigating officers had already heard that the antagonism between Yoshimi and Daigo was not just a personality conflict, that it stemmed from a difference of opinion regarding the Minami Foods scandal. No doubt they had also already learned that Daigo was being threatened with exile at the university in Alaska. From the moment Daigo heard that Yoshimi had been murdered, he realized that he would have to convey to the police a sense of the deep gray monotony of his own life. Consequently he forced himself to talk about his relationship with Yoshimi in a rather detached manner, even when speaking to Furukawa.

Furukawa, however, had said that he just wanted to get a few details straight in his own mind, and had asked Daigo if he had an alibi for the hours between two and five yesterday. At that point, Daigo felt he was beginning to lose his composure. This was not because he was without an alibi, but on the contrary because his alibi was so flawless. Since up to this point he had not known precisely when the crime was committed, he had not given any thought to the matter of an alibi. At the same time, he realized that his perfect alibi was not a lucky accident. His alibi had been carefully planned in advance by someone.

"Are you saying you were in the library from two until

after four? Were you by yourself?'' asked Inspector Furukawa with disquieting calmness.

"Yes, I was alone, and I spent the whole time in the
local history archives."

"Ah yes, that's the small room on the left just as you
go in, isn't it? I've been there two or three times myself to
look things up. I go there to get various statistics and information to use when we do orientation for new recruits."
Furukawa paused a moment, evidently calling to mind the
features of the archive room. "Did you come straight home
after you left the library?"

"No. I dropped in at a lounge in one of the hotels down-
town and had a drink." Daigo smiled cynically to himself
that his own behavior had deviated from the perfect script
that had been so carefully prepared for him. Since it had
still been early in the day there was no one else in the
lounge except for several foreign couples, so he thought
there was a good chance that the solicitous bartender would
remember his face. If it became necessary for him to have
an alibi extend that long, Daigo would still be fairly lucky.

"That's interesting. Do you regularly go off drinking by
yourself like that?"

"No. That was a very rare exception. I just felt particularly tense and tired yesterday after working at the library.
In fact, I just had a single Scotch and water, which I did
not even finish, before going back to my car."

"Naturally. I don't suppose there was any special reason
why you needed a drink?"

With some asperity Daigo replied with a question of his
own. "What time was it yesterday when Yoshimi took the
poison and died?" The newspaper reporters apparently had
not been able to find out the time of death, because the
time frame given in the news was quite extensive.

"We are looking most closely at the period between two-thirty and three-thirty. I suppose that at the very latest the murderer would have done the deed by four.''

''And his wife was away from the house that whole time?''

''That's right. She had gone to Hiroshima to visit her married daughter. There is no question about that. By the same token, we have to suppose that the murderer knew Yoshimi was at home alone, and took the opportunity to visit him.''

''That means the chances are that it was someone he knew. That it was someone who knew about the comings and goings of the Yoshimi family.''

''But the previous evening Professor Yoshimi had attended a wedding banquet. It is entirely possible that during the course of the evening he may have said something about his plans for the following day, and anyone could have overheard such a thing. Or, for that matter, the culprit could have telephoned earlier in the day, and having ascertained that Yoshimi was alone, gone to the house.''

Inspector Furukawa stopped talking for awhile and looked intently at Daigo's face, causing the nervous tic near the eye to begin again.

It was a clear fact that Daigo had not been anywhere near Yoshimi two nights ago. The same was also true for his alibi for the previous afternoon. That little archive room at the library was so small he could surely prove that he had been there the whole time. That being the case, it seemed strange that Furukawa as an investigator did not lose interest in him.

In any event, he seemed to have run into a dead end in his attempt to check out the wedding reception angle. For one thing, two hundred people had been invited, and besides, many of them had gone out into the hotel garden for a stroll. The only good news he had was information brought to him by the lab assistant, Yamada. He had re-

called that just before the party ended at eight he had seen
Yoshimi standing in a corner of the veranda talking with a
young lady. There was nothing particularly unusual about
such a thing, but it had seemed to Yamada that the girl
was definitely not an academic type. He had a distinct feeling that she seemed out of place at the party. But at the
time Yamada had not paid much attention and could not
recall any definite details of the woman's features or her
hairstyle or anything like that.

Furukawa was having some of his men check with the
people who had sent out the invitations to see if he could
identify the girl in question.

When Furukawa mentioned the fact that Yoshimi had
attended the wedding reception, it caused Daigo to recall
his own experience on that Friday night. Just at the time
in question, Daigo had been going around in the company
of a salesman and driver from the Emerald Estates looking
at a vacation home he had no intention of buying. Suddenly
he remembered something so shocking it numbed his mind.
That whole sequence of events involving Emerald Estates,
which had seemed so puzzling at the time, had all been
carefully choreographed in advance. Nothing had been left
to chance about how he spent Friday night and Saturday
afternoon. He had been manipulated like a puppet on both
occasions.

Furukawa moved his body slightly, and once again the
light flashed off his glasses. In the deep recesses of his
memory, Daigo was reminded of the lightning at Barbizon.

# 5

# The Emerald View

Seductions, whether they are many or few, are surely always dangerous. Nevertheless, Kohei Daigo did not seem to realize the danger implicit in his seduction. He was not merely hoping to meet Fumiko Samejima one more time. After all, he had no way to get in touch with her. While they were together in the darkened salon of the Château Chantal, all he had learned of her was her name and the fact that she lived in Tokyo and spent most of her time at home doing translations. Even in the case of her name, he could not be certain it was her real name. As things stood now, he was inclined to believe that she had used her real name.

On the other hand, everything Daigo had said about himself had been the truth. With curious clarity he recalled that at the time he would have felt that deceiving her in these matters would have been tantamount to self-deception. He had told her his true name and that he was a professor of hygiene at J university in Fukuoka. He had wanted to tell her more about himself, but she had stopped him by putting a finger to his lips. "Please don't tell me any more. I already understand you better than anyone else."

Certainly she had a very frank understanding of Daigo, but was that all, or had she moved from understanding to direct action? He had told her that he hated Yoshimi so much that he would like to kill him. This desire lay in the very bottom of his heart, and he had never admitted it to anyone other than Fumiko. At that time, due to cowardice or timidity, Daigo was actually suggesting that he wished someone would kill Yoshimi for him. Perhaps Fumiko had read the true intention of his words and had done the job for him. At the same time she had also created a perfect alibi for him.

On that dark night at Barbizon the word "courage" had been uttered by Fumiko. "Tonight heaven has endowed me with a special form of pure courage." Those were the words she had spoken. After she had left him that night, Daigo had pondered her words and wondered what they meant. No doubt from that night, from that very moment, Fumiko had been determined to carry out this direct action.

All the events that had taken place, from the time he received the special delivery letter two days before Aki-shige Yoshimi's death, through the telephone call that had put him in the prefectural library at the time of the actual murder, this entire string of events constituted a single message from Fumiko to Daigo. Daigo could think of no other explanation for this extraordinary series of happenings. If this was correct, then Fumiko was surely expecting to receive a response of some sort from Daigo. He wanted to tell her that he had received her message and understood it, and that probably . . . well, that he appreciated what she had done. But surely this wish was a dangerous seduction. Surely it was far more dangerous for Fumiko than it was for him. The connection between Daigo and Fumiko was a faint one, but if it became known, no doubt Fumiko would be the one the authorities would seek. After all, she was the one who had taken direct action. Perhaps it was precisely to discourage Daigo from taking any reciprocal action that she had not told him much about herself that night.

At last Daigo felt he was able to read the heart of this silent woman. He realized anew the secret sadness and melancholy that had steeped his soul following their encounter that night. In order to reassure himself he consulted the Tokyo telephone directory to find the name Fumiko Samejima. When he did not find her name listed there, he did not know what to do next. The end of the year with its holiday season was approaching, and although he went through his normal routines both at the university and at home, his mind was in a turmoil.

During all that time, the investigation into the murder of Professor Yoshimi continued, but it seemed clear that they would not find a primary suspect before the end of the year. The range of suspects was very diverse. There were many at J university who had been antagonistic to Yoshimi, both faculty and students (and of course Daigo was at the head of the list). Another pool of suspects were those involved in the analysis of the cookies produced by Minami Foods, including the parents of the children who had come down with cancer, who surely hated Yoshimi. There was also his complicated relationship with the company itself; many felt that that relationship had not been completely harmonious either.

Nevertheless, not a single firm lead had developed. Inspector Furukawa, of course, had set Daigo down as the one having the best motive, but his alibi had been unshakable, and he could not be budged from it. Eventually the investigation had come full circle, and all they had was a hint of the existence of a woman who might have visited Yoshimi on the afternoon of the murder, but there was not even a description of her. All they knew was that she had been wearing a black coat. There might be a connection here with the nonacademic-type woman Yoshimi had been deeply in conversation with at the wedding reception the night before the murder. The investigating team had begun with the people who sent out the invitations and ended up interviewing each of the people who had attended the reception and had done some checking on their own, but in the end they were not able to turn up anything about the woman or her position. Apparently she had not been invited to the reception but had mingled with the guests and had gotten close to Yoshimi. The woman's identity became the focus of the investigation, and even Daigo was questioned once by Inspector Furukawa about her, but he insisted that he knew nothing about the matter.

The new year arrived, and Daigo celebrated his fourth holiday season in his home in Washiro. The new housing development was surrounded by golf courses and farms, so New Year's Day was very quiet indeed. The winter sun was pale, and darkness came early, and even his students were reluctant after the first day of the year to drop in and say hello.

On New Year's Day the family enjoyed a late breakfast of the traditional *zoni*, and then his two daughters, one in the first grade, the other in the third, went to the field behind their house, where they flew kites with the other neighborhood children. Apparently in recent years it had become usual for girls to fly kites as well as boys. Since it was a large open field there were not many electrical lines, and the children could let their kites fly high.

While Daigo busied himself with looking over the New Year's cards they had received, Shihoko served some roasted tea and chatted with him. In her heart, Shihoko was probably the person who, more than anyone else, welcomed the death of Yoshimi. The conflicting opinions surrounding the Popico cookies were only the last straw. She was also furious about Yoshimi's attempts to railroad Daigo off to some university in Alaska. She, for one, would be very depressed if she had to leave Japan.

From the very beginning, Inspector Furukawa had not been blind to this possibility, and Shihoko herself had been a possible suspect, but luckily her alibi was supported by the woman who lived next door.

"For the time being Yoshimi's position is vacant, and I have been asked to take it over," replied Daigo as he continued to look through the greeting cards.

"But sooner or later they will choose a permanent replacement, won't they?"

"That's right."

"When do you suppose that will be."

"Well, I suppose a decision will be made sometime this year."

"I wonder if it has occurred to them that if a professor dies, it is reasonable that an assistant professor already on the faculty should succeed to the position."

"That's not the way it works. The other professors already have their own ideas about who ought to fill the position. Ultimately, the candidate will be chosen by the selection committee."

For one who was raised in the home of a professor in a rural university, such a system rankled. "Is there any chance that you will ever become a full professor?" Concern showed on her face as she raised the question.

"It's probably a fifty-fifty chance." Daigo himself felt that the matter was in the balance, and this was a cause for much reflection. There were about forty full professors on the faculty of the medical school, and they held the authority to make appointments in the department of hygiene. Among them, of course, were some who would support Daigo, but there were others who would support someone from the education department or from the hygiene department in the associated junior college, and there were others who wanted to bring someone in from the outside. The real dynamics of the committee were not clear, and Daigo himself had no inkling what decision they would make. But this was probably not the time for Daigo to make his move.

Shihoko continued to question him as she handed him a cup of tea. "Has any progress been made on the issue of Minami Foods?"

"I guess so." The victims of the case had already been inspired to take action. The father of one of the children who had been hospitalized had taken on the role of representative of all the victims' parents and was beginning negotiations with both the company and the prefectural department of hygiene. The man had telephoned Daigo just before the end of the year and said that they would begin talks in earnest just after the beginning of the year.

With regard to the corporate responsibility of Minami Foods, as far as the victims were concerned it was important that people know that Daigo's opinion differed from that of Yoshimi, and now that Yoshimi was no longer there, they intended to make sure Daigo's opinion was heard. Daigo's resolve was firm.

Perhaps it was necessary to allow some time to elapse before a new written statement was issued, but in the end they were determined to make public the results of Daigo's analysis on the cookies, the analysis he had done before Yoshimi tried to block his results, and this time they were determined to make clear who was responsible in this matter. In that case, litigation was probably inevitable. Daigo was determined to side with the victims at all costs. If he could prove a link between the children's cancer and the

Popico cookies, the company would have to pay each of the victims or their families a large settlement. It would be a good deal more than the token sum the company had been offering up till now, and it would lead to a resolution of the problem.

It was unclear whether Daigo's involvement in this matter would be a plus or a minus when it came time to choose a new professor to replace Yoshimi. It was quite possible that he would find some support even among the faculty of the medical school where Yoshimi had been very influential. Still, this issue alone would probably not turn the tide in his favor.

"It is inexcusable to cause cancer in children." Fumiko had choked back a sob as she said this, and the recollection of it once again came to Daigo. She had told him about a young girl in her neighborhood whom she had been tutoring in French who had died of cancer. Probably that night as she listened to Daigo's story she had come to hate Yoshimi as much as Daigo did. As a result, she had secretly taken action.

Daigo realized that his wife was watching him with sullen suspicion.

"The Minami Foods case is going to take some time yet," he answered irrelevantly, and took a gulp of tea. He quickly turned his attention to the next New Year's card. He glanced at the address and turned the card over. He was going through the cards more or less automatically when he came to a picture postcard that was mixed in with the others. The photograph on the front of the card depicted a mountain and a lake. His eyes swept quickly over the photo, which showed an excursion boat on the lake.

"Oh, that's Hakone," murmured Shihoko under her breath. Daigo also, of course, recognized the scene. Looming in the background over the lake was the snowcapped peak of Mount Fuji. The lake was obviously Ashinoko.

When Daigo turned the card over, a name and address were written in well-formed script. The white space reserved for a message was left blank. Beneath the postage stamp was merely a rubber stamp saying, "Happy Holidays." The name of the person who had sent it was missing, but the words "Emerald View Hotel" were printed on the left-hand edge of the card in a Gothic script. On the side of the card were printed the address and telephone number of the hotel. The photograph really depicted the hotel. Apparently the sender had merely scribbled in the addressee's name and address and dropped it in the mail.

Seeing the name Emerald View Hotel brought Daigo to a sudden stop, it seemed as though he was stunned by the memory. That night, Fumiko had said something about "Midori Nagahara, the eldest daughter of the owners of the Emerald View Hotel. Two years ago she killed someone, and ever since that time I have told myself that I would have to kill her."

Daigo felt he recognized the handwriting in the address on the card. It was very similar to the educated hand he had noticed on the envelope of the special delivery letter that had arrived in his office from Emerald Estates. Daigo realized that he was breathing fast, and tried to calm himself. As he slowly let his breath out, he thought, Up until now I have intended to show that I have received Fumiko's message and that I have understood it, but now it seems I have only understood half of it.

At this point Shihoko said, "I wonder why a Hakone hotel sent us a New Year's card? Have you ever stayed there?"

"No. Never. But I may have to go there in the near future. They are hosting a symposium there."

Nine days later, on Monday, January 10—

Kohei Daigo elected to stay at a small Japanese-style inn

somewhat south of the mountain, even though it was near Ashinoko. It was called the Fumotokan and was about a ten-minute walk to the Emerald View Hotel. From his room, Daigo could see the white, rather old-fashioned front of that hotel.

Hakone itself was experiencing a quiet period after all the New Year's holiday guests had left. Even now the clouds hung low, as though they were bringing snow, and the temperature was down, so there were very few cars on the roads around the lake.

The forest pressed close to the rugged shoreline of the lake, and the open areas were covered with leafless bushes. The whole scene was encircled by mountains, and the landscape shaded from ash gray to a cold ice blue. Here and there throughout the forest were mounds of old melting snow. Northeast of the lake, where one would expect to see Mount Fuji, its outline was only faintly visible in the mist.

Daigo arrived at the inn at about three o'clock and was now sitting on the ledge of the window of his second-floor room, his elbows resting on the railing. For a long time he just sat gazing at the chilly landscape.

He had not expected to be given a room from which he could actually see the Emerald View Hotel, but since he was able from this room to see a corner of the building, it was easy to engage the maid in some conversation about it. The young maid had talked endlessly ever since Daigo had arrived, for he had made an effort to make her feel that he was a guest who was fond of such chatter, but when he was alone his expression returned to one of gloomy nervousness. After he had gazed at the Emerald View for a time, a frown appeared on his face.

When he had thought about Hakone while still in Fukuoka, it had seemed very far away, but, using a combination of airplane and train, it had taken him less than five hours to arrive here. After flying to Tokyo, he had taken the bullet train to Odawara, and from there a bus to Kojiri. Some may think five hours is a long trip, but because of the numerous transfers, Daigo had been left dizzy by the speed of his travel. It was still hard for him to grasp the fact that he was really in Hakone. Even though he could actually see the Emerald View Hotel, he wanted to take another look at the postcard. It seemed as though very little time had elapsed between the time he decided to take this action and when he actually did it. The very fact that he had come here seemed unbelievably out of character for him.

From that moment on New Year's Day when he had first seen the postcard from the Emerald View, he knew it was another message. Until he saw the name of the hotel, he had thought Yoshimi's murder had been an isolated incident. Thanks to someone's careful planning he had an alibi, and the mystery woman in the case had not been apprehended, and as the unsolved murder faded further and further into the past, he had supposed that the matter was finished. In thinking that, he had gone only halfway; the Yoshimi murder was only half of the total incident.

That night in the salon of the restaurant at Barbizon, he had actually confessed that he wanted to see Yoshimi dead, but prior to that Fumiko had said that there was a certain woman who must die. "My heart will have no peace until that woman is dead," said Fumiko. Even if Fumiko had only been speaking metaphorically, it made Daigo realize that he himself could not get on with his life until he got Yoshimi out of the way. Had not the realization that they were conspirators in crime been a powerful force on both of them, both physically and emotionally?

Indeed it had. Apparently at that time Fumiko had already formulated her plan to make them fellow criminals. Perhaps she had been working out that plan in her mind while Daigo had been sitting in silence. At the very least it was certain that she now expected Daigo to eliminate Midori Nagahara. Fumiko had never met and did not know Akishige Yoshimi, but she had found out who he was, created a perfect alibi for Daigo, and had committed the crime without making a slip. That is, assuming that Fumiko was the mystery woman in the investigation. Daigo had come to believe that this was the only possible explanation for what had happened. His receipt of the Emerald View card was her way of saying that it was now time to implement the second half of the plan.

Midori Nagahara was someone Daigo did not know and had never met. For that very reason it would be possible for him to get close to her without her knowing it. At the same time, he hoped this might bring him into contact with Fumiko Samejima. He supposed that Fumiko was one of Midori's acquaintances and that some significant link must exist between the two women.

The expectation that he might actually discover who this Fumiko was provided a great motivating power to spur Daigo to immediate action. In any case, the first thing he had to do was collect some information on Midori Nagahara in secret.

As far as his trip to Hakone was concerned, Daigo was still on his winter holiday from school and his lectures for the next term had not yet begun, so this was a convenient time for him. He had consulted a guidebook on his own and selected this inn. He had given Shihoko some vague explanation to the effect that his laboratory and a laboratory from a university in Tokyo were getting together for a joint symposium. She thought the meeting was being held at a hotel in Tokyo, and he said he would call her when he got there. He had not mentioned anything at all to his wife about Hakone. Shihoko was not the sort of wife who pried into the details of her husband's business traveling, and by all appearances, she had already forgotten about the post-card from the Emerald View Hotel.

"May I come in?" Daigo heard the voice of the maid outside the door to his room. Daigo quickly fumbled a pair of sunglasses from his pocket and put them on. The sunglasses had thick black frames and pale green lenses; he had found them in an optical shop in Fukuoka the other day. Daigo ordinarily had a long nose and an ordinary-looking face, but the sunglasses made him look younger and sportier.

The maid was a smallish woman in her forties who clearly gave the impression of being an old-timer. "Have you had a chance to bathe yet?" As she knelt by the door-way the maid asked her question as she eyed the padded kimono intended for the use of guests, but which Daigo had ignored.

"Uh, no. I'm afraid I have been so absorbed in the beauty of the scenery here that I've just been sitting here gazing out at the lake. I generally visit Hakone in the spring and in the autumn, but this is the first time I've been here in over a year." Daigo tried to use an Osaka accent as he spoke. Although he himself had come from a different part of the country, his mother's relatives lived in Osaka, and since childhood he had had many opportunities to listen to the Osaka dialect, so it was not that difficult for him to imitate it. When he registered at the inn, he had used a false name and had given an Osaka address. He put down that he was a writer.

"I have noticed that Hakone really changes from year to year. It seems that hotels and summer homes are constantly springing up," the maid said.

"Maybe so, but that sort of change is not evident in the view from here. Although I suppose that hotel over there, the one they call the Emerald, is an exception."

"That would be the Emerald View," said the maid with

a curious look as Daigo leaned out the window wearing his sunglasses.

"Yes, I guess you're right about that. I stayed there in the spring more than a year ago. I was with a couple of friends—we were on our way back from Tokyo. One of my friends was particularly fond of the daughter of the owner of that hotel. As it turned out, I didn't have a chance to meet her, but I wonder if she really is attractive."

"Oh yes, they have two daughters there."

"I suppose they help run the hotel."

"Well, I don't know about that. They don't live at the hotel, and they spend most of their time at home."

"You are talking about the home of the people who own the Emerald View, aren't you?"

"Yes, I am."

The maid seemed well informed about things that were happening in the neighborhood. She was not very talkative, but he had given her a suitable tip when he had first arrived, so she was willing to be quite sociable.

"I suppose she is quite attractive. You would expect that of a person who made a living by running a hotel in lovely surroundings such as these. I personally am very fond of Hakone. I always end up staying here longer than I had planned. But for a young lady like that, this must seem a very boring and dreary place."

"Both the daughters of that family went to school in Tokyo, and now they have returned here to their home."

"I would like to have a chance to meet them, but I suppose they are very busy with their friends. I suppose if I went to the hotel and looked, I might meet one of them."

He learned where the family lived, and, deciding that was enough information for one time, he changed the subject. He thought it would not be a good idea to be too persistent. He had broken out in a sweat just from hearing this information.

Then, as though the maid had suddenly remembered something, she said, "I did hear that the older daughter sometimes plays the piano in the restaurant at the hotel. Apparently she graduated from a musical conservatory in Tokyo."

At that point Daigo asked when dinner was served, and asked the maid to bring it to his room at that time.

As she was leaving, the maid gave Daigo a doubtful look. After all, it was a very cold day, and he was sitting there with the window open looking out, and that seemed peculiar to her. Daigo, as though reading her thoughts, suddenly stood up, closed the window, and seated himself on the floor.

The maid pursed her lips, as though she found this also strange, then opened the door and left the room. Even though he tried to behave in a perfectly natural fashion, Daigo felt he always seemed to inspire some look of strangeness in the eyes of others. After the maid left, Daigo realized that he was bathed in sweat. From now on he would have to be more careful about how he acted.

The inn served a light dinner at an early hour, and afterwards Daigo walked down the road that followed the lakeshore toward the Emerald View Hotel. Along this route the road passed relatively close to the lakeshore.

The hotel itself was at the foot of a private road leading down toward the lake from the highway, and the hotel was screened by a grove of Himalayan cedars. It was a square, white-painted, three-story building, and it was really quite small compared to the resort hotels that are being built today. It's white paint was peeling, and it had an old and shabby look, yet it seemed to have a special character all its own.

The front of the hotel was in shadow, and he could make out the shapes of two or three cars parked there. The lobby was also very quiet.

As he passed through the lobby, which was decorated with a stuffed eagle, he found that the main dining room was right in front of him. The dining room, with its elegant chandelier, was in the classic style, and there were perhaps four or five groups of guests seated at the tables. In the far corner of the room was a dark, wine-colored piano, but no pianist. Daigo walked over to the piano.

He looked out the window through a lace curtain. The lawn of the garden spread out in a casual manner, and at the foot of the garden was the lake itself. He also caught a glimpse of a small jetty with several boats bobbing around it. Off to the right was a low hedge, but it was quite a large garden.

Daigo seated himself at an inconspicuous table near the piano, and when the waiter came, he ordered Scotch and smoked salmon.

When the waiter returned with his drink, he casually glanced toward the piano and asked, ''Will the young lady be playing this evening?'' Of course he spoke in an Osaka accent.

''Maybe,'' said the waiter.

''No, listen, I mean it. The young lady of the house sometimes plays the piano here. I've heard her, she is really good. Will she be entertaining us tonight?''

''Well, unfortunately she does not play every night.''

''When is she scheduled to play next, don't you even know that?''

''I don't know for sure. Please wait a minute.''

A short time later the waiter placed a plate of smoked salmon before Daigo and said, ''The chief told me that the young lady you asked about will be playing tomorrow night. Apparently some of her acquaintances will be staying here at the hotel tomorrow night. You might want to give us a telephone call tomorrow to confirm it.''

''No, I'll just come back tomorrow.''

The following day there were occasional breaks in the clouds, and in the late afternoon there were even periods of sunshine. But the cold chill of the winter mountains was nevertheless in the air. The surface of the lake was calm and leaden.

Before noon Daigo left the inn and walked in the direction of Midori Nagahara's house. It was located about two kilometers north of the Emerald View Hotel and was a Western-style house situated on a sloping piece of land near Togendai. He had learned the location of the house both from the waiter at the hotel and from the maid at the inn. He was able to find his way right to the house without difficulty. For a time the road to Togendai moved away from the shore of the lake and made its way up the slope to the east, running through forests and open spaces. In this neighborhood the homes were surrounded by hurricane fencing or by natural hedges, and he could see the naked walls of the homes surrounded by their withered lawns and gardens.

Daigo walked on for some distance past the house and noticed that there were a number of other unique houses in the area, but none of them could be mistaken for the one he was looking for. Daigo verified the house by seeing the plaque on the doorpost that had the name Nagahara on it. He took a good look at the place to familiarize himself with it and then returned back down the road.

Tonight he would have a chance to get close to Midori herself. He felt a certain amount of tension and anxiety about the encounter. Nevertheless, he returned to the inn and passed the time reading a book. By 5:30 he had finished eating the dinner provided by the inn and had set out for the Emerald View. Tonight the lobby was more lively than it had been the night before.

As he walked toward the dining room, Daigo happened to notice a young man and a young woman talking in a corner of the lobby, and before he realized it, he had come to a stop and stood taking in the woman's figure.

At first glance she appeared to be in her mid-twenties. She had pale golden skin, and her features resembled those of a Westerner. She was quite tall, and her lithe body was draped in a long, chic dress of emerald green. An opal necklace hung in the cleft of her breasts. But what originally attracted Daigo to the woman was the fact that she clutched a sheaf of sheet music. It suddenly occurred to him that this must be Midori Nagahara.

The man she was talking to was in his thirties, dressed in a well-tailored dark suit. He was smiling casually and talking to the woman, but he did not seem to be listening to what she was saying.

Daigo cast a brief glance at the man, but his attention was focused on the woman. She appeared to be very elegant. Yet beneath her high cheekbones there was a gray area, and even when she smiled, there seemed to be something cold about her. Apparently the man was telling a joke, for the woman's face cracked momentarily and she smiled, and in that smile one could see her haughty arrogance.

*She is arrogant, and her heart is as cold as ice. It was because of that arrogance and pride that two years ago she killed a person.* Fumiko's words echoed in Daigo's ears.

Daigo absorbed the shock of this encounter by telling himself that it was just fate that he should see her this way. He was sorry he was not able to get a glimpse of her profile.

# 6

# The Objective

MIDORI NAGAHARA PERFORMED A CASUAL PROGRAM, IN-cluding such popular classics as Chopin waltzes and Bee-thoven's "Moonlight" Sonata, as well as some contemporary folk music. Tonight most of the tables were occupied, and the room was filled with a mood of quiet intensity. She had chosen to perform tonight, not because of the crowd, but because one of her former professors from the music conservatory was staying at the hotel with his wife. Daigo had learned this much from the waiter the previous night. He also learned that in addition to this din-ing room, the hotel had a nightclub located just off the garden, where a professional band played.

The special guest was easily spotted. He was a frail old gentleman with long, silver hair, and with him was his rather flabby wife, dressed in a faded brown velvet dress. Seated next to the old couple was a third person, a young lady in a dazzling blue pantsuit. They were all seated at a table just to the right of Midori, and as she finished playing each piece they politely clapped longer than necessary.

The man who had been talking to Midori at the entrance of the dining room the previous night was now seated near the wall on the opposite side of her, where he smoked and watched. From where he was sitting he could have seen nothing but Midori's back. Daigo was seated two tables away from the first group, and of course he was alone. He could see Midori's profile through the crowd of people.

When the applause burst out at the conclusion of each piece, Midori acknowledged the audience with a smile and a slight nod. Nevertheless, there was a cold, calculating look in her deep gray eyes, and she never had eye contact with anyone, but preferred to look slightly over the heads of the audience. Daigo had already noticed that it was not possible to catch Midori's eye. From the first glimpse he had of her, he was overcome by a mysterious feeling of dread that here was a woman he had been destined to encounter at some point in his life. The dread came from his expectation that here was a case where the murderer would be murdered. He already instinctively understood that Midori was his target.

No. He had to relax a little. He had to give himself a little more latitude. He still had not made up his mind for certain that he was going to do it. He thoughtfully picked at his fish and sipped a little white wine. There was an intermission in the performance.

Leaving the sheet music on the piano, Midori came down from the low platform where she had been performing and went to the table of the three guests. Daigo looked down at his plate but pricked up his ears to overhear their conversation. They exchanged amiable greetings and compliments. Daigo could not quite make out the words, but he did get a sense of the mood of their talk. Once in a while he would catch a word, such as "professor," but that was all. Midori's voice was not all that high-pitched, but it was penetrating. Later came the voice of the professor, which was the voice of an elderly man. He seemed to be speaking to her in a fatherly manner. As far as the other two women were concerned, they had their backs to Daigo, so he could hear nothing of what they said.

The older woman coughed from time to time. She had coughed occasionally during the performance, but now that it was intermission she coughed more frequently. The young lady who was with her would pat her on the back each time she coughed. With each spell of coughing, the others would stop talking and look at the old woman.

After this happened two or three times, the young woman stood up and said something, but all Daigo heard were the words "grandmother" and "medicine." Apparently she was going to their room to fetch the old woman's medicine. The young lady began to thread her way between the tables, and Daigo felt her pass behind him. He could smell the fragrance of her makeup. Just after the girl had passed Daigo's table, the older woman turned around and called, "Fumiko," and the young lady stopped.

"Yes?" she replied in a low voice.

"I believe it would be better if I went to my room and lay down for a bit. I will have to apologize for not being able to attend the rest of the concert." Even before she had finished speaking, the old woman coughed slightly, pushed back her chair, and stood up.

Midori and the old man each made some remark, and the young lady returned to the table. They continued their discussion for a moment, then the young woman put her arm around the older woman's shoulder and together they set out across the dining room. As they passed behind Daigo for the second time, the old woman's elbow brushed against Daigo's neck and the younger woman said, "Excuse me."

Even though he looked up, the two women were still beyond his line of vision behind him, so he turned the upper part of his body. Daigo's heart was beating wildly. Fumiko. The older woman had definitely called her that. Up to this point all of Daigo's nervous attention had been focused on Midori, and he had paid no attention to this other young woman. He had not even looked very closely at her face. Was it mere chance that her name happened to be Fumiko?

The moment the pair left the dining room and the waiter closed the door, Daigo was on his feet. He threw his napkin down on the table as he turned away. Midori and the old man where still talking together. If he hurried too quickly, they might realize he was following the two women who had just left. Daigo tried to keep the sound of his footsteps as quiet as possible as he cut across the dining room.

He saw the two women at the edge of the lobby heading for the corridor that led to the guest rooms. Daigo stopped to gaze at a stuffed eagle in the lobby, waiting for the right moment to make his move. When he finally did go to the corridor, it appeared that the women had gone upstairs. He could hear the sound of coughing coming from the stairwell. The elevator was on the opposite side of the lobby in a rather hidden location. Nevertheless, the fact that they had chosen to use the stairs suggested that their room was on the second floor.

Again Daigo timed himself before making his move. He took off the sunglasses he had been wearing all evening and put them in his pocket. When he reached the second floor, he saw the two women just going into a room halfway along the corridor. The older woman went in first, and the young lady in the blue pantsuit followed and closed the door.

Daigo hurried to their door, went a little past it, stopped, and looked back at the door. Above the cream-colored door was the room number, 237. There was no sound, neither in the corridor nor from any of the rooms. Daigo held his breath and waited. Beyond that door were Fumiko and the old lady. What were the chances that this Fumiko was Fumiko Samejima, his Fumiko?

Up till now he had always suspected that the name she had given him that night might be a false one. He felt there was a strong possibility of that. On the other hand, the name Midori Nagahara had been real, so that might suggest that the name Fumiko Samejima was for real also. Perhaps the fact that he still thought there was a chance that Fumiko was a fictitious name stemmed from his own innate sense of pessimism. There was also the fact that this woman named Fumiko had some sort of relationship with Midori. He knew that the old man had been Midori's teacher at the conservatory, and this Fumiko was clearly closely related to them.

At this point it suddenly occurred to Daigo that Fumiko may have anticipated that he would be in the hotel tonight and had chosen this opportunity to reveal herself. Having thought things through to this point, he gathered his courage as he continued to stare at the door. He had been thinking about coming to Hakone ever since New Year's and on January 6 had telephoned to Tokyo to make his airline reservation. Since he had told his wife this was a working trip, he had used his real name for the ticket. Was it possible that Fumiko had been keeping an eye on him, and knowing his schedule had made a point to be at the hotel tonight? When he thought back on the fact that she had cleverly sent him that original message, and later had been able to put in an appearance as the mystery woman in the

Yoshimi murder and then disappear, it seemed that even this was possible.

At that point his reveries were interrupted when he noticed that the door to room 237 was beginning to open. In confusion he retreated several steps. The thick carpet muffled the sound of his footsteps.

Fumiko emerged from the room and closed the door behind her, took a few steps, and stopped in front of room 236. Taking a key from her purse, she opened the door and went in.

Since Daigo had gone past the rooms and was standing in the corridor on the other side, he only saw Fumiko from behind. She was of medium build and medium height, and generally speaking appeared to have a nice figure. Her hair was short, coming to ear length, and was wavy.

She emerged from the second room moments later wearing a wool jacket over her blue pantsuit. Daigo had retired further toward the end of the corridor, hoping she would not notice his presence. He stood paralyzed as she walked away down the corridor toward the stairs. The whole thing seemed unreal to him.

Daigo left the Emerald View right away and followed the highway until he came to a drive-in restaurant where he killed time until nine. Earlier he had seen Fumiko return to the dining room. When he had looked into the dining room he had seen Midori, the silver-haired old man, and Fumiko talking together. There was no question that soon Midori would once again resume her place at the piano. In any case, he decided that he would have to be very careful about approaching Fumiko while the three of them were together. In the meantime, he felt very conspicuous hanging around the lobby by himself. Insofar as possible, he wanted to make sure he was not remembered by the people of the Emerald View Hotel. For that reason he chose to wait at a large drive-in restaurant with a golf driving range attached where he could spend his time unnoticed.

He still did not have any confidence that nine was some sort of magic hour. It was just that he supposed that the old man would have retired by that time. His voice had sounded feeble, and he appeared to be close to seventy, and his wife was surely not in good health.

Apparently the old couple were staying in room 237 and Fumiko was staying alone in room 236. If this Fumiko was the Fumiko he thought she was, and if she had been aware of his presence, then the moment she was alone she would be expecting some sort of contact from him. At the same time, even if everything was as he thought, a young lady would be reluctant about being lured out of her hotel room after nine o'clock.

At the drive-in, Daigo walked over to a public telephone in one corner. Fortunately this restaurant had four pay phones, each with its own enclosure. As it turned out, all the phones were in use, but he waited around one that had no line of people waiting for it, and at 9:06 he made his call.

A man's voice answered, and Daigo asked to be connected with room 236.

"Room 236? That would be Ms. Naruse."

"That's right."

"One moment, please."

In the receiver Daigo could hear the phone ringing again. After two and a half rings a voice said, "Hello?" It was a young voice, and undoubtedly feminine.

"May I speak to Fumiko Naruse?"

"That is I."

"I see. I am . . ." Daigo suddenly repressed an urge to divulge his real name. It was quite possible that there was someone else in the room with her. And it was by no means certain that this woman was the Fumiko he thought she was. After all, her family name was not Samejima.

"I'm sorry, excuse me. I wonder if you are the person I met some time ago while I was traveling."

"While traveling? Where?" asked Fumiko in a puzzled tone.

"France. Paris."

The woman was silent for a time. Then she suddenly seemed to remember. "Ah, yes," she said.

A surge of stressful pain seemed to seize Daigo's chest.

"Were you on the tour we took two years ago?" continued Fumiko in an untroubled manner.

Perhaps she was determined to conceal her identity until she had the opportunity to meet Daigo face to face. This was the thought that passed through Daigo's mind.

"Yes, I was on the tour with you. I saw you this evening in the dining room at the hotel and it brought back memories."

"Oh, really. I have received other phone calls from people who were on that tour."

"I'm sorry to bother you, but I wondered if we could get together?"

"Where are you now?"

"I'm very close to your hotel."

Again there was silence as Fumiko did not respond. Finally, "All right. I'll meet you in the lobby in a few minutes."

"Great. Well, no. It will be hard to relax in the lobby. How would it be if we met in the nightclub. It is off to the right of the lobby, and it is quiet there."

"Yes. I know the place."

Daigo took this response to indicate that she was indeed familiar with the Emerald View Hotel. This, of course, would be expected if she was the Fumiko he thought she was.

"All right, then. I'll meet you there in a few minutes."
As he hung up the phone, he felt drenched in sweat. But
he realized he did not have a moment to waste. He had
told her he would meet her in a few minutes. He had told
her he was right near the hotel, and she might go immediately to the nightclub. It would take him six or seven
minutes to walk from the drive-in to the hotel.

As he stepped out into the chilly darkness, the sweat
gave him an unpleasant clammy feeling. When he reached
the lane leading to the hotel, the wind was blowing in off
the frozen lake through the Himalayan cedars. Daigo broke
into a run.

The nightclub seemed far more spacious than the dining
room. Tables lined the walls on three sides of the room.
In the center of the room was a stage for the band, but it
was deserted now. In front of it was a large clear space
that served as a dance floor.

Daigo paused at the door to catch his breath, and as he
did so, he surveyed the room, which was bathed in orange
light. There were clusters of people at various tables, and
the place had a very quiet mood. It had been the same last
night when he had peeked in. Not only was the holiday
season past, it was a weekday, so the hotel seemed largely
deserted. He could not see anyone resembling Fumiko
among the sprinkling of guests. Apparently she had not yet
come.

Daigo heaved a sigh of relief and slumped down in the
nearest empty seat. Just as he took out his handkerchief to
wipe his face he saw a woman enter the room. She had an
oval face and short hair. She was wearing a dress with a
floral pattern on a black background, but he recognized the
jacket draped over her shoulders. It was Fumiko all right.
Earlier she had been wearing a pantsuit, but he recognized
the way she walked.

Daigo suddenly felt tense. Fumiko stopped in the middle

of the dance floor and looked around the room. When Daigo raised a hand and signaled to her, she approached his table.

She appeared to be in her late twenties and had a surprisingly plump oval face. She had gracefully curved eyebrows and rather thick lips under a large nose, and a narrow jaw. At first glance she gave the impression of being a woman who had not been raised in a first-class family.

Fumiko also looked intently at Daigo. She had an artificial smile on her lips, but she obviously could not place him.

"Good evening. It's been a long time." He tried to greet her as warmly as possible as he offered her a seat. Fumiko looked around, noticed that there was no one at any of the adjoining tables, and took a seat opposite Daigo. Once again she looked closely at him as though trying to remember if she had met him before.

"Let's see, excuse me if I am mistaken, but aren't you the one who was on the tour with a friend? As I recall, the friend is in the advertising business." Fumiko murmured this as she plumbed her memory for a way to identify Daigo. Her voice was low-pitched. Now that he talked to her directly he heard the same peculiar intonation he had heard on the telephone. On that night in France, Fumiko had had a deeper, huskier voice. Perhaps her voice was just different then because she was suffering from a cold and her throat hurt. "And if I remember correctly, you are a schoolteacher."

Daigo was startled. Was she using this roundabout way to convey a message to him?

"As I recall, you teach at a missionary school for high school girls, but I am afraid I don't remember your name."

"My name is Ikegami." That was the name Daigo had used when he registered at the inn.

"Mr. Ikegami. Yes, I think I am beginning to remember. You were very kind to me while we were on the tour."

The waiter came to take their order, bringing hot towels.

"What will you have to drink?" asked Daigo.

"Oh, I don't care, anything will do."

Daigo realized that his throat was very dry. He ordered beer and some snacks. As he wiped his sweaty palms with the hot towel he felt himself begin to tremble.

Up till now he had been confident that if he met Fumiko, or rather the woman he had met before, he would know immediately that it was she. This was not a rational thing, but some sort of instinctive self-confidence. But now that this Fumiko was sitting in front of him, he could not be sure whether it was the woman he had met that night in France or not. There was something in her features that seemed familiar to him, that reminded him of someone, but he could make no immediate connections. After all he had not seen either the face or the figure of the woman he had met on that dark night in the salon of the Château Chantal.

Long ago there had been a time when he was a student when he had gone camping with some friends during the summer holiday. They had enjoyed folk dancing with some other young people. Even though they had a campfire burning, it had been too dark to make out the features of his partner. The strange thing about it was that even though they changed partners often, they knew instinctively when they came back to their original partner. They did not keep count as they changed partners, but it was something they knew very clearly, and it had been a thrilling experience. The next morning he had searched the campground looking for the girl who had been his partner, but he could not find her. The memory of that distant experience came back to Daigo now with surprising clarity.

In a sense, his awareness of things in the dark had a

certain sharpness that could not be obtained by direct sight. But no, that is not right. What had passed between Daigo and Fumiko that night had been an ultrahuman sort of deep and direct understanding of each other. Daigo still believed that it was a once-in-a-lifetime sort of communication. It was for that reason he had been confident that he would recognize Fumiko at a single glance. On the other hand, if this was not the right Fumiko, she would think he was a pretty bizarre individual.

If this was the right Fumiko, she was being far more cautious than Daigo, and if she was not absolutely certain of his identity, she might not reveal her own true self. Even though she may have been able to learn his travel plans, she might still not know what he looked like. More than anything else, he must not forget that this woman had already carried out her part of the plan. It was even possible that the woman might suspect that Daigo could be a detective.

Daigo began to respond with a natural and noncommittal patience. The only thing he could do was proceed cautiously and show his hand. Their drinks and snacks arrived, and the waiter filled their glasses with beer. Daigo raised his glass to face level, and Fumiko responded with a similar salute.

"So, are you and Midori old friends?"

"Oh, do you know Midori?" asked Fumiko, thrusting out her jaw.

"No, not really. I just heard that she is the daughter of the people who run this hotel and that she sometimes plays the piano here, so I thought I would come tonight and listen to her play."

"Yes. She is really very good on the piano. Tonight she did a special performance for my uncle."

"Your uncle? Is he the man I saw you with in the dining room?"

"Yes. When Midori was at the music conservatory she was a student of his. Since then my uncle has retired from teaching, but he is still on the board of trustees for the conservatory. I suppose Midori was one of the very last students he taught."

"And that is his wife who was with him?"

"It is a tradition with them to come to Hakone for some peace and quiet every summer and winter holiday, and I usually come with them. My aunt is in poor health, and besides, I work as my uncle's assistant at the conservatory."

"I see. So you and Midori are pretty good friends."

"No, I wouldn't say that. I have only met her three or four times either here or at my uncle's house." The woman's answer seemed completely natural.

Nevertheless, Fumiko seemed to have something in mind, and that feeling only made Daigo all the more uneasy. Even though he felt on the defensive, he decided to go one step further.

"How many times have you been to France?"

"Three times, including the time we were on that tour."

"Have you ever been there by yourself?"

"No, I've always gone with friends. Once I went with my aunt and uncle."

"Where do you spend most of your time when you go to France? Personally I prefer the southern outskirts of Paris better than the city itself." He caught Fumiko's eye as he spoke and lowered his voice. "I like the Loire region— Fountainebleau and Barbizon."

Fumiko blinked her eyes and said, "The old châteaux in the Loire region are wonderful, aren't they. But so far I have never been anywhere outside of Paris. I always plan to do some traveling, but end up spending all my time shopping on the Champs-Elysées." Fumiko tightened her mouth and laughed silently.

A surprising thought occurred to Daigo when he saw the expression on her face. A deep feeling of gloom swept over his heart. He knew that Fumiko vaguely reminded him of someone, but up till now he could not remember who: it was a girl classmate of his in high school. The school he had attended was in a town of about 30,000 in the rural part of Kyushu where he had been born and raised. His family had been poor farmers, and the girl was the daughter of a family that had owned a hospital for several generations. In school she was part of a clique composed of other rich kids. Consequently Daigo did not have much contact with her, and neither of them paid much attention to the other.

On one occasion the girl fell ill with something or other and missed two weeks of school. When she came back, she asked to borrow Daigo's notes. Although she usually didn't talk to him, the reason she now asked for his notes was that he was widely considered one of the brainiest kids in the class. Daigo, of course, could hardly refuse, and in fact he not only agreed to copy the notes for her, he also promised to bring them to her house. He carried out the promise, and on a cold and rainy afternoon in early winter he took the notes to her house, where he was shown into the living room and served tea. She gave him a rectangular box wrapped in department store paper, saying it was a gift for him. After that he got the feeling that she wanted him to leave, so he did, after being there less than fifteen minutes.

When he got home, Daigo opened the package and saw that it was a foreign-made Cross pencil set. If that had been the end of the matter it would not be worth remembering, but later he learned that the day he took the notes to the girl's house had been her birthday, and that at the time of his visit she was entertaining a number of classmates at a birthday party in another part of the house. The party included both boys and girls. Since the party was in progress when he arrived with the notes, she had quickly given Daigo the gift and gotten rid of him. It would have been much nicer if she had invited him to the party rather than just giving him a Cross pencil set, and the experience left Daigo feeling bitter toward her. He did not particularly want to be included in her circle of friends, but he would have felt much better about the whole thing if she had been decent enough to invite him to the party. He felt discriminated against. She probably felt she did not want to associate with people who did not belong to the same social class she did.

After graduating from high school he had heard that she had gone to a women's college in Nagasaki, and no doubt by now she had met some nice young man from her own social class, married him, and he would inherit her family's hospital.

Daigo's family was so poor they could not even afford to send him to college, even though he was the eldest son. But he had attracted the attention of one of his teachers, who urged his parents to send him to college, and finally after promising to pay for his room and board by working his way through school, he was able to get into college.

His parents were both dead now, and their small farm had been inherited by Daigo's younger brother, who worked in a factory and tried to run the farm at the same time.

This Fumiko who was sitting in front of him smiling reminded Daigo of the girl who had asked for his notes. With her large nose, pursed lips, and high-toned way of speaking, she resembled his former classmate to a remarkable degree. This sort of face for Daigo was symbolic of a certain type of woman, a type that called to mind a whole range of negative feelings, including revulsion, irritation, and humiliation. Perhaps he had realized this from the very first moment he had confronted Fumiko. He had known it, but unconsciously he had turned his eyes away from that fact.

At that moment the lights in the nightclub suddenly went out. In their place a bright white spotlight hit the center of the room. Four or five band members and a woman singer in a sequined gown appeared in the circle of light. The show was about to begin.

The area around Daigo's table was in complete darkness. When he looked across at Fumiko he was startled again. She had moved her chair around in order to see the show and was now sitting with her back to Daigo. Against the background of the spotlight her face and legs glowed whitely. They were surprisingly beautiful legs: slim, taut, and without a bit of slack on them. Again he recalled the stormy night and the woman who had been sitting in the wingback chair in the French salon. Etched in the back of his memory was the vision of her seen in a momentary flash of lightning when he had seen her profile and legs in just this same way. Once again he was filled with uncertainty about whether or not this was Fumiko. She had the same elegant manner of speaking that Fumiko had and the same artificial smile. Could this be someone impersonating her? Now that they were isolated together in the darkness he wondered if she might give some definite sign that she was Fumiko. The pure passion of that night in France was revived for Daigo.

Even though he recognized intellectually that the woman's features and manner of speaking reflected the inner woman, he doubted, even if this was Fumiko, that they could recreate the intoxication of that stormy night in France. Indeed, there was no reason to suppose they could. By recreating the physical and emotional unity of that moment, the woman's face and voice were transformed into those he most desired, and he felt a new attitude toward her. No matter how abundantly blessed with time and opportunity, there would always be a question of how well a man and a woman understood each other until they knew they were mutually in love. In any case, the darkness had enabled him to see this woman in a new light. Even as Daigo watched, the woman swung her legs around and turned to face him.

"I'm afraid it's about time for me to be leaving." She held her arm up toward the light in order to see her watch. "It's time for my aunt to take her medicine. She suffers from asthma, and it seems to be particularly bad today."

Something in her tone seemed to suggest that maybe tomorrow . . . The thought flashed through Daigo's mind that he might have another chance to meet this woman. "Well, thank you very much. I'm afraid it was very rude of me to call you away like this on the spur of the moment." He tried to keep his voice calm and neutral as he spoke. "How long will you be staying here?"

"I think we will be here till the day after tomorrow."

"I see. I'm staying farther down toward Moto Hakone at an inn called the Fumotokan. If there is anything . . . I mean, I'll come here again tomorrow night about this same time."

A pleasant smile appeared on Fumiko's face, and she nodded slightly to him. Again he was reminded of the rich girl who had given him the Cross pencil set.

"Take care," said Daigo, and as she turned to walk away he said, "Oh, just a moment, there is one other thing I wanted to ask you. What characters do you use to write your name?"

"*Fumi* is the character meaning 'word,' and *ko* is the standard 'ko.' "

"I see. For some reason I had the impression that you used the *Fumi* that means 'history' for your name."

She looked at her watch once again and hurried away.

Daigo spent the whole of the following day in his room at the inn. The day he had arrived in Hakone had been heavily overcast and gloomy, but since yesterday the weather had been steadily improving. On his third day there, the sky was blue and the coldness had abated.

It made the maids at the inn nervous that he would stay shut up in his room on such a day, but he had various thoughts and feelings to contend with, and preferred the solitude. If Fumiko had been reluctant to reveal herself and her plans last night, then he expected he would have to give her some proof that he really was Kohei Daigo and that then they could have some secret communication.

Last night when they parted he had mentioned the name Fumiko with the proper characters. He had intended that as a definite sign that he was looking for the woman he had met in France. And yet, though he waited until evening, she still had not telephoned. At nine o'clock he set out for the nightclub at the Emerald View.

On his way through the hotel he stopped to take a look in the dining room, but he saw no sign of either Midori or Fumiko. He did see the man sitting at his table along the wall, just as he had been the previous night, whom he had previously seen talking to Midori in the corridor.

The nightclub was even quieter than it had been the previous night. He had created another opportunity for meeting Fumiko, but now Daigo regretted that he had not chosen another place to meet. Although he was not a guest at the hotel, he had been coming here so often during the past few days that people might notice and remember him. In fact, now that he thought about it, it probably would have been better if he had booked a room here in the first place. And yet, even last night he had not been able to immediately think of a suitable meeting place elsewhere. He decided that if Fumiko showed up again tonight he would invite her to go with him someplace where they could be alone.

So far it seemed as though he was doing everything wrong. But perhaps he need not worry too much about his excessive comings and goings at the Emerald View. After all he had not yet committed himself to doing anything wrong. He tried to turn his thoughts in directions that would help him relax. Tonight all he wanted was to get in touch with Fumiko.

Again tonight at 9:30 the lights went out and the show started. Daigo stayed in his place until 10:30, but Fumiko did not show up. He felt that during that time he was gradually able to regain a measure of sound judgment.

This woman clearly was not the Fumiko he wanted. It was only a coincidence that their names were pronounced the same way. After all, Fumiko was not such an unusual name.

He had thought his Fumiko was a magician and had ascribed supernatural powers to her in thinking that she would show up here at the hotel. He had definitely over-reacted. Just because this new Fumiko had nice legs did not mean she was the same woman he had met at Barbizon. Certainly he could not rely on his memory of a brief glimpse he had had of the woman's legs in France. In any case, it had been a hasty judgment to imagine that Fumiko Naruse was the woman he was looking for.

Although he could not construct in his mind the face and features of the Fumiko he was looking for, he was quite certain she was not like this woman he had met in Hakone. Having reached this conclusion, he felt a welcome sense of relief. When the show ended at 10:30, he left the club.

By the time he reached the corridor, he was already growing impatient. Today was his third day in Hakone. If he did not return to Fukuoka tomorrow his wife would surely grow suspicious. In fact he had called his wife earlier in the day and told her he would probably return to-morrow. Winter vacation was over, and he would soon have to begin his lectures, and it was quite possible that the university would be trying to get in touch with him about something.

At any rate, during his three days here he had gotten a good look at Midori Nagahara and had verified where she lived. The only thing he had failed to accomplish was to make contact with Fumiko. He still supposed that the only way he could go about locating her was through her personal relationship with Midori. He was sure there was an important link between the two women.

Just as Daigo reached the lobby of the hotel his attention was attracted by a figure of a dark-suited man crossing the lobby in front of him. It was the man he had seen talking to Midori two days ago and later sitting alone in the dining room. He had emerged from the corridor leading to the guest rooms and had disappeared in the opposite direction.

Daigo stood still for a moment, watching. He recalled the first time he had seen the man talking to Midori. On that occasion his whole attention had been on Midori, but he had had the impression that the man had told a joke and Midori was laughing. Later when he speculated on his impression he had decided that they seemed friendly and affable with each other. At the same time, it did not seem to be an intimate relationship. The fact that he had sat behind her when she was playing the piano so that he could only see her back seemed to reinforce that notion of their casual relationship. In fact, he recalled noticing a slightly cynical smile touch the man's lips each time Midori made a slight error in playing the piano.

Daigo paused for a moment, then followed into the L-shaped corridor. He stopped in a dark corner to take out his sunglasses. He had not worn them at all since the previous night, when he followed Fumiko to her room. In the

corridor was a small shop that sold magazines and medicines, and a game room, and diagonally across from them
was a door with old-fashioned silver letters saying BAR.
Compared to the dining room, this was apparently the old
part of the hotel. Even in the game room, which had slot
machines and pool tables, and in the small shop he could
see no trace of the man he was looking for.

Daigo pushed his way through the door leading to the
bar. It was a long narrow room with barely enough space
for the bar that spanned its length. The dim light gave the
place a forlorn look. At the far end of the room was the
man in the suit, talking into a public telephone. There were
only two other men in the place, and they were together in
the middle of the bar talking and drinking.

Daigo moved to a position between the two men at the
bar and the one talking on the telephone and sat down next
to the man on the phone. He noticed that this bar, like the
dining room, looked out on the garden, which sloped down
to the lake. Behind the man and facing the bar was a door
that opened onto the garden. Through an opening in the
curtains he could vaguely see a bit of the garden and the
lakeshore by the light of the garden lights. From time to
time a gust of wind rattled the door.

The bar was tended by a single, aging man in a white
shirt and apron. He took Daigo's order with his normal
bored expression. A quick glance to the side informed him
that the man beside him had a shot glass and a bottle of
Old Parr whiskey set out. That seemed to suggest that he
was a heavy drinker. Was it his normal practice to come
here for a few drinks after dinner before retiring to his
room?

Daigo ordered a whiskey sour. He was not opposed to
alcoholic beverages, but he was not much of a drinker.
Besides, right now he felt he needed all the self-control he
could muster.

The man beside him seemed to be making a business call; he was giving instructions to the person on the other end of the line. He used a lot of technical terms and foreign words and was talking about dollars and marks, but it was not clear what sort of business was being transacted.

Eventually the telephone conversation came to an end, and apparently the talk had dried the man's throat, for he raised his glass and took a long drink. Only then did he seem to notice that Daigo was sitting next to him and turned in Daigo's direction.

He had a broad forehead, slightly wavy hair, and large eyes. The flesh on his face was sleek and fat. His plump body was clothed in a dark suit, and his tie was dark red with silver dots. He appeared to be one who paid close attention to his clothes.

The man turned toward Daigo, and as their eyes met, Daigo smiled as though to say "Excuse me." The other man responded with a friendly nod.

Daigo's immediate assessment of the man was that he was one who would rather drink than eat. In a very short time he had knocked back three drinks, and Daigo remembered observing him in the dining room the previous night. He had smoked a lot but had not eaten much. Now he was signaling the bartender for a fourth drink.

That drink emptied the bottle of Old Parr, but the bartender quickly replaced it with a fresh bottle. There was a tag with the man's name on it on the empty bottle, and the bartender now transferred the tag to the new bottle. Unfortunately, from where he was sitting, it was difficult for Daigo to get a good look at the name on the tag. Nevertheless, it was clear that the man was a frequent guest at the hotel.

He sat facing straight at the bar, lit a cigarette, and with obvious pleasure blew the smoke straight out in front of him.

"Pardon me for intruding, but . . ." Daigo had tried to time his move. The man turned and looked at Daigo with his large eyes. "Didn't I see you standing in the lobby the other night talking to Midori Nagahara? Do you know her quite well?" Daigo spoke with a Kansai accent and fingered his sunglasses.

"Yes, I've known her for quite some time."

"I see. She is really very good on the piano. I was hoping I would be able to hear her play again this evening, but I was out of luck. Then I happened to see you in the lobby, and thought we might be able to talk a little, so I followed you here."

Had he gone too far in saying this? Daigo was terrified, but he felt he had to go on, and so he continued, making his Kansai accent as thick as possible.

"You want to talk to me?" The man laughed, but it seemed to be a pleasant laugh. He did not appear to be a snob, and with superficial pleasantness he waited to see what Daigo would say next.

"Yes. I'm the manager of a nightclub near Lake Biwa. My name is Yamashita. And yours?"

"I'm Umezaki. I'm from Tokyo."

Daigo reached for his business card. At the same time the other man also reached into an inside pocket and drew out a business card. As he placed it on the counter, Daigo said, "Oh, I'm sorry. I seem to have left my cards in my other jacket."

Umezaki's card read, "Sadao Umezaki, Managing Director, OS Trading Company."

"What sort of work do you do? I couldn't help overhearing you on the telephone a few minutes ago, and you were using some very difficult technical words."

"Not at all, it's just a trading company. We import farm machinery from West Germany—mostly specialized equipment."

"Oh, that's interesting. But to go back to what we were talking about before, I wonder if I might be able to book Midori to play for my club?"

"I wonder if she would be willing to go to Lake Biwa? I really don't know." Umezaki tilted his head and smiled as he brought his glass to his lips.

"Yesterday when I was here I cornered one of the waiters and asked her name, and I also learned that she is the daughter of the people who run this place, and that she graduated from the conservatory of music, and that she only plays here when she feels like it."

"That's pretty much the way it is. She is a very proud woman, and she certainly doesn't need the money. She might decline an invitation to come to the Kansai area to perform."

"I suppose if it was Tokyo, it would depend on the club."

"After graduating from the conservatory, she played for a while in a number of private clubs in Tokyo. Her father was opposed to it, and eventually he got her to come back here, where she now giving private lessons to a few children. For her it is almost like living in exile."

Umezaki spoke about Midori in an enthusiastic way, but it was apparent that there was some distance between him and Midori. Perhaps it was because he was slightly drunk, but when he spoke of Midori he had the same cynical expression on his face that he had had the previous night whenever she had made a mistake on the piano.

"I understand that she also has a younger sister."

"Yes. She is two years younger than Midori, and I have heard a rumor that they are actually half sisters, but they resemble each other."

"How old are they, would you suppose?"

"Midori is twenty-seven, so her sister is twenty-five."

"Is the younger sister also a musician?"

"No, the younger sister's name is Akane, and she is an artist. She paints."

"Those two are the only children?"

"That's right." Umezaki nodded, with his familiar bitter smile.

"I would suppose that charming young ladies like that are probably already engaged to be married." Even as he asked, Daigo realized that this question was too impatient; Umezaki would probably get the wrong impression of him. But Daigo felt he was on the right track. He did not know anyone else in the area whom he could ask for detailed information about Midori. Daigo ordered a second whiskey sour and continued the conversation about Midori.

"Excuse me for being personal, but what is your relationship with her?"

"No, no. You're off base there. I may look like a free spirit, but I have a wife and family of my own." Umezaki lifted the plump ring finger of his left hand and displayed a platinum wedding band. He waved the hand around several times in a grandiose motion. "To tell the simple truth, Midori is one of the few people I can talk to with utter frankness about anything whatsoever."

Daigo laughed at this and kept his eyes on the man.

"It's true, I tell you. Ask her for yourself and see."

Umezaki had had too much to drink, and he was a bit unsteady as he turned toward the entrance to the bar and gestured. He seemed to be hinting that he had an appointment to meet Midori here. It was all right to talk about Midori when she was not present, but now Daigo would have to be very careful what he said in case she should appear on the scene. He was moved by some sort of special caution in case he found himself face to face with the woman herself. Her features were already clearly engraved in his memory.

"I see. In that case, is Midori engaged to someone?"

Daigo noticed that his companion had begun to relax and decided that now was the time to make his move.

"No, I don't think there is anyone at the present time. There may be someone waiting in the wings that I don't know about, but she has been raised in a wealthy family, and it would be a rare individual who could maintain her in the manner to which she is accustomed."

"Even now?"

"I understand there was a young man who was in love with her some time ago. Unfortunately, he already had a wife, so they could not get married. Nevertheless, she seemed to have fallen deeply and truly in love with him." Umezaki's cynical smile disappeared from his eyes, and his gaze seemed to be shadowed by the past itself. He turned his gaze to the counter behind the bar. "As it turned out, the man she loved died. It happened about two years ago."

Daigo suddenly released a deep sigh of relief and, raising his glass to his lips, asked, "You say he died two years ago, but you make it sound as though there was something strange about his death. Was there?"

"He gassed himself, if that's what you mean. He generally worked at home. For the most part he translated French literature, but he also did some work in modern theater, and he had something of a reputation in that area."

"What was his name?"

"Michiya Kume. He was only thirty-three or thirty-four years old at the time of his death."

Daigo seemed to have some vague recollection of this name. He remembered reading about the matter two years ago in the local newspaper in Fukuoka. "Oh yes, I remember now. In the end they decided that it was an accident, didn't they?"

"At the time they carried out an investigation to determine if it was a suicide or an accident or a murder. When his wife returned in the evening to their apartment in Yot-suya, she found him lying on the floor in his study. The fire was off in the gas heater, and the room was filled with gas. Since there was no proof and no evidence in any other direction, they decided it was an accident, but Midori was extensively questioned in the matter."

Umezaki seemed to smile indulgently, and a blast of breath whistled through his nose. "He already had a wife, so they could not make their relationship public. Some thought the murder might have resulted from blind love."

"Ah . . ." Without realizing it, Daigo sighed a deep sigh. Was it possible that Umezaki could have understood the significance of that deep sigh? And yet Daigo remembered Fumiko as having said, *Two years ago that woman killed a man. The police carried out an investigation, but there was no evidence that he had been killed by some other person; but I know who it was who killed him.* Presently Daigo got hold of himself and responded, saying, "Does the widow of that Michiya Kume still live in Tokyo?"

"I'm sorry, I'm afraid I just don't know."

"I wonder if his widow is following in his footsteps and is continuing to translate French literature?"

Kohei Daigo left the mountains of Hakone after spending three nights there. When he stopped to consider the situation he realized that he had indeed accomplished his original goals. Those goals had been to check out the Emerald View Hotel, to get a look at Midori Nagahara, to find out what he could about her, to make certain she was the sort of woman Fumiko had described to him, and finally to try to seek out Fumiko herself.

He now knew the layout of the Emerald View Hotel, and he knew the location of Midori's house, which was some distance north of the hotel. He had had an opportunity to get a good look at Midori on several occasions. He had seen her in the lobby talking to Umezaki, and he had seen her again while she was playing the piano. The impression he had gotten of Midori corresponded exactly with the way he had pictured her from Fumiko's brief description. She had a glamorous, flamboyant air about her, and inside her there seemed to be a certain arrogance and a heart of ice. All of this was well reflected by the high nose, the cheekbones, and the gray eyes.

There was also the fact that a man with whom she had been intimate had died two years ago under suspicious circumstances. Having learned this much, Daigo parted with Umezaki and left the bar. Umezaki was pretty drunk by that time, and Daigo was afraid that if he kept asking questions about Midori he would become suspicious. Even now Daigo could not be completely sure that his own unusual inquisitiveness had gone undetected. And then the news that Midori herself might put in an appearance had driven him off. He was afraid that Umezaki might already have some faint suspicion that would cause him to remember Daigo. Still, he was hoping that in the event that Umezaki was ever questioned by the police, all he would be able to say would be, "He is a man who speaks with a Kansai accent who runs a nightclub at Lake Biwa."

On his way home Daigo took the bus From Hakone to make connections with the Odakyu Special Express, and he was in the Shinjuku district of Tokyo shortly after noon. From the station he took a taxi to the local library and asked for the old newspaper archives. The previous October in France, Fumiko had said it had happened two years ago, and since a gas heater had been the cause of death, he looked first at the papers for late October and November.

He soon found the article. It was in a morning edition dated October 29 two years ago. Perhaps there had not been a lot of news on that day, because the article took up two columns and announced the death of the translator Michiya Kume. The content of the article was relatively succinct. Around 7:00 on the evening of October 28, the victim's wife, Yuko, aged twenty-seven, had returned to the couple's Yotsuya apartment from work. She had found the study filled with gas and her husband sprawled on the floor. The valve on the heater was 80 percent open, but there was no fire burning. Yuko had immediately turned off the gas and called for an ambulance, but Kume was already dead. The cause of death was gas poisoning. The estimated time of death was 6:00.

According to Yuko's account, there was no obvious reason why Kume would commit suicide, and he left no suicide note. Since there was a kettle of water on the stove, it was thought that the kettle had boiled over without Kume noticing and the fire had been extinguished. The cause of death was under investigation. Following these facts was a brief biography of Kume.

He was thirty-four years old and had been born in Tokyo in the nineteen-forties. After doing graduate work in French literature at S university, he had worked as a teaching assistant at that same university, and later as an instructor. Later still he had been invited to join the Jourdan theater group and had become a theatrical producer. In addition to his translation of stories and plays from French, he had also published some of his own poetry.

In the morning edition two days later there was a small follow-up article saying simply that it was not clear whether Kume's death had been suicide or murder, whether it had been an accident or premeditated.

Daigo murmured to himself, "His wife, Yuko, was twenty-seven at the time."

Yuko Kume. It was a pretty name, he thought. Suddenly he recalled the fragrance of Fumiko's perfume.

# 7

# The Hourglass

By early February the department at the university was beginning to make some progress in developing plans to select a successor to Yoshimi. The stiffest competition Daigo faced for the position was from a faculty member in the medical school and from a hygiene person whom one group wanted to bring in from another university.

Regarding the Minami Foods scandal, the victims group had publicly announced toward the end of January that they wanted to have the tests repeated under Daigo's supervision to see whether or not there was a link between the Popico cookies and the outbreak of cancer among the children. Daigo had accepted the assignment and on his own had already very carefully reproduced his original results. There could be no doubt that the cause of the cancer in the children was due to a mold that had developed in the potato starch that had been used as one of the basic ingredients in the cookies. At the same time, since the original tests had been done by Daigo the previous August at the request of the Prefectural Health Office, there was no fear that a counter-argument might be made that the samples used in the tests were too old. The only delicate point was the timing for making the test results public. As far as the victims were concerned, of course, the sooner the better, since the sooner they could file a law suit and win a favorable court judgment, the sooner they would receive compensation from the company.

At the same time, if it became known that Daigo and Yoshimi had disagreed on the study, and if it became known that Yoshimi had suppressed Daigo's opinion, it might mean difficulty for those who had supported Yoshimi. The tension that resulted from all this took Daigo's mind off his interlude at Hakone. What brought it back as an urgent and unavoidable problem was a second visit from Inspector Furukawa of the Fukuoka police.

February 11 was a holiday, and in the late morning, at the urging of his two daughters, Daigo left the house to go to a neighborhood sporting goods store to buy a badminton set for the family. As he walked out of the front yard, he saw Inspector Furukawa halfway up the hill on the deserted street in front of his house.

Apparently today was a holiday for the police as well, because the inspector was wearing a casual jacket and checked slacks. When he saw Daigo, a smile lit up his ruddy, healthy face, and he walked toward Daigo. "Say, look who's here. I haven't been in touch with you in a long time. Are you going out for a walk too?"

"Uh, yeah. Sort of."

"My house is just over that hill. I often come along this way when I go out for a walk." With his chin the policeman indicated a nearby hill, and again he smiled.

The same thing had happened on that Sunday morning in December shortly after Yoshimi's murder when he had suddenly stopped in to visit Daigo, saying that he was just passing the house on his way to the office and wanted to ask a few questions. It had ended up being a very long and detailed interrogation. Again this morning it seemed likely that he had been hanging around with the specific intention of running into Daigo. It appeared that he had been observing the house from a distance, as though looking for something.

Daigo had sent his children on ahead to the sporting goods store, and seeing the policeman put him in a defiant mood. "How's it going? The investigation, I mean?"

"Frankly speaking, it's not going too well. The investigative team hasn't been disbanded, but there are only a very few officers working on the case now. The holiday season always brings a lot of new cases for us, so there just aren't enough officers to go around."

"Have you come up with any prime suspects?"

"In most cases there is usually only one prime suspect."

The police officer looked off toward the edge of the terrace, which was lit by the weak winter sunshine, but as he answered, he suddenly turned back to Daigo, who felt a thrill of fear pass through him. It was almost as if the policeman had said, *You are the only prime suspect in this case*. Despite his jovial features, the policeman's eyes behind the lenses of his dark-rimmed glasses were penetrating and relentless.

"Just one?"

"Yes. There is a woman. There was a young woman who was seen talking to Professor Yoshimi at the wedding reception on the night before the murder. Likewise, a young woman in a black coat was seen entering Yoshimi's house at two-twenty on the afternoon of the murder. We have evaluated all the other suspects one by one, and none of them seems to be the murderer except her.''

"Yes, of course.''

"The problem is that from among all Yoshimi's friends and acquaintances, no one can identify the woman for us.''

"But aren't there a great many women who could fit that description among the mothers of the children who came down with liver cancer? Of course many of those mothers hated Yoshimi, whether or not he fudged on the results of the chemical analysis.''

"Our investigation went into every possibility of that aspect of the case. We turned up absolutely nothing. The only conclusion we can some to is that this mystery woman is someone who is not among those people we know to be associated with Yoshimi.''

The policeman gazed steadily at Daigo the whole time he was talking, until Daigo could virtually feel the pressure. He realized that the best course of action would be to say nothing, but he felt he had to say something just to relieve the tension.

"In that case how does the investigative team intend to solve this case?''

The policeman's features took on a pleasant intimacy, and he smiled casually.

"You ask how we're going to solve this case; we're going to ask you to help us do the job. But I should also tell you about one theory we have.''

"What is that?''

"It might have been a contract murder. There are any number of people who might have liked to see Yoshimi dead, and there is the possibility that one of them asked a woman who had no direct involvement with Yoshimi to poison him. When we look back at cases in the past, I can find no precedent for this sort of thing outside of gangland-type killings. And since the one who was asked to commit the murder was a woman, we can suppose that she might have been the mistress or otherwise related to the person who asked her to commit murder. Somehow through this sort of connection we hope to turn up the woman we are looking for. At the moment, however, our case is rather weak on this point."

Furukawa took a deep breath and pulled a pack of cigarettes from his jacket pocket. Daigo asked if he would like to come into the house and have a cup of tea, but with some apparent consternation the police officer declined the invitation and said he would continue on his walk.

"But of course we have not yet given up hope of locating the woman. Even though we have interviewed the more than two hundred people who were at the wedding reception, we are not yet prepared to write off the investigation. And if you can think of anything that would help us, no matter how small a detail it might be, please don't hesitate to call me."

As he was adding this final comment on the point of departure, his eyes behind his glasses seemed relentlessly watching for Daigo's response.

So, the policeman had suggested the possibility of a contract murder.

Daigo was shocked and simply stood there for a moment trying to take in this news. If that was the position they took, then his watertight alibi would no longer mean anything. Anyone who had a strong motive would now be suspect. It seemed as though the blood was rushing to his head, and he became very uneasy.

There was no doubt in his mind that Fumiko Samejima was expecting him to take some direct action regarding Midori Nagahara. Until now Daigo had been uncertain about what to do and had put the matter off day after day, but what if Fumiko now decided that Daigo lacked the will to actually do something? Surely she would respond to this treachery on his part and would perhaps give the police some reason to suppose that Daigo had put out the contract on Yoshimi, and he would surely be implicated.

In the next moment he was overcome with a nauseous feeling of self-loathing. Why had he suddenly come to suspect such terrible things about Fumiko? He owed so much to her both physically and emotionally, did he now intend to besmirch her? No, surely Fumiko would never doubt that he would carry out his part of the plan. Once again he recalled the quiet, tranquil darkness of that night at Barbizon, and once again he was able to renew his faith in Fumiko. No doubt she also had faith in him.

And yet he already felt that within him there was a certain boundary line beyond which he did not think he could cross, and once again he began to shudder. People are capable of doing unimaginable things, and there are parts of themselves they are not even aware of. It seemed that if he was going to act, he should do it right away. He brought this last decision to the foreground of his mind and began to think it over.

Inspector Furukawa had spoken of the possibility of the crime having been committed on a contract basis by someone who had nothing to do with the victim. Yet he had also suggested that the possibility of this sort of murder was remote except for gangland slayings.

As long as their thinking was limited to this framework, Daigo decided they probably would not make a connection between this case and a similar, unrelated murder in distant Hakone. But when should he make his move? It seemed that at some point he had already made a decision to act. And what should he do about preparing an alibi for Fumiko? Just as Daigo had automatically been a suspect in the murder of Yoshimi, so too Fumiko would surely be included in the list of suspects if Midori Nagahara was murdered.

At that point he noticed his two daughters coming down the hill. Apparently they had given up on waiting for their father and had come to urge him along. Daigo turned his attention to them and began to walk in their direction.

Fumiko had arranged for Daigo to have an alibi before the murder had taken place. But Daigo had no address for her that would enable him to arrange a similar sort of alibi.

"Today's a holiday, isn't it?" said his younger daughter as she took his hand.

"A holiday?"

"The sporting goods store is closed on Fridays, and today is Friday," added the older daughter.

"That's too bad. I had my heart set on playing badminton with Daddy today."

At last Daigo realized what they were talking about. The sporting goods store where they had intended to buy the badminton set was closed today. Since it was a holiday, it felt like Sunday, but of course it was only Friday.

"We could go to the Mineya, they sell them there." The elder daughter mentioned the name of the nearest department store as a way of testing to see how far her father was willing to go to get a badminton set.

"Aren't they also closed today?"

"No. Mineya is closed on Wednesdays."

"Oh, well then let's go there."

With shrieks of delight, the children ran to the house to make preparations for going out. On the way to the house they talked to each other and laughed about something. Recently Papa had been too good to them. Indeed, since his return from Hakone he had been very much involved with the affairs of his wife and children. But if he changed too radically, they might suspect something. While this thought occupied one part of his mind, he seemed a bit distracted as he bade them farewell.

He had to get some grasp of Midori Nagahara's lifestyle.

Umezaki had laughed and said she seemed to be a very retiring sort of person who spent most of her time at home. But surely she went out on certain days, and he had to find out when.

Daigo set out once again on a walk, but came to a stop almost immediately. Unconsciously he gripped his left hand in his right hand. Slowly he brought the left hand close to his face and twice he looked at it carefully. That was it. Fumiko had not left anything to chance.

That night after she had mentioned the name Midori Nagahara, he had asked her to tell him something about herself. She had told him that her name was Fumiko Samejima, and then she had taken Daigo's left hand and with her finger had traced the characters she used for her name. Then she had said, *I live by myself in Tokyo, and for the most part I stay home and do translation work there, but on Tuesdays and Fridays I go to my office from noon to about six.* So Fumiko's alibi was secure from noon until six on Tuesdays and Fridays.

The first thing he needed to do was make a telephone call. He felt that this would be a good first step for implementing his plan. He knew that Midori Nagahara's home was about two kilometers north of the Emerald View Hotel, and of course he had made a point of finding out her telephone number and making a note of it.

He decided to make his move after dinner that evening, when his wife and children were in the family room watching TV. He used the bedroom telephone extension and dialed the Hakone number. The phone rang four and a half times before it was answered by a young woman's voice.

"Hello," said Daigo. "Is this the Nagahara residence?"

"Yes it is." The voice that replied was low and innocent-sounding. Was it Midori herself?

"Is Midori in?"

"Yes she is. Who may I say is calling?"

"Actually this is the first time I have called her, but my name is Okuda, I live in Hakone."

It was fortunate that even though he was calling all the way from Fukuoka, the connection was good, so no one would suspect the call was long distance. "I am trying to find someone who gives private lessons on the piano, and I would like to speak to Midori."

"I see. Just a moment please." The woman seemed unsuspecting as she put the telephone receiver down. So it was not Midori who had answered. Although he had thought he could handle this casually, Daigo could already feel the sweat running down his back.

"Hello. This is Midori."

The shrill, high-pitched voice rang in his ears. Earlier when he had been to Hakone, he had not had an opportunity to hear her speak at close range, but the sound of the voice fitted perfectly with the image he had of her.

"I'm sorry to be calling you so abruptly like this, but my daughter is in the fifth grade, and I am looking for a piano teacher for her. Someone mentioned your name, and I wonder if you would be willing to give her private lessons."

Midori was silent for a moment, then said, "Is she just beginning the piano?"

"No. She has completed the third volume of the Pleyel series, but her present teacher has suddenly moved to Tokyo, so we are looking for a new teacher."

"I see. On which day of the week did you want to schedule the lessons?"

"Oh, that doesn't matter, we can arrange it for whenever is convenient for you. By the way, excuse me for asking, but I wonder, how many students are you teaching at the present time?"

"I have two students."

"I suppose the students come to your house for the lessons? Or do you go to the student's house?"

"Generally I prefer that the students come here. Right now I have one student who comes here on Wednesdays, but the other student recently broke her leg, and since it is hard for her to get around, I go to her house on Friday afternoons."

Friday afternoons. The mention of it sent Daigo's mind racing.

"As I said, my daughter is in the fifth grade, so she gets home from school late every day except Friday. If it would be all right with you, I wonder if we could arrange for lessons sometime on Friday afternoon that won't conflict with your other student."

"Oh, she lives quite close by—just over the hill from my house. I go there for her lesson from four until five, so if your daughter could come either before or after that we might be able to work something out. If she would come once so I can meet her, perhaps we can make some arrangement."

"Yes. That sounds good to me. I will have my daughter talk to you, and then I will call you again. I wonder if you are at home on other days?"

"Usually I am at home. I go to the golf driving range on Tuesdays, so I am usually not around then."

"Oh, you play golf. I play a bit myself. Which golf course do you use?"

"I'm really not that good. I am just taking lessons from the professional coach at the Lily Hill Country Club."

Judging from the tone of her voice, Daigo had the feeling she felt her privacy was being invaded, so he quickly concluded the conversation and hung up.

Wiping the sweat from his forehead with a handkerchief, he went to the sideboard and poured himself a glass of brandy. His underwear was so soaked with cold sweat, he was tempted to change it, but he decided to put that off until after he had had a swallow of brandy. As the warmth of it spread through his body, along with it went the feeling of satisfaction that he had completed the first part of his project.

Now he knew that on Tuesdays she played golf and on Fridays she went out for a late piano lesson. Suddenly it occurred to him that the two days a week that Midori was away from home corresponded exactly to the two days when Fumiko went to the office to work. He took another gulp of brandy and went to the study, which adjoined the bedroom. There he got out a map of Hakone and searched for the Lily Hill Country Club. It was a short distance into the mountains, directly north of Hakone—far enough away from Midori's house to suppose that she did not walk there, so presumably she went by car. If that was the case, then Friday would be his best opportunity.

His eyes fell to the map, and in his mind he recreated the background for Midori's house. He remembered it as he had seen it when he had been to Hakone. The Emerald View Hotel was situated by the lake, and above it was the highway, which ran off to the east at an angle for about two kilometers before reaching the boarding area for the excursion boats that plied the lake, as well as the entrance to the cable car that went up the mountain, and some camping grounds. If one returned by way of Hakone Park, there were numerous large hotels and traditional inns, but the area between the Emerald View Hotel and Midori's house was a closed valley that had not been built up with summer homes and that sort of thing.

Midori had told him that on Friday afternoons between four and five o'clock she went to her student's house just over the hill from where she lived. No doubt she walked. He could guess that both from the lay of the land and from the way Midori had spoken about it. It was a quiet, isolated area. The only problem was that there might be an eye-witness. He had to make sure there were no witnesses from the highway below. If he chose a time when the weather was cold, as it had been before, then everything would be in his favor. Just a month ago on, January 11, when Daigo had gone to observe Midori's house, there had been nothing moving in the area, not even a stray dog.

Daigo gulped down the last of the brandy and fell across the bed. As he closed his eyes, he seemed to see in his mind a vision of an hourglass whose time was running out. Today was Friday, February 11. Five more Fridays would have to pass before he had his spring vacation and he could once again legitimately make a trip to Hakone. He made up his mind on the spot that he would have to make some definite decisions before much more sand had run through the hourglass.

# 8

# The Phantom Woman

FEELING HE WOULD NEVER HAVE A BETTER CHANCE, DAI-
go made arrangements for the visit. It was Friday, March
4. For the past two days the entire nation had been gripped
in a late winter cold snap. The previous night he had called
the public access weather information number and had
learned that the forecast was for cloudiness with occasional
light snow. Daigo had planned his trip for this time because
the three days from March 3 to March 5 had been set aside
for administering admissions examinations for J university.
That was done by instructors, so the professors and assistant professors were able to have a holiday.

Having made reservations the previous day, Daigo set
out on March 4 for Tokyo. He told his wife he was going
to do some comparative studies of water pollution in a
different part of the country. From Tokyo he took the bullet

train to Odawara, and from there, as on his previous trip, he took the least conspicuous bus to Hakone.

It was near three o'clock in the afternoon when he got off the bus near Midori Nagahara's house. As he had expected, the trip from Fukuoka had taken nearly five hours. Still, this distance was probably a good thing if it helped to insure the safety of himself and Fumiko.

Since he had no desire to remain in Hakone overnight, he did not bother about making a reservation. He wanted to stay in the area as short a time as possible, and he planned to return to Tokyo immediately after committing the crime.

The broad, sloping hillside occupied by the homes of the wealthy was even lonelier and more desolate than Daigo had remembered. Occasionally a few large flakes of snow swirled down from the leaden sky. The twilight gloom was rapidly gathering, and although there was no wind, the chill mountain air pierced to the very marrow of his bones.

Daigo first located Midori's house, then circled around outside the quince hedge that surrounded it, looking down from the slope of the hill behind the house. There was a hillside covered with a thin scattering of forest, and a narrow lane leading away from the back door of the house. The lane curved, gently rising to the top of the hill, then down the other side, where only two other elegant homes were visible. No matter which of the homes it was where Midori gave the piano lesson, she would surely walk along this lane.

The forest that covered the slope was composed of cedar, cypress, cherry, and birch, both deciduous and evergreen trees, and although it was not really a dense forest, it would be a sufficient screen to keep Daigo hidden from view. Here in the forest on this gloomy, overcast afternoon, the shadows seemed to flow among the trees like a thick, viscous fluid. The only question was, would he be visible from the road below?

To find out, Daigo climbed halfway up the slope. From there the road that ran along the edge of the lake was not visible, but there was a narrow side road directly below Midori's house that seemed to join the main road a little farther on. The place where Daigo stood could be seen from that narrow road if one looked directly up. Still, it seemed that the road was rarely used, and even the main road along the lake appeared to have very little traffic today.

Daigo was further reassured when, after watching the narrow road for a good ten minutes, he saw only one car and no pedestrians. He thought it unlikely that anyone inside a car would notice movement taking place on the hillside above the road.

Daigo looked at his watch and saw that it was 3:40. He took up a position in the shadows across the road from the hedge surrounding Midori's house. From there he could see the lane he had just been walking along, the whole slope of the hillside, and the frozen lake below. From where he stood he could just see the top of the terminal building for the cable car lift. He could see a gondola beginning its slow descent.

The cruel cold of the place seemed to go all through Daigo's body. His toes were numb inside his shoes. His heart felt equally numb, and he felt no emotion whatsoever. His actions and his emotions seemed to be two separate things, and he was overcome by a sense of unreality. Rather than feeling the stress or fear one normally feels before taking a decisive action, he only felt empty and alone. He tried to recall how he had felt on that dark night at Barbizon. *That's enough, please don't tell me any more. These things are not important. I think I already understand you better than anyone else.* He could hear Fumiko saying these words in his ear like a mother admonishing a small boy.

Ah, he wanted to see Fumiko again. He wondered if meeting her again would somehow bring meaning back into his life. In any case, it was clear that he had to undertake this next step. Unless he did this, there would be no chance of ever meeting Fumiko again. After all, she had been surprisingly strong-willed and courageous in carrying out her part of their secret agreement.

In his mind he saw Yoshimi's protruding eyes and thick lips. He recalled the man's unceasing drive for power and money. Yoshimi had not worried about crushing other, weaker people like insects and destroying their lives. In the matter of the chemical analysis of the Popico cookies, he had not hesitated to reject Daigo's results and substitute his own. Daigo recalled the thin smile Yoshimi had had when he urged Daigo to accept a position at that Alaskan university. He recalled the ceaseless moaning of the young children who had been Yoshimi's victims, and the frantic manner in which one of the mothers had grabbed his arm and begged to know the truth. Yoshimi had been a person who had absolutely no right to live.

For Fumiko, the same applied to Midori Nagahara. Perhaps when Fumiko had killed Yoshimi she had pretended she was killing Midori. With this in mind Daigo decided to pretend he would be killing Yoshimi.

He was not about to murder Midori because he was afraid that if he did not Fumiko might implicate him as the one who had arranged for Yoshimi to be killed. Daigo struggled to persuade himself that he was not acting out of any shameful motive of self-protection. And yet, when he tried to convince himself that he had done his duty in ridding society of the likes of Yoshimi, he knew that in fact he had not been quite so heroic. But there was also another Daigo, perhaps his innermost self, who went beyond convention and normal standards—a man with a poetic nature that yearned for something pure and eternal—and he wondered if it was not this part of himself that was urging him now to take some direct action.

How often in one's life do we have the opportunity to experience the eternal? When such an opportunity arrives, if we do not have the courage to embrace it, we find ourselves buried under the trivia of daily concerns and our lives are impoverished. Without that courage, we cannot become one of the chosen few. For Daigo, Fumiko represented this eternal value. He felt condemned to eternal aloneness until someday he would be able to embrace the eternal with his own arms. The image of Fumiko which Daigo created in his mind was an image that filled his heart and transformed his loneliness to a bittersweet feeling of melancholy longing.

At this point in his reverie, the tension returned and gripped him. The white iron gate in the hedge opened and a woman emerged wearing a coat with a black hood. She was a tall, slim woman. Beneath the coat she wore a rose-colored pantsuit and black boots. On her hands she wore gloves that matched her pantsuit, and she clutched a folder of sheet music to her breast.

As the woman turned to close the gate, Daigo caught a glimpse of her profile, which revealed the high cheekbones and sharp eyes of Midori Nagahara. She glanced up at the sky, and with a cold shiver pulled up the collar of her coat as she began to walk up the hill.

Unconsciously Daigo glanced at his watch and saw that it was 4:02. The shadows of the evening twilight were already beginning to gather. A few flakes of snow settled on Midori's black hood and the back of her coat. Daigo took three or four quiet steps and looked down at the road below. All he could see was the cold strip of asphalt. He

had the impression that no person or car had passed along
that road all day.

Midori hurried up the gravel lane with long strides. She
was already about a third of the way up the slope. He
would have to get close enough to call to her before she
reached the halfway point on the slope. If she went any
farther than that, they would be visible from the highway
that ran along the edge of the lake. He would have to
approach her and lure her into the brush while it was still
safe to do so.

He knew what he was going to say to her: "Excuse me,
but a large amount of mail has been thrown away in the
bushes over here, I wonder if some of your mail might be
in with it. Would you mind stepping over here to take
a look? It will just take a moment." He had read about
an incident like this while riding on the bullet train this
morning.

He hoped that when he tried this line on Midori, she
would glance unsuspectingly at the bushes, and Daigo
would walk into the brush as casually as he could. He
believed there was a good chance Midori would follow
him. Today Daigo was wearing a dark blue overcoat, and
although he had discarded his dark glasses, he was wearing a simple pair of horn-rimmed glasses with plain glass
lenses.

Daigo would try to get Midori into a small hollow on
the hillside that could not be seen from the road, and then
positioning himself behind her would say, "You see, the
mail has been scattered all around here." When she leaned
over to look, he would take the nylon stocking he had in
his pocket and knot it around her neck. He figured she
would not even have time to cry out.

As it turned out, what really happened was quite different. Daigo started up the lane behind Midori. She had not
yet noticed his presence. He moved forward one step, two

steps, three steps, and just at that moment there suddenly came the sound of a car horn from the road below the house. Midori stopped and turned.

There in the driveway was a small yellow sports car, and a young lady was leaning out the window on the driver's side. Daigo swallowed his heart. In confusion he tried to conceal himself, but he realized it was far too late for that. The woman in the car could surely see Daigo just as plainly as she could see Midori. Perhaps if he just remained motionless he would at least be inconspicuous.

"Midori." The faint sound of the woman's voice rose through the darkening forest. It was a deep, slightly husky voice.

"Yes, what is it?" replied Midori.

"I just got a telephone call from Keiko's mother. She has come down with a cold and fever and has asked that today's lesson be cancelled. She only just now realized that the child was running a fever, so she did not get in touch with you earlier."

The young woman spoke rather quickly and directly. This was the same voice Daigo had heard earlier when he telephoned from Fukuoka. Even though Daigo was looking at her from a distance, there was more light down in the road and he could see quite clearly that she was darker complected than Midori and her features were more Western-looking. No doubt this was Midori's younger sister, whom Umezaki had mentioned.

"Oh, that's a relief," said Midori, hunching her shoulders. She seemed less perturbed by the cancellation of the lesson than by the lateness of the message. Her voice was so soft, the woman in the car had surely not heard it; nevertheless, she continued to lean out the window and watch them. Midori waved her hand to show that she understood, and started back toward the house. At that moment she came face to face with Daigo.

Perhaps it was only Daigo's fear that made him think he saw some hint of recognition in Midori's eyes as their gaze met. In any case, Daigo did not know how to interpret the look—if it was there at all. Daigo instinctively turned his face away. With his eyes on the ground he brushed past her, trying to act like an ordinary pedestrian. Presently he heard the sound of Midori closing the iron gate behind her, and at the same moment he heard the sound of the car motor starting up.

Daigo paused for a time all alone on the hillside lane feeling a surge of dizziness and weakness. A faint fragrance of Midori's perfume, the fragrance of crape myrtle, lingered in the darkening air.

It was seven o'clock by the time Daigo got back to Tokyo, where he took a room at a business hotel in Shimbashi where he usually stayed when he was in Tokyo for meetings. Tokyo was also in the grip of the cold spell, and all afternoon there had been flurries of snow that had accumulated here and there on the streets.

The window of his hotel room looked out on the dark wall of the adjoining building, and he had only the slightest glimpse of the dark, starless sky, to which a nearby neon sign gave a reddish tint.

Daigo felt confused and stood gazing at the scene from his darkened window as though it was some sort of shadowy painting. Just as he had finally gotten close to Midori and was about to make his move, her sister had showed up in a car; it was just bad luck, and there was nothing he could do about it. Probably the younger sister was just getting ready to go out somewhere in the car when the call came from Midori's student canceling the lesson, so she had passed the message along to Midori. His first thought had been that too many things had gone wrong for all of this to have been accidental. The younger sister, for example, had waited in the car watching until Midori was safely back inside the yard. Perhaps she had some intuitive understanding of why Daigo was there. At least it was fortunate that they were interrupted before he had spoken to Midori.

In one sense he had been lucky today, but unfortunately he was going to have to find another opportunity. He had taken a hired car to the foot of the mountains, and on the way he had thought through the sequence of events over and over. He concluded that it could have turned out much worse than it had. The only thing he could do was to try again.

He could not turn his mind away from the site he had chosen for the murder. Time and again he pictured the slope of the hill in his mind. Why was that? Well, he knew the reason. Even before he had begun following Midori up the hill, during the time he was hiding in the shadows of the hedge, the sadness and loneliness that had oppressed him, and the memory of Fumiko, had left a lasting impression on his heart. He felt he must at all costs meet her once again; there was nothing in the world he wanted more. It was too bad, really, that today he had failed to keep the "promise" he had made to Fumiko. He had thought that after today everything would be done and they could look forward to a long cooling-off period. What he desparately needed was another meeting with Fumiko.

His reasoning was that he would be seduced as before, and that this time his emotions would be raised to an even higher pitch. It was the problem of how to find Fumiko that had caused him to fall into his present state of emotional turmoil and confusion.

Daigo sat on the edge of the bed in his tastelessly furnished single room and realized that he was very hungry. On the way to Hakone he had eaten a light lunch at the buffet on the bullet train, and on the way back he had stood

on the platform and drunk a cup of coffee, but other than
that he had not eaten.

After rinsing his mouth out in the bathroom, he went to
the restaurant on the seventh floor of the hotel. Although
this was only an ordinary business hotel, the ginger-fla-
vored steak he ordered was remarkably good, and he
washed it down with half a bottle of red wine. Afterward
he felt greatly restored both physically and emotionally. It
was almost as though he had recharged his batteries, and
he felt new reserves of courage and determination welling
up within him.

The cold wave that gripped the nation was widespread
and promised to continue. The forecast was that spring
would be late this year. The same weather they had experienced today would continue for the next few days. This
meant there was a good chance that on Tuesday Midori
would make her usual trip to the indoor driving range for
her golf lesson.

No good plan occurred to him, but when he thought of
the frozen, isolated landscape around Midori's house and
the lonely highway along the lakeshore, he felt there would
surely be future opportunities for him. He was sure he
would be able to carry out his plan safely. The certainty of
this flooded his heart. Next he wanted to give some thought
to the matter of Fumiko; his mind was naturally drawn to
her.

Feeling remorseful, he took out his wallet, which contained his driver's license and a small memo notebook.
From between its pages he extracted a copy of a news
article and spread it on the palm of his hand. That day at
the public library in Shinjuku, he had made a copy of one
of the articles he had found in the old newspapers.

The article reported the death of the translator and drama
producer Michiya Kume. It also gave the name of his wife,
Yuko, and it mentioned the address of their apartment. It

was a private apartment building located at 1 Chome in Yotsuya. After reading the article, he had tried calling the apartment building, but as he had feared, he learned that about one month after her husband died, Yuko Kume had moved. The woman who had answered the telephone at the apartment building said she had left no forwarding address. All she had were unpleasant memories of the fact that Kume had killed himself in the apartment. Although the telephone conversation had told him that Yuko no longer lived there, Daigo had decided there was nothing he could do but try to find the apartment building anyway. When he had located it, it was an inconspicuous-looking two-story apartment building located between a small run-down temple and a large, expensive-looking condominium.

Daigo loitered for a time in the rear courtyard of the temple and looked at the dark walls and stairwell of the building. Then he returned to his hotel, imagining that the Kumes had not been well off in terms of money, but that they had a stoic love that bound them together.

With some impatience he returned the newspaper clipping to its original place and took out his handkerchief, but not in time to ward off an outburst of coughing.

Diagonally across from the restaurant was a glass-enclosed telephone booth. He entered it and looked in the directory for the name Jourdan. This was the name of the theater group for whom Kume had worked as a producer before his death. Eventually he found the number of the drama group's office among a large number of bars and coffee shops that had the same name.

No sooner had he finished dialing than a young man's voice answered. It was already nearly nine in the evening, but Daigo had a clear impression that there was a lot of activity going on in the background. Daigo asked if they knew how he might be able to locate the widow of Michiya Kume.

The young man at the other end of the line seemed uncertain. "I heard that after she left her apartment in Yotsuya she moved someplace where she could be close to her parents, but I don't know where that is. She hasn't kept in touch with the theater group. Hold on a moment and I'll see if any of the others knows anything."

There was a pause, then: "Mrs. Kume was apparently a good friend of one of the women in our wardrobe department, so if you can hold on for a minute, I've put out a call for her."

After waiting a time longer, a melodious woman's voice answered, saying, "Yuko is living in Kita Kamakura now. Her parents live there, but she's not living with them. She has rented a house of her own nearby. She lives alone. Let me see if I can find the address." After rummaging around for a time, she gave him the address and precise directions about how to find the place from the train station. Daigo wanted to continue the conversation and find out a little bit about Yuko Kume, but the woman asked, "Excuse me, but are you a friend of the late Mr. Kume?"

"Why yes, I am. But you see, I have been living overseas for the past few years and I had not heard about what happened. I thought I should visit his widow to pay my respects." He continued on with a bunch of nonsense and finally hung up.

When he returned to his table he transferred the note of her address that he had scribbled down into his notebook. He enclosed the copy of the newspaper article with it, dropped the notebook into his jacket pocket, and sat for a time pressing it with his hand. It helped to ease the throbbing of his heart.

The following day Tokyo continued in the grip of cold, but when the sun did shine through occasional gaps in the clouds it was surprisingly bright. When the sun was shining, it really did feel like March and as though spring had finally arrived. Daigo checked out of his hotel at 10:00 and boarded the Yokosuka Line at Shimbashi. Since it was Saturday, and since he was going against the flow of commuter traffic, the first-class car was virtually deserted. Surprisingly, he felt almost relaxed as he looked out the window and watched the urban and industrial landscape flow past. It was 11:30 when he stepped down from the train at Kita Kamakura.

The train station there is very small and surrounded by forests, making it seem like a rural station. On both sides of the station are rustic-looking traditional Japanese homes enclosed by trees and hedges. Diagonally across the tracks was the path lined with towering cedars that leads to the great temple of the Enkakuji and the large mountain behind it.

Daigo blended in with the crowd of other passengers. Leaving the station, he set out along the road according to the instructions he had received the previous night. Here in Kamakura the air seemed much purer than in Tokyo, but it also seemed colder. In Shimbashi the snow had been melting to slush, but here in the dark shadows of the ancient farmhouses it was continuing to accumulate.

For a time he followed a main arterial street with much traffic headed for Kamakura, but when he turned the corner at the woodcarver's shop he abruptly found himself in a residential district. He walked along an old cobbled street lined with moss-covered stone and wooden fences. Occasionally he would come across a modern house among the older ones, but for the most part the neighborhood was composed of large, old, traditional Japanese homes. With the ranges of snow-covered mountains in the background, the setting was very peaceful. It was easy for Daigo to maintain the mood of serenity he had experienced on the train.

Last night he had considered calling Yuko Kume directly by telephone, but after intense hesitation he gave up the idea. Although he did not know Fumiko's real name or address, it was unthinkable that she would simply refuse to talk to him if he could locate her, even though he still had not carried out his part of the plan. Also, there still remained the uncertainty of whether or not Yuko Kume and Fumiko were the same person. He doubted if he would be able to tell just by hearing the sound of her voice. On that night in Barbizon, Fumiko had explained that her throat was sore and that she was coming down with a cold, and she had seemed to have trouble controlling her voice.

The question was whether or not Fumiko and Yuko were the same person. He told himself that he would soon find out. He had failed in the case of Fumiko Naruse, and the memory of that blunder was still painful. Yet from all the checking and scouting he was able to do, among the women who had anything to do with Midori, this Yuko seemed to be the most likely candidate to be the Fumiko he was looking for. He wondered if he would recognize her the moment he saw her. There had been some uncertainty with the other Fumiko because she was not the person he was looking for. He had always instinctively believed that he would recognize Fumiko if he met her again. He had felt this way ever since that next morning in Barbizon. He was sure he would recognize her even if he only caught a glimpse of her at a distance. He did not necessarily need intimate contact with her.

Today he would be satisfied if he could verify the residence of Yuko Kume and get even a fleeting glimpse of her. Perhaps he would have to wait until he had completed his part of the plan before he could meet her again, and he had to be cautious about his relationship with Fumiko. Still, he had a strong sense of anticipation, since she had told him that with the exception of Tuesday and Friday afternoons, when she went to the office, she spent virtually all of her time at home doing translations.

The woman at the theater company had been very precise in her instructions, and Daigo had little difficulty finding the narrow, little-used street on which the house was situated. She was living alone in a small detached house that she rented from a family named Itaya who lived in the main house in the same compound. Daigo soon found an old-fashioned gate set in a bamboo fence, and on the gate was a plaque with the name Itaya on it. The gate was closed. The house behind the gate was a large, old-fashioned mansion. He followed the bamboo fence a bit further and soon came to another entrance.

After checking to see that there was no one else in the street, he opened the gate and stepped inside. There was no question that this was part of the grounds of the larger mansion, but there was no garden or lawn, only flat, bare earth. In one corner of the compound was a small, apparently two-room, detached building in the traditional Japanese style. On the other side, beyond a clump of trees, he could see the gray roof of the main house.

Although a pale winter sun was shining, his first impression was that everything seemed faded, but now he realized that this was due to the pall of smoke from a fire that was burning in the middle of the yard. With a feeling of dread Daigo approached the detached house. He had to consider the danger of being seen by the people in the main house, but fortunately he was at the rear of the main house and there was a clump of trees that screened him from the house. If necessary he could probably come up with some excuse for being there.

Suddenly Daigo stopped and went rigid. A small woman wearing a persimmon-colored kimono appeared near the bonfire, walked to the detached building, and entered it. She did not notice Daigo's presence.

As he stood there, his heart beating furiously, the woman reemerged from the house. She had a large wastebasket and a paper bag in her hands. Her complexion was pale, and her features were refined and elegant in the traditional style. All this Daigo noticed at a glance and retained.

After adding the wastepaper to the fire, the woman stood for a time gazing at the blaze. She was small and well-proportioned, though a bit plump around the hips. She had a relaxed manner, and Daigo felt that it bespoke a certain tenaciousness of spirit in the woman.

Daigo felt paralyzed. He was completely entranced by the woman's figure. She certainly did not fit the image of Fumiko he had in his mind. He had been expecting some-one a bit less traditional, more modern. But now as he stood watching Yuko Kume with the smoke rising behind her, he saw that she radiated the bearing and tranquility he had been expecting. She was very beautiful.

This was exactly the sort of woman Fumiko would be; he knew this instinctively, and now he had to grasp it in-tellectually. Probably this was the woman he was looking for. This was his Fumiko.

In his heart he felt overcome by powerful and confused surges of emotion. But he would have to be careful about speaking to her. Until everything was done and settled, Yuko Kume would probably not admit to being Fumiko. Perhaps if he met her unexpectedly like this he might find her lacking the purity and courage that Fumiko had spoken of on that night in France.

The real problem was that Daigo had already attempted murder, and if by any chance someone happened to see them together, it could lead to disaster for both of them.

At the same time Daigo felt a terrible need to send Fumi-ko some sort of message. From the pocket of his overcoat he took a magazine. It was a special issue of a nutrition magazine devoted to baby food. He had left his overnight bag in a coin locker at the station, and all he had with him was this magazine.

At once Daigo approached the entrance of the detached house, where the front door was still open. He laid the magazine down face up on the floor inside the door. If this woman really was the Fumiko he thought she was, once she saw this magazine she would know that Daigo had paid her a visit and would have some idea of what he was about to do. And even if Yuko was not the person he thought she was, she would simply be puzzled by the magazine but would not make any big thing about it. After all, she was obviously getting rid of some old papers. Naturally Daigo's name was not on the magazine, so he felt he could safely send this much of a signal.

He left the magazine and hurried away. As he did so, he took one last look at the woman standing before the fire in the pale spring sunlight.

# 9

# Sapphire Mink

DAIGO PRESSED HIS BODY FLAT AGAINST THE FROZEN CE-
ment wall and felt the chill of it penetrate to the very marrow of his bones. He had been crouching in this narrow,
cramped space for ages; his feet and legs were numb from
a combination of the cramped position and the effects of
the cold. Once when his legs became too numb, Daigo
took a chance and did a few deep knee bends to restore the
circulation. If he raised his body all the way up, he could
see before him the squat, sleek body of the Porsche 914.

Each time he breathed, his breath came out in white
clouds. The faint glow of the yard light dimly lit the narrow
space between the cement wall of the garage and the side
of the car. The light vaguely illuminated the gravel driveway sweeping down the slope and disappearing in a grove
of trees that could only be seen in silhouette. He had spent

140

the last twenty minutes crouching here in the garage with only this for a view.

With difficulty Daigo tried to bring his watch close enough to his face to see what time it was in the dim light. Eventually he was able to make out that in another five minutes it would be 6:20. Since it would take about five minutes to get to the Emerald View Hotel by car, and since Midori was scheduled to play the piano there at 6:30, she should be coming out to the car in the next few minutes.

Even in the remote possibility that they sent a car from the hotel to pick her up, and she did not use the yellow Porsche, she would still have to return home after the performance, and he would have a chance then. But he had no way of knowing at what time she would return home, and it was always possible that someone would bring her home. At the same time, he had to consider the fact that Fumiko Samejima worked at her office on Tuesdays and Fridays from noon until six. Since he assumed that her office was somewhere in Tokyo, even if he committed the murder after six, as long as not enough time had elapsed for Fumiko to make the trip to Hakone, her alibi would still stand, but if he waited too long, he might jeopardize her alibi. For him it made no difference whether he committed the murder on Tuesday or Friday, but if he was not able to guarantee Fumiko's alibi, then the whole murder plan, including the murder of Yoshimi, would be meaningless. If possible he wanted to have his chance before Midori went to play at the Emerald View. Besides, if he missed his chance tonight, this second failure would shake his confidence in his ability to carry out his plan.

Today was Tuesday, March 8, and although there would be at least three more Tuesdays and Fridays before the spring tourist season at Hakone really got under way, Daigo was afraid that his wife and colleagues might become suspicious if he made too many of these overnight trips.

He wanted to complete the second murder as quickly as possible and wait for the heat to die down, and then he was looking forward to the opportunity to see Fumiko again. At some point he had become convinced that on that fateful night in France, he and Fumiko Samejima had definitely made a pact to murder both Akishige Yoshimi and Midori Nagahara.

On the previous occasion, after returning to Tokyo from Kita Kamakura, Daigo had telephoned the Emerald View Hotel before catching the plane back to Fukuoka. He had inquired if they knew when Midori Nagahara would next be performing on the piano. He said he had stayed at the hotel once and had been quite enchanted at hearing her play. He went on to say that in the near future he would be coming to Hakone again, and he would like to arrange to come at a time when Midori would be performing.

The person he talked to on the phone was the elderly desk manager, who said, "I don't know if you are aware of it or not, but Midori is the daughter of the owner of the hotel, and she only performs when she feels like it. She is not a professional entertainer, so it is hard to say exactly when she will be performing." Typical of an old-fashioned hotel man, he felt compelled to give this elaborate explanation before informing Daigo, "Nevertheless, you will surely be able to hear her perform next Tuesday evening. She will be playing for a private party, but I don't think there will be any objection if you want to listen."

As it turned out, the owner of the hotel was giving a party for a local politician with whom he was heavily involved. The party would be held in the hotel's main dining room, and Midori would be performing from 6:30. Finally, the manager had informed Daigo that since there was sure to be a festive atmosphere about the place, if he merely told the organizers that he just wanted to hear Midori play, he would be able to sit in.

Daigo had considered this for a time, then said, "Do you know if Midori will be attending the party all evening?"

"Oh no. I expect she will just come to the hotel for her performance and then leave."

That seemed right. It was unlikely that a young woman like Midori would want to hang around with a bunch of elderly politicians. He wanted to ask if she would be driving from her house to the hotel, but he was afraid that would be too dangerous, so he just hung up with the words that he would arrange his reservations later. Even though he could not be sure, he believed there was a strong possibility that Midori would drive to the hotel from her home in her own car.

The last time she performed she had worn a green evening gown. It was unlikely that she would be going anywhere else before her performance dressed like that, and of course it was much too far from her house to the hotel to walk dressed like that on a cold evening. Certainly if she went every week to play golf, she must be able to drive.

Taking all these things into consideration, Daigo made his plans based on the assumption that Midori would leave her house alone sometime after six on the night of March 8. This time he expected to be successful.

He had left Fukuoka this morning shortly before noon, telling his wife and his colleagues that he had an elderly aunt who lived all alone in Osaka who had been ill, and that he was going to check on her condition and arrange to have her hospitalized if necessary. On the previous occasion when he had gone to Hakone, school was in recess for the entrance examinations, so Daigo had only had to make a false excuse to his wife, but he had not had to worry about explaining his absence to his colleagues and assistants at the lab. Nevertheless, he was afraid he might slip up and say something that would give him away. Certainly the assistant, Yamada, who had been Yoshimi's flunky, maintained a sullen attitude toward Daigo and was always looking for him to make a slip of some sort.

It was true that he had an elderly aunt living in Osaka. She was his mother's sister-in-law, and since they had no children and her husband had already passed away, she was living alone; but she was only in her sixties, and could not be said to be all that elderly. Daigo had not seen her in ten years, and since his mother and father died, the only contact maintained with his aunt was to exchange New Year's cards. Nevertheless, the aunt's existence provided a convenient excuse he could make to his wife. For some time now Shihoko had been saying they ought to do something to help her, and now, when she heard Daigo say he was going to visit her, she was pleased.

When he arrived in Tokyo, Daigo telephoned the aunt in Osaka from the airport. The old woman was quite surprised, since he had not even telephoned her for some years, but she was in good health and was pleased that he had called. She was living simply but adequately on the pension her husband had earned from the steel company for which he had worked.

Daigo told her he had come to Osaka on business and was just calling to find out how she was getting along. He apologized that he would not have time to actually stop in to see her. Nevertheless, she expressed her great joy at hearing from him. Daigo felt that in case he needed an alibi, this phone call would go some distance toward providing one.

It was after four when he approached Midori's house. The pale, early spring twilight gloom was just beginning to gather. The distant mountain slopes with their barren trees could be seen only dimly, but there was a hint of color in them that suggested that the new leaves were about to bud. It was March, and the days were getting longer. Fortunately it was overcast today, and the twilight gathered early.

The garage at Midori's house was located a bit down the slope from the front gate and was a cement structure dug into the hillside. The garage was large enough for two cars, but Daigo had heaved a sigh of relief when he saw that there was only the one yellow Porsche 914 in the garage. This was the same car Midori's younger sister had been driving the other day when she had called to them from the driveway. When he had peeped into the garage that day on his way back, it had been empty. He assumed that the vacant space was for their father's car and that the Porsche was used by both the sisters.

Until around 5:40 Daigo loitered beside the road where he could keep an eye on both the garage and Midori's front gate. He stayed in the shadows, watching the only thing in view—the elegant old mansion of the Nagaharas. As usual there were no pedestrians along this narrow, isolated road. No one entered or left the Nagahara home. At a quarter to six he entered the darkened garage. The Porsche had been backed into the garage, and he squeezed himself into the narrow space between the back of the Porsche and the wall.

He figured he would probably have to spend about thirty-five minutes there. Already it had grown quite dark outside. By now he figured it was about time for Midori to come out. He did not think she would be going to the hotel from some other place, but if she did, he would just have to wait here until she returned home. But what if someone brought her home?

If he missed his chance this time, it would be difficult to get away from Fukuoka again next week. Even his easy-going wife would begin to have suspicions if he stayed away from home another weekend. Besides, next Tuesday there was an important faculty meeting he was expected to attend. He had to take Yoshimi's place at these meetings now. Next week would not be a good time for him to get away.

As the hands on his watch moved past 6:20, Daigo felt the sweat begin to form on his back, and he began to tingle with intensity. Everything around him was wrapped in darkness. From time to time he could hear the sound of the wind in the trees across the road, but it seemed tranquil, too tranquil. He began to wonder if all his effort had been in vain. What if Midori was already at the hotel, sitting at the piano performing for the party?

Moments later, however, he heard footsteps. It sounded like high heels coming down the steps from the house. For a moment he lost the sound entirely, then suddenly there was looming over him a shadow of a woman standing between the wall of the garage and the Porsche. The profile was familiar, as was the wave of the hair. From the features he could make out, it was surely Midori. Today too she was wearing a floor-length gown. Over it she wore a half-length coat of silver-gray fur. In one hand she carried what appeared to be sheet music and in the other a small handbag suitable for such a party.

Midori turned sideways and entered the space between the car and the wall. She grimaced as she tried to make sure she didn't touch the dirty car with any of her clothing; she was unaware of Daigo's presence. Indeed, even if she had looked in his direction, the light was so dim and he was so well hidden in the shadows that she would have seen nothing. He crouched by the trunk of the car, his hands ready, hardly daring to breathe.

Midori used the key in her hand to unlock the door of the car. She put the sheet music and other things she was carrying on the seat.

At that moment, Daigo rose up and pulled the nylon stocking from his pocket, but for a terrifying moment his legs failed to respond to the urgency of his command. Was he really going to be able to do it? Did he have any choice? Suddenly he was gripped by a paralyzing wave of fear. He could hear the blood rushing in his ears.

Midori adjusted the front of her coat in preparation for sliding into the driver's seat. Just at that moment, however, she seemed to sense his presence and turned toward him. She held her breath and searched for him with her eyes.

At last she made out the figure of a man crouching in the darkness of her garage, and she shattered the stillness with a scream. The sound catapulted Daigo into action. He lunged forward, and as she started to dodge away, he reached for her neck with the nylon stocking. Daigo staggered as he tightened the stocking around her throat, using all his strength. Midori had seen him coming and managed to get both hands up to her throat, but she could not stop the bite of the stocking as it dug into the flesh of her throat. Her bright red fingernails clawed at the neck of her jacket.

Later, Daigo could never remember whether she had tried to cry out or not. The only sound he heard was the blood roaring in his own ears. He seemed to lose consciousness for a time, and when he came to himself, he found Midori at his feet with the stocking around her neck. It occurred to him that she had put up very little resistance, but perhaps it had just seemed so since he had gone into a trance during the last part of their struggle.

The dim outdoor light glazed the pale features of Midori's face. It appeared that she was no longer breathing. Her eyes were closed, but there remained a cold, arrogant look on her face, and her features seemed surprisingly serene. A faint fragrance of Midori's perfume, crape myrtle, lingered in the air.

Suddenly Daigo felt a surge of remorse for this woman. He recalled the first time he had seen Midori standing in the corridor of the Emerald View, and the air of mystery he had felt about her. He had to wonder what strange fate it was that had linked him to her. Even though they had never met or spoken to one another, they had experienced that intimate relationship of murderer and murdered. Could anything be more pathetic for a human being than this?

Daigo suddenly felt a tightness in his throat and bit his lip. It was only later that he realized his legs were trembling.


The yellow Porsche had been abandoned in a grove of cedars surrounded by fields of dry pampas grass. These were the fields and meadows on the slope that spread out below the driveway of Midori's house. Beyond the fields were those dark cedars that are unique to Hakone. Although Daigo had attempted to hide the Porsche in the trees, it was of such a striking yellow that during the daylight hours it would surely attract the attention of anyone who was looking for it. In the darkness, however, even the headlights of passing cars would not penetrate this far. This would give him some time before the murder was discovered.

Inspector Kazuo Eda of the Odawara police stood in the chilly night wind looking at the car illuminated by the bright spotlights and reviewed the situation in his mind. They had discovered a Porsche 914 with the driver's side door hanging open, and he could still see the green leather of the seat covers. It was a brand new sports car, so new it could have just come from the showroom. The powder they had used to check for fingerprints on the dashboard and seat had left the outline of the young lady's body, which had already been removed from the car.

Midori Nagahara's strangled body had been left just as it was found until the team of investigators from Odawara arrived on the scene. Eda and his men had got there about 9:30, and now they were just completing their initial examination of the site, looking for clues.

"We got a call from the Emerald View at about seven-fifteen asking us to start a search for the victim," said the local police sergeant, who was standing next to Eda. He was older than Eda and had his shoulders hunched against the cold. "The owner of the Emerald View is the girl's father. He called about seven-fifteen and said she was supposed to play the piano at six-thirty for a party they were having at the hotel, but that she hadn't shown up. He called her home and found that she had already left for the party and that her car was not in the garage. He decided she must have gone somewhere else on some sort of errand, so he waited, but she never showed up. He checked with several of her close friends, but none of them had seen her this evening. Finally, on the off chance that she might have had a traffic accident, he contacted us."

At that point two local police officers had gone to the hotel, where they mobilized a couple of the clerks to begin a search for the missing girl. They saw no signs of any accident, but continued the search for nearly an hour. Around 8:30 they rigged up a spotlight and repeated the search. This time, said the old officer, they found the abandoned Porsche down among the trees on the slope directly below the driveway of Midori's house. The local officer was indignant at being displaced as chief investigative officer in the case by the younger Eda, who was only in his thirties. As it turned out, the district chief had been hospitalized for overwork, and the assistant chief was out of town on business, so, like it or not, Eda had to take charge of the investigation. This was the first investigation he had supervised.

"When you discovered the car, Midori was in the driver's seat and had been strangled from behind by a silk stocking. The key was in the ignition, but the motor was off." Eda repeated these facts quietly as though talking to himself. "What time did Midori leave home?" he asked the local officer.

"Her younger sister said it was about six-twenty or so."

"I see."

Eda recalled that earlier one of the veteran investigators on his staff had guessed that the murder had taken place no later than 7:00 at the latest. That suggested at that some point between the house and the hotel, the murderer had gotten into Midori's car, driven it to this spot, and strangled her. If that were the case, then there were only a limited number of people who could have done such a thing. In the morning, of course, he would send out teams of detectives to see if they could turn up any eyewitnesses. There were not many people in Hakone at this time of year, and it would probably not take long to check out the girl's circle of friends and acquaintances.

Eda was in rather good spirits. Thrusting both his hands deep into the pockets of his overcoat and burying his chin in his muffler, he returned to his car. It was shortly after 11:00. He left behind the teams of investigators who were searching the area for footprints or other clues and headed for the Nagahara home. He left the driving to his young assistant, Igusa.

When he arrived at the Nagahara home he found the left-hand side of the garage occupied by a black Opel sedan; the right side of the garage was vacant. Apparently this was where the Opel was normally kept. He parked his own car in the garage beside the Opel.

The old-fashioned living room was overheated, and a gas fire burned brightly in the fireplace. Bathed in the light of the fire but nevertheless pale from stress and fatigue were Midori's father, Makoto, and her younger sister, Akane. Both had participated in the search for Midori, and after the Porsche had been found, they had remained at the scene until Eda and his men arrived. They only returned home after the police began their on-site investigation. Consequently, Eda had already spoken with them briefly.

Nagahara invited both Eda and Igusa to come close to the fire, saying, "We appreciate all the effort you are making." He was an elegant gentleman who appeared to be about sixty, with silver hair, and who gave the impression of being an English gentleman. "I am afraid my wife has been quite shaken by all this. She is upstairs resting. I have asked our family doctor to come and take a look at her. I am sorry she is not able to talk to you just now." The fact that he could be so polite even under these circumstances surely was the result of his many years as a hotel owner.

Next he introduced his younger daughter, Akane, a tall woman wearing orange slacks and a sweater to match. Akane remained seated and merely nodded slightly when she was introduced. She resembled her sister in that she had very pronounced, almost Western-looking features. She seemed to be a naturally active and vivacious sort of person. At the moment her eyes were red and her face lusterless, but it appeared that usually her skin was bronzed and vibrant.

Eda briefly expressed his regret for what had happened, then began asking the elder Nagahara for basic background information about Midori.

"Last November she turned twenty-seven. After graduating from the music conservatory in Tokyo, she spent three years studying in Europe and then worked as a performer in a private club in the Akasaka district of Tokyo. She pretty much lived as she pleased, but when she turned twenty-five I asked her to come back here to her home. I was thinking it was about time for her to think of getting married." Nagahara answered Eda's questions, but his voice quavered and broke from time to time.

"Was she already engaged to be married to someone?"

"No. We had considered several candidates, but one way or another, she did not like any of them."

"Did she have a lover?"

"No. Not to my knowledge."

"Did she have a boyfriend or anyone she was particularly interested in?"

"There may have been some men she was interested in, but she didn't introduce me to any of them, so I really can't say."

At this point the telephone began to ring in another room. A moment later the middle-aged housekeeper who had shown Eda and Igusa into the living room appeared and said that the call was for Mr. Nagahara from the hotel. Nagahara said, "Excuse me," and left the room. They could hear the muffled sound of the lengthy conversation, but not clearly enough to understand what was being said.

Eda studied Akane's profile as she sat gazing into the fire. At last he spoke. "You heard what your father said, but as Midori's sister, I expect you know a lot more about her friends and relationships than he does."

Akane returned Eda's gaze with her own green eyes, giving the impression of being a woman with a strong will of her own.

"How about it? Did your sister have any lovers or any especially intimate boyfriends? You understand, of course, that the reason I am asking this so persistently is that it is hard to imagine that Midori was murdered in an attempted robbery or assault. Neither her money, her jewelry, nor her mink coat were taken, and there seems to have been no sign of a struggle. It seems likely that the murderer knew Midori by sight and that he had some opportunity to get into her car. This leads us to suspect that the murder was committed by someone who knew her."

Eda had a genial way of talking when he questioned people. This was not a calculated approach but his normal way of talking, and he used it no matter how elevated or socially important the person he was questioning was. On the other hand he had earned the enmity and scorn of his fellow investigators and police officers for this casual manner.

Akane replied, "I expect there was someone like that in her life."

"You think she had a lover?"

"I'm afraid I really couldn't say."

"Can you give me the name of any boyfriend she might have had?"

"As far as I know . . ." At Eda's urging Akane gave the names of a professional golfer, a painter, and a student, all of whom lived in the area of Hakone.

"I expect she also had friends in Tokyo?"

"I suppose so, but she never said much about Tokyo." For the first time a faint shadow of melancholy darkened Akane's face, and she stretched her hands out toward the fire.

"Did you also live in Tokyo at one time?"

"Yes, when I was a student. But my sister and I did not live together when we were in Tokyo." Suddenly Akane squeezed her eyes shut with a spasm of grief before continuing. "I suppose of the circle of friends my sister had in Tokyo, Umezaki was the one she knew best."

"Who is Umezaki?"

"He's the manager of a trading company in Tokyo. Apparently Midori got to know him when she was playing the piano at the private club she worked for in Akasaka. He came and stayed at the Emerald View on several occasions. I guess he is more like a friend of the family. But I really can't say whether or not he and my sister had any special sort of relationship."

As she spoke, the tears welled up in Akane's eyes as she once again realized the reality of her sister's death.

"Can you tell me this Umezaki's address in Tokyo?"

"Yes, of course, but if I'm not mistaken, I believe he is staying at the Emerald View tonight."

"You mean he's right here in Hakone?"

"Probably. He is involved with the people who were sponsoring the party at the hotel tonight. I think I remember my sister saying something about his being invited."

Eda nevertheless got the name Sadao Umezaki and the name of his trading company, and his assistant made a note of this information.

Presently Mr. Nagahara completed his telephone conversation and returned to the room, and after the housekeeper had served coffee, Eda resumed questioning. He asked Akane what sort of mood Midori had been in when she left the house to go to the hotel, and she replied that everything had seemed normal.

"Mother felt she was coming down with a cold, so she was upstairs resting, and I was alone in the living room." She went on to explain that the housekeeper lived nearby and normally went home at 6:00, so she was not in the house at the time. She had returned to the Nagahara home tonight because of the tragedy. "Midori had been in her room getting dressed, and she only peeked into the living room for a moment on her way out. I was here reading a book and hardly noticed that she looked in and certainly did not pay any attention to her." Akane explained that she seemed to recall that Midori had gone out the front door, and that a short time later she had heard the Porsche engine start in the garage below, but she wasn't really sure.

"Was there anything about Midori recently that gave you the impression she was upset or disturbed about anything?"

The elder Nagahara simply sat with his shoulders slumped and an anguished look on his face. Akane thought for a time, then said, "A while back, I believe it was last

Friday, Midori was on the lane that goes up the hill behind the house, and I called to her from the driveway below. I was relaying information about one of her piano lessons. There was a man in the lane right behind Midori, and he seemed startled when I called out. It was unusual because ordinarily no one uses that lane.''

''What sort of man was he? Can you describe him?''

''I was pretty far away, so I couldn't see all that well, but he was wearing glasses and wore a suit.''

With only that information it was impossible to say whether or not the man might be connected with the murder.

At around one in the morning, Eda and Igusa finished their questioning and departed. At this point it seemed there were no further leads to be pursued in the case, and it was best to leave the family to assuage their grief the best they could without interference from the police. Tomorrow morning Eda would go to the Emerald View and have a talk with Sadao Umezaki. Eda was both excited and tired as he descended the stone steps in front of the Nagahara home. After the excessive warmth of the house, it felt good to be in the chilly embrace of Hakone's cold night air.

Eda walked to the passenger side door of the car, and as he did so, he happened to look down at the ground. The outdoor light on the front of the garage dimly lighted the area in front of the black police car. Just beneath the passenger-side door he saw a small tuft of fur gleaming dully in the faint light. When he picked it up and looked closely at it, he could see that it had that special quality of elegance.

He held it out to Igusa who had gotten into the drivers seat and said, ''Take a look at this. I believe it's mink.''

''Yes, I think you're right. I know a woman who has a mink coat, and the fur looks just like this,'' said Igusa after taking a close look at the fur.

This was just where the Porsche had been parked earlier. "I wonder if mink is the sort of fur that sheds easily?" Eda murmured to himself, and suddenly he felt a fresh wave of excitement.

# 10

# Pursuing the Investigation

"THIS NEW CLUE MAY GIVE ME A FRESH ANGLE ON THE murder case" was the first thought that occurred to Eda when he discovered the mink fur in Midori's garage. Thoughts such as this filled Inspector Eda's mind as he drove through the crowded residential suburbs of Tokyo the next day.

He had been right about the fur. It was from the half-length sapphire mink coat that Midori had been wearing at the time of her death. He had gone back to the house, and the fur had been positively identified by both the elder Nagahara and Akane. It seemed unlikely that this cluster of ten or twelve hairs should have fallen from the coat accidentally.

Akane had murmured to herself, "I wonder if Midori was attacked in the garage before she even got into the car? The killer could have been waiting for her in the garage,

157

attacked her from behind, strangled her, then loaded her body into the car and driven it to the field where it was found. That would have given the killer time to get away before the body was discovered." The elder Nagahara agreed that this scenario was possible.

"In that case, then, the murderer is not necessarily a man Midori knew, as you conjectured earlier. Even a woman would be strong enough to attack from behind and strangle a victim."

Eda, of course, felt that he would have to take this possibility also into account as he pursued the investigation. He suddenly had the unpleasant feeling that if he checked out all Midori's male friends and failed to turn up a prime suspect, then this case which at first had seemed so straightforward might turn out to be quite difficult.

The assistant chief had been informed of the murder and had returned from his meeting in Yokohama aboard the first bullet train of the morning. He encouraged the investigative teams to continue their work on the basic investigation. In all, he had mobilized nearly a hundred officers to search the site where the body had been found and to question all Midori's friends who could be located.

All the officers had gathered for a strategy meeting that morning, and as soon as it was over, Eda had set out for the Emerald View Hotel, where he met Sadao Umezaki in the lobby; he had made the appointment earlier by telephone. It was a warm, sunny day that belied the chilling cold that had gripped Hakone the previous night.

With his carefully tailored clothes and condescending manner, Umezaki was not the sort of person Eda liked to deal with, but he quickly learned that Umezaki had a perfectly good alibi. From five the previous evening he had been at the party in the hotel dining room that had been given for the local politician.

"My family used to have a summer home near here, but

we sold it years ago. Nevertheless, my father knew this politician quite well in the old days, and even after my father died I maintained the contact, and so I was invited to the party last night. That is why I was staying here at the hotel last night, but I can assure you that there was absolutely nothing between Midori and me.''

The front desk clerk and the bellhops all attested to the fact that Umezaki had not left the hotel last night between 5:00 and 7:30, so his alibi seemed sound. Apparently Umezaki had joined in the search for Midori once there was some concern for her whereabouts. As he continued talking, he further strengthened Eda's feeling of the previous evening that this case might become very complicated.

''You ask about Midori's circle of friends in Tokyo, but I really didn't know her very long when she was living in Tokyo. I guess I knew her for about a year before she returned here to Hakone a couple of years ago. I am a member of the club in Akasaka where she played the piano.''

''If you had known her for a year, you must have known her pretty well. Did she have a lot of male friends besides yourself?''

''I guess you could say that if you mean casual friends. But in those days she did not seem too interested in that sort of thing.''

''Do you mean that she was so involved with her work that she did not have time for other interests?''

''No, it was not that.'' Umezaki gave Eda an appraising glance. ''Didn't Akane tell you what happened?''

''She just said that you knew more about Midori's life in Tokyo than she did.''

''I understand. It is probably difficult for a family member to talk about such things.''

''Are you suggesting that something messy happened?''

"Oh, I'm not suggesting it, I'm *telling* you it was a real messy affair." Umezaki lit a cigarette and took several puffs on it while looking out over the misty lake. Eda had the impression that he was considering how to tell the story, rather than whether to tell it.

"In those days she became involved in a very emotional love affair. The man was a scholar of French literature who already had a wife, and he was just beginning to make a name for himself as a drama producer. When I first got to know Midori she was just beginning to get involved in this thing. It happened very quickly, and before I knew it this guy was the only thing she could think about. I was able to look on as a dispassionate observer, but it seemed that Midori just radiated some marvelous inner beauty as a result of this involvement."

"It sounds wonderful. How did this little affair turn out?"

"It turned out the way these affairs always turn out—it didn't work. The man already had a wife, and Midori was a very proud and possessive woman, so there were problems almost from the beginning. In the end, the lovers were physically separated."

"What you mean, they were physically separated?"

"I mean the man died. I suppose it was the trauma of her lover's death that prompted Midori's father to bring her back here to Hakone."

The circumstances surrounding the death of Michiya Kume were shrouded in mystery, and this in itself added impetus to the investigation being carried out by Eda's team.

As he told the story to Eda, a puzzled look formed on Umezaki's face and he muttered, "I seem to recall having told this story to someone else recently."

After lunch Eda set out for Tokyo. Since the initial phase of an investigation requires by far the most manpower, Eda made the trip to Tokyo alone. Actually, he felt more comfortable doing this sort of thing by himself, and he often came up with some sort of excuse to get away from his subordinates and work alone. It was not necessarily that he thought he was better than the others, but it was easier to follow up a hunch or to rely on some sixth sense if he didn't have to explain and justify what he was doing to his colleagues. Indeed, he was convinced that the best police work is usually done by people who have enough imagination to be unorthodox.

It was after one when he arrived in Tokyo. Eda went directly to the Yotsuya precinct station to see what record they had concerning the death of Michiya Kume some two years ago. Since the death had been judged an accident, the records concerning it were very scanty.

At about 7:00 on the evening of October 28 that year, Yuko Kume returned to her apartment in Yotsuya and discovered the body of her husband, Michiya, sprawled on the floor of the small room he used as a study. The gas heater had been turned on and the fire was out. The room was filled with gas fumes, and Kume was already dead.

An autopsy had confirmed that the cause of death was gas, and that the time of death was about 6:00 P.M. There was no evidence of drugs or poison. Neither his wife nor close friends could suggest any reason why he would have wanted to commit suicide, and no suicide note was found.

At that point an investigation was undertaken to determine whether the death had been by accident or murder, and although many of his acquaintances were questioned, there was no evidence pointing to homicide. The conclusion finally reached by the coroner was that the death was an accident. It was known that Kume had been working feverishly on a translation and had not been getting much sleep. It was assumed that he had fallen asleep at his desk, the teakettle on the heater had boiled over, putting out the fire, and that he had died without waking up. The record included a list of the people interviewed in connection with the case. These included his wife, Yuko, the members of his theatre group, people who had known him when he was a student, and even Midori Nagahara.

From reading the record of the interviews, it seemed evident that a certain amount of suspicion fell on Midori. For approximately one year prior to his death, Midori and Kume had been lovers, and shortly before his death Midori was known to have been angry that he would not leave his wife. It also turned out that Midori did not have a solid alibi for the time around 6:00 when Kume died. Nevertheless, there was absolutely no evidence to prove that Midori had been responsible for his death.

The warm spring sunlight came through the window of the Yokosuka Line train and fell on Eda's cheek. He dozed for a while. It had been 3:00 A.M. by the time he had returned home last night, and he had left for work at 7:30 this morning. Waking from his doze, he could see the large statue of Kannon, the goddess of mercy, in the distance and knew that the train had reached Ofuna station. The next stop would be Kita Kamakura, his destination.

Eda got up from his seat and made his way toward the front of the train. As he walked, he pulled a wadded handbill from his overcoat pocket. It had been an insert in the morning newspaper which he had thrust into his pocket as he left the house, and he had used it to write Yuko's address on when he had telephoned earlier.

"Who gave you my address?" asked Yuko with an unhappy expression on her face. She had invited Eda into her tiny, detached house and was giving him a cushion to sit on.

"I called the offices of the Jourdan theater group and

asked them. If they had not been able to give me the information, I would have gone to the city offices to get your forwarding address, but fortunately one of the women who works in the wardrobe department of the theater group was nice enough to tell me where you live.''

"Ah yes, that must have been Saeki. We went to high school together, and she even came to the memorial service that was held for my late husband." But the tight set of the lips and the look on her face made it clear that Yuko did not care to have people telling other people where she lived.

Yuko Kume was now twenty-nine years old, and everything about her, from her serene, formal features to the straight set of the collar of her kimono, confirmed that she was a woman of good taste and upbringing. Perhaps her youthful good looks were due in part to the fact that she had not borne any children. She was a small woman dressed in a traditional Japanese kimono, and her good looks were enhanced by the air of tragic loss that cloaked her like a veil. No doubt this was the result of having been widowed at a young age.

"I am sorry to intrude on you like this, but I am curious to know why you have hidden yourself away in such a remote and unlikely place. I understand that you moved out of your apartment in Yotsuya less than a month after your husband died. Isn't it terribly lonely for you here?" Eda asked this question with true inquisitiveness as he looked out at the garden, which was surrounded by shrubbery rather than a fence. The leaves had not yet come out on the trees, and the setting sun glowed red just over the top of the traditional gate.

"It's not really that lonely. My parents live quite close by, and they urged me to live around here. My elder brother and his family live with my parents, so I decided to rent this little place and live alone." The tone of Yuko's voice and the features of her face all accented the sense of tranquility and serenity she seemed to exude.

"Besides, you had quit your job in Tokyo, so you really had no reason to stay there."

"That's right."

Probably while her husband was still alive they had gotten very little money for his translations and plays and had a hard time making ends meet, so she had had to go out and find a job, but after he died, she probably received enough financial help from her family that she did not lack anything. She had the air of a woman of good breeding, and this had helped Eda reach his conclusions about her.

Yuko prepared tea for Eda, served it, and then shyly kept her eyes on the floor, obviously waiting for the interrogation to begin. First, however, Eda wanted to ask some more questions about her intensely private lifestyle.

"You said when you came in that you are investigating some sort of case."

Eda, of course, had identified himself and had shown his badge when he first introduced himself to her. "Yes. The case I was referring to is the strangulation murder of Midori Nagahara at Hakone last night."

Eda noticed that Yuko's features froze and she shut her eyes when she heard those words, and yet in some sense it seemed almost as though she had been expecting this.

"Were you aware of the murder?"

"Yes, I saw it both on television and in the newspapers," she murmured, still keeping her eyes on the floor.

"We have been doing a background check on the victim, and of course this led us to the death of your husband two and a half years ago. As you know, that was eventually judged to have been an accident, but at one time there was considerable suspicion cast on Midori, and she was questioned extensively. This led us to wonder if there might be some connection between Midori's murder and your husband's death.''

"I'm afraid I don't understand. What sort of connection do you think there might be?" Eda sensed a note of deep mistrust in Yuko's voice.

"Well, to put the matter quite bluntly, there are some who feel that Midori may have murdered your husband and made it look like an accident, and that opens the possibility that Midori's murder was an act of revenge.''

"I see,'' said Yuko taking a deep breath. Then she knitted her brows and once again gazed at the floor.

"Please excuse me for being rude, but I wonder, at the time of your husband's death, were you aware of the nature of his relationship with Midori?''

After a slight pause, she said, "Yes'' with a slight nod.

"Were you personally acquainted with Midori Nagahara?''

"I met her on two occasions. It was quite by accident each time.'' Yuko kept her eyes on the floor, and though her voice was barely audible, she managed to reply. Then her lips tightened and her brow knitted again and she seemed on the verge of tears. She was clearly reliving a painful part of her past.

For a time Eda gazed out the window at the front part of the garden and tried to formulate a plan. Presently he looked back at the woman and said, "My next question may alarm you, but I want you to understand that today I am only trying to establish the context for our investigation. Can I assume that you were here at home at around six-thirty last night?''

Yuko slowly lifted her gaze to meet his, and a wave of emotion seemed to sweep across her eyes. "Yesterday I went to Kamakura. I was there at six, and I returned here at about seven.''

"May I ask what you were doing in Kamakura?''

"Yes, of course. Every Tuesday and Friday I go to Kamakura, where I work for a publishing company. I work for the husband of a friend of mine who has a company that specializes in art books."

"In other words, you went there yesterday and worked as usual?"

"That's right. I worked there from noon until about six o'clock."

Naturally Eda made a note of the name and address of the publishing company, but for his own part, he was sure she was telling the truth. If Yuko had been in Kamakura at 6:00 there was simply no way she could have been in the garage of Midori's house to strangle her at 6:30. It was out of the question. Eda experienced a feeling of disappointment, but this did not mean that he had entirely lost interest in this tragic young widow.

"Apart from Tuesdays and Fridays, what do you do?" he asked as though speaking across a great chasm that separated them.

The opposite wall and the wall by the veranda were literally hidden by bookshelves. They contained complete sets of classic French theater, modern theater, poetry collections, and individual works of literature; apparently they had belonged to her husband.

"Recently I have been putting my late husband's books and papers and writings in order." Yuko had seen his gaze and had responded to it in her usual serene fashion.

Eda tried to focus his gaze on the spines of the books, but had difficulty reading their titles. Then, suddenly, he looked away. He had seen a title that appeared out of place. There between collections of Byron and Verlaine was a book spine with the title *Studies in Nutrition*. It appeared to have been hastily stuffed between books on classical literature, and was the only volume of its kind on the shelf.

This had attracted his attention, and it struck him as being quite extraordinary.

Yuko followed Eda's gaze and said, "Oh, I see you have noticed that magazine. It's most peculiar. It seems out of place here, but I found it when I was arranging my husband's things." She nodded her head slightly, and on her mouth was a smile that was partly childish, partly perplexed.

No doubt this was an out-of-place magazine that Yuko had come across when she was arranging her husband's books, but she seemed expecially sensitive to its discovery. When Eda looked at the magazine more closely, he noticed that the date printed on the spine was for April of this year.

# 11

# The Picture Postcard

When the telephone began to ring, Daigo was astounded, wondering if it could possibly be another call for him. As he listened to it ringing, he was almost certain it would be for him. No doubt the call had something to do with yesterday's announcement in the newspaper reporting the new analysis that had been done on the Popico cookies produced by Minami Foods.

His assistant, Yamada, answered the phone, but as expected, he turned to Daigo and said, "It's for you. From Tokyo."

Taking the receiver, Daigo said, "Hello."

He heard a woman's voice on the other end of the line. "Is that you, Professor Daigo? I am on the editorial staff of the magazine *Studies in Nutrition.*"

For a moment an unpleasant shock clutched at Daigo's heart. Automatically he thought of the magazine he had

168

left at the entrace of Yuko Kume's house in Kita Kamakura. For an awful moment he wondered if they had been able to trace him from that and link him to the murder of Midori Nagahara?

The woman apparently handed the phone over to a man who was the assistant editor of the magazine. He said that he had seen the reports in several newspapers of Daigo's announcement concerning the link between the Popico cookies and the liver cancer in children, and he wanted to congratulate Daigo on a good piece of scientific research.

"In fact, I wonder if you would be interested in doing an article for our magazine? As I am sure you know, our April issue was a special issue devoted to the question of children's foods. We would like to continue along that line in our next issue and would certainly appreciate it if you could do an article for us."

The editor went on to say that they would like to have about a thirty-page manuscript explaining the background of the news reports and why, even though he was working in the same laboratory as the late Professor Yoshimi, his results had been exactly the opposite of the earlier study.

At first as he listened to the editor explaining what he wanted, Daigo was terrified that his secret had been discovered; in order to buy himself a little more time to decide how to deal with the situation, he agreed to do the article. Having hung up the telephone, he returned to his desk, where his eye came to rest on the morning edition of yesterday's newspaper. The results of the study Daigo had completed last August had been painstakingly redone, and two days ago the results were sent to the prefectural hygiene office. Yesterday those results had been reported in the morning edition of the newspaper. Although he had expected the story to make the newspapers, he had not been prepared for the extent of the coverage it had received or the extent of the public outcry that followed it. And yet, when he stopped to think, it seemed appropriate.

Since last September the incidence of liver cancer among the children who had eaten the Popico cookies made by Minami Foods had been played down, but it had not died out entirely, and in fact at one point it had received national coverage. That in addition to the fact that the results Daigo published in his report were directly contrary to those published by the late Professor Yoshimi; a report that directly linked the ingredients used in Popico cookies with the A toxin that was responsible for causing cancer, and the resulting conclusion that the responsibility for this tragedy went back to the manufacturer, was played up extensively by the media.

This report, however, ignored the results produced by Yoshimi's assistants and had suggested that there had been a cover-up in the interpretation of the results. Consequently, the telephone in Daigo's laboratory had been ringing continuously since yesterday afternoon. The news media wanted interviews, and the general public wanted answers, and there were calls of support from the victims themselves. There were even a few unpleasant callers who accused him of merely promoting himself.

Behind his back he heard Yamada mutter, "You've really become a celebrity, haven't you?" His tone was half ironic, half joking. This seemed to be typical of the response he could expect to receive from his colleagues and co-workers at J university. This also fanned the hostility between those who wanted Daigo to succeed to Yoshimi's position and those who opposed him.

Daigo glanced at his watch; it was 11:40. It was a bit early to be leaving for lunch, but he decided to break away from reading the results of river pollution studies. As long as he stayed in the lab, the telephone would continue to ring and he would have to deal with it, so he decided to get away.

"If the phone rings again, tell them I'll be out all afternoon. I'll be back in an hour, of course, but tell them that anyway."

"I hear you," said Yamada with a sneer on his thin lips.

For the past few days the spring sun had been warm, and all across the university campus the trees were coming into full bud. It was a brilliant contrast to the hard cold of winter that had persisted until just last week. Nevertheless, despite the warmth, Daigo could still sometimes feel the deep chill he had experienced on that cold night when he had crouched in Midori's garage at Hakone. Emotionally and physically he felt sick and confused about what had happened.

Where, he wondered, had Fumiko Samejima been when she heard the news that Midori Nagahara had been murdered? She had probably been at home alone in that isolated detatched house in Kita Kamakura when she had heard the news.

Perhaps the police had come to interview her later. No doubt the police would quickly learn that Midori had been suspected in the death of Yuko's husband two and a half years ago, and would be very interested in talking to her. But Yuko Kume should have an airtight alibi. The news reports of the murder had said that Midori Nagahara had been strangled in her garage at about 6:20 on the evening of March 8.

In order to give himself time to escape and at the same time to throw suspicion on those who were acquainted with Midori, Daigo had taken the car down the slope and hidden it in some trees, but obviously the police already knew that the murder had been committed in the garage within minutes of the time Midori left the house. Consequently, if Fumiko had been right in telling him that she worked at the office from noon until 6:00 on Tuesday and Friday afternoons, she would have a firm alibi.

No doubt Fumiko would also have seen the news report about the new lab results that had been published yesterday. The report had been spread by the national wire services. The thought of Fumiko reading both these news reports left Daigo with a deep sense of satisfaction. He could not help but hear once again in his mind Midori's tearful voice as she said, "It's horrible to think of all those little children with cancer." It had been obvious to him on that fateful night in Barbizon that Fumiko had shared his hatred for Yoshimi and his collusion with the company that had caused the children to have cancer, just as she had shared his sympathy with the children.

In fact, now that he thought about it, hadn't that been the very beginning of everything? It was this that had brought them together and created their shared bond of human concern. When Daigo had said that there were some people in the world who were not fit to live, Fumiko had agreed with him and had said it takes a lot of courage to insure that such people do not exist.

Certainly it was only after that that Fumiko had been inspired to take direct action. But Daigo had also been a part of the agreement. Consequently, he had not been deterred, and had not his publication of the true test results been the final act in their conspiracy?

At this point he could probably expect to be involved in a lot of publicity and promotion, and once the company had paid compensation to the victims his position would become all the more elevated. He did not, however, permit himself to revel in a prestige he did not enjoy. Nevertheless, nothing could deny him the deep sense of satisfaction he felt.

Daigo was beginning to feel that this sort of heroism made him more youthful. His heart was full of the notion that he would not mind sacrificing his own future if he could help relieve the agony of innocent children and their parents. At the same time he felt self-conscious at being in the position of the scientist who has received notoriety for doing some social good.

Because he was afraid of his intermittent and terrible memories, he tried to protect himself from them somehow. If he could do that, he would be able to live a new and satisfying life. He felt as though a fragrant wind was blowing around him, and he was sure that sooner or later he would be able to meet Fumiko again.

He had also felt relieved when the news of his lab reports finally pushed the stories of Midori's murder out of the newspapers. Apparently the investigation in Hakone had come to a standstill. Even the local newspapers in Hakone were no longer giving the murder detailed coverage, but no doubt the level of interest was still intense among the police investigators in Odawara, and they were surely still combing the area for suspects.

Daigo began to wonder how long he should wait to let all the furor die down before he tried to see Fumiko again. Eight days had passed since Midori had been murdered. He remembered reading somewhere that in such a case the investigation was intense for the first two weeks, then it was put on the back burner for about a month, and if it still was not solved by that time, it was generally listed as an unsolved crime. By next Tuesday it would be two weeks since the killing.

The spring vacation from school was beginning, and he no longer had many lectures to prepare. Daigo set out along the street behind the campus immersed in his own thoughts. For some time he walked slowly along the busy street. A warm sun was shining down, and it seemed he could feel its warmth transmitted to his feet from the pavement. A short distance ahead was a bowling alley where they had a nice snack bar that served a good lunch and where he could get a cup of coffee.

Another meeting with Fumiko . . . Daigo pictured in his mind what the meeting would be like—running toward each other across a rose-dappled meadow after having passed through the valley of the shadow of death. But when he tried to think realistically how he could bring this about, the problem seemed insurmountable. Some of his uneasiness came from the fact that he had never actually met Fumiko. All he could remember from their night at the Château Chantal was a brief glimpse of her coffee brown hair, her shoulder, her profile, and her slim legs sheathed in dark stockings. He remembered the feel of her firm, resilient flesh and the fragrance of her perfume, which gave the impression that she was an elegant person. After that, there was her voice, but of course he could not be sure he had heard her real voice.

But Daigo had more than just his memory of that night to use in his search for Fumiko. For one thing, she was a woman who had spent a week in Paris last October. There was also the fact that she had been in Fukuoka on the evening of December 3 and on the afternoon of December 4. On the evening of the third Yoshimi had attended a wedding reception at a hotel in the center of the city, and she had also been there, as well as on the fourth, between 2:00 and 4:00 in the afternoon, when she had gone to his house and poisoned him. And finally, more than anything else, she was a woman who hated Midori Nagahara intensely.

Certainly Yuko Kume seemed to fit this description. It would be wise for him to try to find out whether or not Yuko had been to Paris last fall, but it would be very difficult to check on something like that without her finding out about it. He recalled seeing Yuko wearing a kimono, standing before the smoke of the fire at her home in Kita

Kamakura. He wondered if she realized that he was the author of the message he had intended by leaving a copy of the nutrition magazine on her doorstep? Suddenly a dark suspicion began to form in a corner of his mind. Perhaps it merely stemmed from the unpleasant shock he had received earlier when he had gotten a phone call from the editorial offices of that same magazine.

Daigo came to a halt on the sidewalk. He saw something on the street in front of him that made his heart recoil. There, not twenty feet in front of him, was parked a large black car. As he watched, a heavyset man emerged from it. The man closed the car door, raised his hand in some sort of sign, and the car sped away as the man walked toward Daigo. A uniformed man was driving the car.

Daigo resumed walking again. Even if he stayed put, Inspector Furukawa would soon be upon him with that same smiling face, pretending that he had just run into Daigo by accident, the way he always did.

"Well, how are you? I haven't seen you around for a long time." Inspector Furukawa's ruddy, cheerful face was just as Daigo had remembered it. His smiling features seemed a bit obscured by the dark frames of the glasses he wore. Behind those glasses, his eyes glittered relentlessly, and he appeared full of enthusiasm to learn everything he could about the people he encountered. He radiated good cheer.

"You must be on your lunch break, eh, professor?" Furukawa took a look at his watch and noted that it was 11:50.

"Well, the fact is, I'm a little early today. I've been getting so many telephone calls, it's impossible to get any work done." He was sure the police officer already knew this much about him and that he was giving away nothing.

"I can understand that," said the officer with a deep bow. "I'm just a layman, and from the beginning I have never really understood this specialized stuff, but I really feel like giving you some applause for your latest achievement. It was really something.''

"I suppose you are referring to the matter of Minami Foods.''

"Of course. That company has not only made huge profits on their cookies, but also on their bread and various instant foods. There is no reason why they shouldn't pay a handsome settlement to their victims. After all, they have their corporate image to maintain if they expect to continue doing business. They can't expect to do that if the public associates them with their crying victims.''

"Well, all I did was prepare an objective report in which I stated my findings.''

"Are your free for a bit right now?'' asked Furukawa.

"Do you want to talk to me about something as official police business?''

"Yes, that's right. I tried to call you earlier on the telephone, but the line was busy and I couldn't get through.''

Daigo felt himself tremble, but there was nothing he could do. The pair entered a nearby coffee shop. It was a small, forlorn, and forgotten place that looked out on the national highway. Even though it was just noon, the brilliant sunshine outside did not penetrate here.

"Let's see now, the last time we met was on a holiday, February 11, in front of your house.'' Furukawa began speaking after the waitress had taken their order and after he had lit a cigarette. Because of the smoke, he squinted his eyes as he looked at Daigo. "Since then our investigation has been stumbling along, but at last we have located a woman of the sort we were looking for.''

"A woman of the sort you were looking for?'' Daigo was suddenly very alert, but he tried to sound casual.

"That's right. You remember we were looking for the woman who was seen talking to Yoshimi on the terrace at the wedding reception on the night before the murder. We believe she was the same woman who was seen entering Yoshimi's house on the afternoon of the murder. We believe she is a key to solving this case. At any rate, we have been making every effort to learn something about her. We talked to the people who planned the reception and went over every single name on the guest list, but we found no one matching her description.''

''In other words, the woman just crashed the party, isn't that what you told me before?''

''Yes, that's right. We have been intensely interested in this woman, and in the end, the only thing we could do was interview all of the more than two hundred guests at the reception and see if anyone remembered anything about her.''

When they had met on the previous occasion, Furukawa had said that they had not been able to locate the woman among the circle of Yoshimi's known friends and acquaintances.

''Were you able to find someone who attended the reception who knew who the woman was?''

Furukawa gave him a curiously intent look when Daigo asked this question. The waitress, threading her way between the tables, saw the policeman's smile and thought it was for her. Daigo's jaw tightened with the tension.

''From the very beginning there were a number of people who vaguely remembered seeing her. People like Yoshimi's lab assistant, Yamada, remembered her. That's how we first became aware of the woman's existence. But from there on we ran into difficulties in trying to identify her.''

They had interviewed each and every one of the two hundred eleven people who had been invited to the reception, people who had come from as far away as Tokyo and Kagoshima. To make matters worse, a group of them had left the following day for a trip overseas. These and other problems caused unexpected delays, but eventually they had interviewed everyone and asked them if they knew anything or remembered anything about the woman, and they had come up with nothing. But the woman was not just a phantom. Nearly twenty of the people they had questioned had some vague recollection that the woman had been there. On the basis of the vague and fragmentary information available to them, they had determined that the woman was in her late twenties or early thirties, that she had long hair and a medium build. She had been wearing a tastefully designed long dress in either blue or gray, and part of the time she had been wearing blue-tinted sunglasses.

There was nothing in this description of the woman that conflicted with the description of the woman who had been seen entering Yoshimi's house the following day. "Nevertheless, that was the only information we were able to get from the people who had attended the reception." Furukawa grimaced as though his coffee was bitter, added sugar to it, and sat in silence for a time.

Daigo recalled the look of determination he had seen on Furukawa's face when they had met in February and the policeman told him that they had not given up trying to identify the mystery woman. He was the tenacious sort of investigator who would leave no stone unturned.

"But didn't you say a moment ago that you had found some leads after all?" Daigo could not conceal his anxiety.

"Yes. In the end we tried to get as much cooperation as we could from the other guests who were staying at the hotel that night, or from people who had been at the hotel. There was some chance that the mystery woman had actually spent the night at the hotel, so it seemed possible that one of the other guests might have had some contact with her."

"That makes sense. Did you learn anything?" Daigo's

coffee was cold, but he raised it to his lips as he asked this question.

Furukawa's face burst with a self-satisfied smile. "Eventually we found what we were looking for. There was a woman who had bumped into our mystery woman in the ladies room, which is located between the banquet hall and the lobby."

"Bumped into her?"

"Quite literally. This woman is from Tokyo. She had accompanied her husband to Fukuoka that day; he works for some company. Her son and his wife had moved here in September, and they had come to see how the young couple was getting along. Since the young couple only have a small apartment, the parents stayed at the hotel."

"So I suppose all you had to do was check the hotel registry."

"Well, of course we did that. We got a list of the people who stayed at the hotel that night, and we even talked to some of them—at least to the ones who had listed their real names and addresses. It was quite a project. We had policemen in Tokyo and Osaka and all over the country tracking down people."

Daigo was appalled at the scope and organization the police could bring to bear on the case, and began to think they might find him out after all. "So you said this woman bumped into your mystery lady?"

"It was about seven-forty that evening. The woman we talked to and her husband were just leaving the hotel when the woman decided to go into the ladies' powder room just off the lobby. She ran right into a young lady who was coming out. The young lady was just in the process of putting something away in her purse when the collision occurred. The young lady's purse fell to the floor and its contents went everywhere. The older woman was embarrassed about the whole thing and helped the other woman collect her belongings. The younger woman did not seem too indignant about the accident, but she did behave in a peculiar manner. She did not say anything, and she tried to keep her face averted. This young woman was dressed in a long skirt of blue-gray material and she was wearing blue-tinted sunglasses.''

Daigo suddenly felt a dull, leaden pain begin to spread through his body. Without quite being aware of what he was doing he picked up his coffee and drank without realizing that he had not yet even added sugar to it. After some time had passed he said, ''So this great lead you were telling me about is the fact that your mystery lady wears blue-tinted sunglasses?''

''Well, no, there's more to it than that.'' There seemed to be a look of cunning in Furukawa's eyes, almost as though he had expected Daigo to ask that question. ''The contents of the purse that were scattered all over the floor included what you would expect in a woman's purse: there was a compact and a handkerchief and so on, but among the other things there was also a picture postcard. The older woman picked it up and did not really pay much attention to it, but she seemed to recall that the picture showed a mountain and a lake, and a white excursion boat on the lake. She had the distinct impression that it was probably a picture of Hakone or Fuji Five Lakes.''

A desperate shiver passed through Daigo as he realized that it was surely a picture of the Emerald View Hotel. It was probably exactly like the card that had been delivered to his home on New Year's Day with all the other New Year's greeting cards. Probably Fumiko was carrying it around with the intention of sending him a message when her part of the job had been completed, and then for some reason she had decided not to send it.

''Actually, it was in connection with this card that I wanted to talk with you today. We were wondering if Professor Yoshimi had any friends or acquaintances living in the area around Hakone or Fuji Five Lakes, or if he had any special connection with that part of the country. Do you know anything about that?''

At least they had not yet made a connection with the Emerald View Hotel, and Daigo forced himself to return the inspector's steady gaze. Still, he wondered if he had acted too quickly in committing the second murder so soon.

# 12

# The Second Meeting

"In other words, as far as you can tell the man did his initial stalking of Midori on January 10 of this year. He spent three nights in a Japanese inn called Fumotokan just south of Hakone, and on his first day there he took one of the maids aside and questioned her about the elder daughter of the owners of the Emerald View."

As Detective Eda of the Odawara police force summarized his report, he was busy fishing crumpled notes and memos from the various pockets of his suit. The scribbles on them seemed to be some sort of code, but he carefully arranged the scraps of paper on his desk as he spoke. Of course all the notes of the interviews he had conducted had been annotated in his official notebook, but when he wanted to compare bits of information or synthesize it, he would tear pages out of his notebook and arrange them on his desk. Over the years he had devised a system where it was more convenient to write his notes on separate sheets of paper from the very beginning. Nevertheless, the scribbles on the paper and their wrinkled and torn appearance from having been crumpled in his various pockets were eloquent testimony to his disorganized nature.

Nevertheless, the information he imparted as he surveyed his disarray of notes was significant enough to capture the complete attention of Department Chief Sasaki, who was sitting on the other side of the desk. The chief disliked Eda's disorganized and unorthodox methods and his refusal to work as a part of the team, but he also knew that there was no one on the force who was more tenacious and determined once he got on the scent of something. It was the morning of March 17, and they were awaiting the arrival of the detective in charge of the investigation. Just before one of the investigation meetings was always a stressful time.

"The inn where he stayed is an old-fashioned, traditional Japanese inn. It is rather inconspicuous, but a first-class place, and the people who work there are all old residents of the area, so they know what is going on. It may just have been a matter of chance, but this guest stayed in a room on the second floor from which you can actually see a corner of the Emerald View, so he would have had plenty of leisure to observe the place. Even though the weather was quite cold at the time, he had the windows open."

"I understand he was about forty and spoke with an Osaka accent," Sasaki said, reviewing the previous information he had received. He was a heavily built man with intense eyes and large ears. What he lacked in intelligence he more than compensated for with his force of will and his intensity.

"That's right. When he checked into the hotel, he registered under the name of Komao Ikegami. He listed an

Osaka address and indicated that he was a writer by profession, but no one in the writing world has ever heard of anyone by that name. I'm afraid he missed the mark on that one.''

''Yes. And there is a strong possibility that this is the same man who listened to Midori perform on the piano at the Emerald View on February 11 and who approached Tadao Umezaki in the bar on February 12.''

''I have a hunch you are right about this. He was the right age, he was wearing the same sort of sunglasses, and he spoke with the same Osaka accent. But according to Umezaki, the man he talked to runs a nightclub of some sort on the edge of Lake Biwa, and although the man gave his surname, Umezaki has forgotten it. But when I questioned him again later he seemed pretty sure that the man's name was not Ikegami.''

Whoever this man was, he was like a shadow that had crept up on Midori Nagahara and Yuko Kume. Eda had had this feeling ever since the day after the murder when he had stopped at the Emerald View and questioned Umezaki. He had felt this way ever since Umezaki had told him about the death of Kume Michiya two and a half years ago and the subsequent suspicion that had fallen on Midori Nagahara.

He had also heard Umezaki murmur, ''I seem to recall having told this same account to someone else recently.''

Eda did not miss the chance to ask him what he meant by that. Although Umezaki had only a very hazy recollection of the incident, through Eda's persistent questioning the story began to unravel. On the previous occasion when Umezaki had come to Hakone, probably on the evening of January 12, he recalled that a man with an Osaka accent had approached him rather aggressively in this very hotel bar and had asked him about Midori. At the time Umezaki had already drunk quite a bit, but he had related to the stranger what he knew about Midori and about Michiya Kume's past.

Having heard Umezaki's account, Eda consciously brought to mind the figure of Midori's sister, Akane. On the night of the murder, she had conspicuously omitted any mention of her sister's love life. At this point he still could not say what all of this meant as far as this case was concerned, but it was something to follow up. When he had first questioned Akane, she had mentioned seeing a man in the lane directly behind Midori. Hearing this, Eda assigned one of his junior detectives to the task of making the rounds of all the hotels and inns in the area to see if they could find any leads. As a result of this inquiry he learned that a man with a Kansai accent who claimed to be a writer had stayed at the Fumotokan.

It would be significant if they could prove that the guest at the Fumotokan was the same man who had talked to Umezaki.

Sasaki stroked his double chins thoughtfully and looked doubtfully at Eda's scraps of paper. "In other words, we have to check and find out whether or not this man lied about his name and occupation both at the inn and when he talked to Umezaki, and whether or not there is any such person who runs a nightclub on the edge of Lake Biwa."

"Naturally we have already done that," said Eda, responding to the tone of his superior's voice. "We have not been able to locate anyone who corresponds to this man's description. Whoever he is, he is concealing his identity, and he has tried to learn all he could about Midori."

On the afternoon of the day he met Umezaki, Eda had gone to Tokyo, where he had first visited the Yotsuya precinct station. There he had inquired in detail regarding the circumstances surrounding the death of Michiya Kume. Although the death had been judged an accident, Midori, as his secret lover, had been investigated thoroughly.

Next Eda had telephoned Kume's theater group, where he inquired about the present address of Kume's widow, Yuko. "I don't believe we yet have enough information to decide whether or not the man who has begun hanging around Yuko Kume is the same man as the one who talked to Umezaki. Certainly the shadow of guilt that has fallen on Yuko is not nearly as serious as the one that was on Midori at the time of Kume's death."

Sasaki still protruded his lower lip suspiciously and said, "Nevertheless, someone left a copy of that magazine, *Studies in Nutrition*, on her doorstep."

"At first I did not even stop to think about it. I went right ahead and asked her to explain the odd magazine. She merely said that she was clearing up some of Kume's effects and this magazine was among some of his nonprofessional books and journals, but when I took a close look at the magazine, I saw that it was dated April of this year, which means that it probably hit the newsstands in late February or early March. There is no reason to believe that it was mixed in with the personal effects of Kume, who died more than two years ago."

Eda had been persistent in questioning her about the magazine, and she had replied, "Actually, I found it on the evening of March 5. I had been burning some wastepaper in the garden, and when I returned to the house, I found this magazine lying on the doorstep. There was no sign of anyone being around, so I felt it might be some sort of sign from my late husband, and I treasured it," she replied with tears springing to her eyes.

"At that point she turned her head away and would say no more. At the time I could not imagine why Kume's widow was telling me such a story." But after pondering it awhile, it seemed that there might be two reasons for the magazine's appearance. The first reason was that the story was true, and that she had simply told it because she really did not know where the magazine had come from. The other possibility was that she had some scheme, some reason for wanting the police to believe this.

The problem was that if he accepted the second possibility, he did not know what to make of the tragic veil of melancholy that seemed to cover this poor widow. Her grief seemed real enough.

"Either way, there is nothing here that will crack her alibi. Every Tuesday and Friday afternoon she goes to Kamakura, where she works for a small publishing company that specializes in art books. On the evening of March 8 she worked in the office until six o'clock as usual. Three people, including the president of the company, testified that she worked at the office that evening and did not leave for home until after six-fifteen. They observed nothing unusual about her behavior, and her story seems right. So we have to reject the idea that Yuko Kume might have been directly responsible for the murder of Midori Nagahara."

"I see."

"Nevertheless, on the way back I had some feelings about the matter."

With one hand Eda gathered up the scraps of paper on the desk and thrust them once again into his pocket as he continued his account in a somewhat casual tone of voice. As he spoke he smiled faintly, which was rare when he was involved in a case. He gave his formal report and larded it liberally with his own ideas and opinions, but the unusual thing was that his audience consisted only of Sasaki. "After interviewing Umezaki, I went to the police station in Yotsuya, where I learned the details about the murder that happened two and a half years ago. Then I found out where Kume's widow is presently living and went to see her. And as I did so, I thought about the man who approached Umezaki in the hotel bar on the night of December 12 and asked about the details of the death of

Michiya Kume. I wondered if he might not have gotten on this same Yokosuka Line that I was riding and made the journey to Kita Kamakura. This is the idea I had begun to toy with. At least one reason I was thinking along these lines was that this man had been asking about Midori's past, and if from the very beginning he knew about this incident and about the existence of Yuko Kume, he would not have had to ask Umezaki about it and thereby leave open the possibility of a trail we could follow.''

"But the fact is, you really have no proof to indicate that this man actually followed the same course you did and that he had been in contact with Yuko, do you?"

"Of course there is no definite proof, or at least there wasn't any in the beginning. In the first place, he could not have gone to the Yotsuya police station and gained access to the old reports the way I did. But he may have had some other method of finding the information, and it is possible that he might just have gotten enough information from Umezaki to tell him all that he needed to know. But if we make the assumption that he wanted to make contact with Yuko Kume, the question is, how did he go about it?"

"Surely he must have figured out some method very much like yours. He could have gone to her former residence and asked about her forwarding address, or he could have gone to the city office where she would have reported her new address, or perhaps he met one of her old friends, who told him where she was now living." Sasaki's comments were not so much an expression of his own thinking as they were intended as a stimulus to keep Eda talking.

"You're right. I decided there was a fifty-fifty chance that he had contacted her, and I quickly made one more phone call."

"To whom?"

"To the costume maker for the Jourdan theater group, the girl named Saeki. Yuko had said that they were high school classmates. I called the theater office and asked if there was anyone there who knew where Kume's widow was presently living, and eventually that woman came on the line and very politely gave me the information I wanted. She has a very melodic soprano voice. Just by listening to it I was sure she must be a beautiful woman.''

''You mean you called this same woman a second time?''

''Yes, I asked if recently there had been any other man like myself who called asking about Yuko Kume's address.''

''What did she say?''

''What do you think she said? She said yes, there was another man. He had called at about nine on the evening of Friday, March fourth. She went on to tell me in great detail why she remembered that it was that particular date and time.'' According to Saeki's explanation, judging from the man's voice, at first he seemed to be middle-aged, relaxed, and polite. But when she had asked if he was a friend of Kume's, he had become flustered and said that he was a friend, but that he had been living abroad for a long time and had only just heard about Kume's death, and right away he hung up. While he was speaking in that flustered manner, she had had the impression that he had lapsed into a Kyushu accent.

''So this time we have a Kyushu accent,'' said Sasaki, stroking his double chin.

''The Kyushu accent and the Kansai accent are quite similar. It would not be that hard for someone with any sort of talent to fool a simple person in the matter of accents. The important point here is that this happened on the night of March fourth.''

''On the night Midori's body was discovered, didn't her sister, Akane, say something about that?''

''Yes, she said that just at dusk on the evening of March

fourth she had seen her sister in the lane behind the house on her way to a piano lesson, and had called to her from the driveway. She noticed that there was an unfamiliar man wearing glasses on the lane just behind Midori.''

''Yes, that's it.''

''There's more to it than that. It was midday on March fifth that Yuko Kume discovered that someone had mysteriously left a copy of that magazine on her doorstep when she was not aware of it. It was also at around three on that day that the front desk at the Emerald View received a telephone call asking when Midori would next be playing the piano. The hotel manager confirmed that.''

''I see. When you line up events like that, it makes it fairly evident that on January tenth through twelfth and again on March fourth and fifth there was a middle-aged man, or perhaps two men, sniffing about trying to find out something about both Midori and Yuko.''

''I expect it was the same man each time.''

''Yes, he murdered Midori, but how does Yuko figure into the picture?''

''I have a hunch this phantom will make another attempt to get close to Yuko.''

''Why would he do that?''

''I'm not sure. At first I thought Yuko might have asked him to kill Midori for her, but if that were the case he would not have been asking Umezaki about Midori and Yuko.''

''That's true. I wonder if he plans to murder Yuko as well?'' There did not seem to be much basis for Sasaki's conjecture, but it alarmed Eda.

''But I don't see what his motive would be for killing both women. Still, for whatever purpose, I expect this mysterious man will make another attempt to approach Yuko, but I don't think he will try to kill her.''

"He's probably in love with her," snorted Sasaki emphatically and stood up.

In that French salon where the raging storm outside could only be heard faintly, he had listened to Fumiko's gentle, passionate voice saying, "And yet, I already feel as though you are my other self, and I certainly hope you feel the same way about me."

"Of course."

"Thank you. The sharing we have had this evening is not something we have to talk about, but it will be a wonderful thing if it helps us face our individual futures." At that moment was Fumiko promising that she would never tell another soul about their shared experience? Daigo wondered if there was some way he could find proof that Yuko was actually his Fumiko if she would not respond to his sign and if he did not break their pledge. Why? Could it be true that even on that night she had already been determined that they would both carry out their part of the dark conspiracy? But what sort of mutual understanding did they have apart from these words? Could he possibly persuade her to meet him, perhaps in a crowded, dimly lit restaurant?

But surely Yuko was far too cautious to expose herself in such a way to the possibility of being spotted by a third person. As he considered this point, Daigo felt a sudden pang of apprehension and looked around the old-fashioned, dimly lit restaurant where he now sat. Each of the tables was lit by a small lamp that threw a complex pattern of shadows about the room, and even though the restaurant was not all that large, it was virtually impossible to make out the features of the people at other tables. The groups at the other tables were chatting quietly, and there was an occasional ripple of laughter; everything seemed pleasant as the diners enjoyed their Burgundian-style dinner.

Three tables away sat two men Daigo had noticed earlier. They seemed to be watching him closely, but that may merely have been his imagination. One of the white-coated waiters took Yuko's plate of coq au vin and ham which she had hardly touched. Another waiter used a small brush to sweep away the breadcrumbs and straightened the tablecloth before setting out apple tarts and espresso coffee.

As usual Yuko kept her eyes on the table, her expression a mixture of restraint and puzzlement, as she sat facing Daigo. She kept her eyes on the tart in front of her, which was richly laden with jam and gave off a fragrance of rum. Her eyes under their fine lashes did not seem to notice that Daigo was uneasy.

Did this slightly built woman really have within her the astonishing boldness and determination of Fumiko? Daigo once again felt his love for her. This dessert, their dinner of chicken cooked in wine, this woman, the ambience of the restaurant were all a part of the texture of his love.

But Yuko had only picked at the food. Was it possible that she did not care for French cuisine? Daigo was about to apologize for his choice, but at the last minute he swallowed his words. If she did not care for French food, why had she taken the trouble to go all by herself to the Château Chantal for a meal? Coq au vin is a typical Burgundian dish, and these tarts were a speciality of the house. And he clearly remembered Fumiko having said that she especially liked the fresh ham.

"As a matter of fact, it took considerable effort to find this restaurant before I called you. As I told you before, I am from Kyushu and not too familiar with Tokyo. There are not all that many restaurants in Tokyo that specialize in Burgundian cooking. I especially wanted to bring you to such a place because I thought it would be helpful in giving you some idea of the context in which I knew your late husband." Daigo spoke formally and chose his words carefully. Yuko was keeping her guard up much longer than he had expected, and as long as she did not admit to being Fumiko, he felt he had to continue the masquerade of being a friend of her husband when he was studying in France. At the same time he wanted to pass along a definite sign to Fumiko Samejima that he knew who she was.

"I'm sure you did many favors for my husband while he was in France," said Yuko with a slight nod.

Daigo took one of the cups of coffee for himself and looked out at the garden outside the restaurant. He could feel the perspiration beginning to gather on his face.

The garden was surrounded by an old-fashioned iron fence and was somewhat overgrown. It was illuminated by pale blue outdoor lights, and the shrubbery rustled in the evening breeze. Directly in front of them was the silhouette of a round brick tower, intended to remind patrons of a wine storage warehouse. Since he could not count on there being a storm and thunder for their second meeting, Daigo had tried to find such a place as this that would be as reminiscent as possible of their earlier encounter.

Three days ago, on the evening of March 18, Daigo had telephoned Yuko in Kita Kamakura from his home in Fukuoka. It had been two days prior to that that he had met Inspector Furukawa on the street near his university. Ever since he had suddenly learned that the mystery woman who had attended the wedding reception was known to have been carrying a picture postcard depicting either Hakone or Fuji Five Lakes, Daigo had been driven by a desperate sense of urgency.

It was essential that he meet Fumiko right away, before their adversaries identified the Emerald View Hotel. Since the police had not yet identified the name of the hotel, they would not yet have made a connection between the murder of Yoshimi and the killing of Midori. Therefore Daigo felt it would not be too dangerous if he could meet secretly with Fumiko before the police linked the two deaths. He felt that if only he could meet Fumiko once face to face and verify her existence, then he would somehow be able to endure the long separation that must necessarily follow.

In Daigo's mind it had been pleasantly natural to superimpose the images of Fumiko and Yuko. The problem had been to select a suitable place for their meeting. He felt that the location was extremely important. The reason for this was that Daigo felt that Yuko would be reluctant to actually reveal herself to him. Maybe this was because of her caution, prudence, or even embarrassment, or perhaps she just wanted to tease him. If the surroundings were right, she might be willing to show herself briefly. After all, women are said to swing wildly from one mood to another.

After deliberating on the matter for a day, Daigo telephoned a friend who was a professor at a university in Tokyo and got from him the name of a restaurant that had the atmosphere of the Château Chantal and which specialized in French cuisine. Another problem was whether or not the restaurant had a hotel attached to it, or if there was a hotel very nearby. That was the sort of place he wanted. After explaining his needs, his friend right away told him about a perfect place located in a very quiet neighborhood in the Azabu district of Tokyo on one of the streets behind the Soviet embassy. Originally it had been quite a prestigious hotel with a restaurant attached that specialized in Burgundian cooking. The hotel itself had fallen on hard times, but the restaurant had maintained its customers, who continued to patronize the establishment year after year.

Daigo's spirits began to rise as he looked forward to a meeting with Yuko. When he telephoned, the call was answered by someone in the main house who transferred the call to Yuko's detached house, and a moment later he heard Yuko's serene voice just as he had remembered it.

"I'm sorry to be calling you out of the blue like this,

but my name is Otamo. Years ago when your husband was studying at the University of Paris, we were good friends. Even though I was on the same exchange program, my own field of study was very different from his; I'm in nutrition. I wonder if he might have said something about me to you."

Daigo had learned from the obituaries that while Kume was a college student he had participated in an exchange program that enabled him to spend a year at the University of Paris studying drama. He was not sure whether or not Japanese students went to Paris to study nutrition at that time, but it was unlikely that anyone would question his assertion. On the other hand, his statement that he was a nutritionist was intended as a key for Yuko to recognize who was really calling.

But Yuko, however, merely responded, "Why no, I don't recall that he ever mentioned you, but we were not married until the year after he returned from France."

"I guess that's natural. I also returned from Paris at the same time, but then I went back and have only just now returned to Japan. That is why I have only now learned of the unfortunate tragedy that befell Kume." Daigo went on to say that while they were in France, Kume had left some books and other personal effects in his apartment, and that even though Kume was now dead, some of the things were quite valuable, and he wanted to pass them along to Kume's widow.

Yuko seemed to be genuinely moved by this news and said, "Yes, by all means, I would like to have them. Where may I pick them up?"

"Well, I hate to make trouble for you, but I wonder if you could come to the Sincere Hotel in Azabu. You see I plan to be going back to Kyushu soon, and am just staying here for the time being."

They made plans to meet on the evening of the twenty-first and set the time. Daigo said she could plan to have dinner with him. "That hotel has a very famous restaurant in it. It has very much the sort of atmosphere as the places where Kume and I used to hang out in France. If it is all right with you, I would like to reminisce a little."

Daigo had thought about saying it was very much like the Château Chantal, but thought better of it. At first Yuko had been quite reserved, but she seemed to relax a little after he invited her for dinner. Daigo took that sense of relaxation to indicate that she knew who was calling. Next he called and made reservations for a room at the hotel, and for dinner at the restaurant.

At six on the evening of the twenty-first Yuko Kume kept her date with Daigo. Since in a sense they did not know each other, Daigo put two or three of his nutrition books on the table so that she would recognize him. He took his seat at a table looking out over the garden at 5:40 and waited. When Yuko entered the restaurant wearing a springlike blue kimono with a flowered pattern, he raised his hand and waved cheerily to her.

Yuko's long dark hair was carefully set, as though she had just come from the beauty parlor, and, in her traditional Japanese-style coat, she had all the freshness of a traditional young wife.

Daigo and Yuko exchanged the usual pleasantries people use when first meeting. On seeing Yuko at close range, Daigo was utterly enchanted by her beauty, and yet something seemed not quite right. He had always been certain that if he ever met Fumiko face to face, he would recognize her instantly and intuitively. But now when he looked at Yuko, he identified her as a very beautiful woman named Yuko Kume, but he was not sure whether or not she was his Fumiko. Still, he was emotionally overwhelmed by the presence of this woman. He realized that intellectually, he was persuading himself that this was Fumiko. Certainly her sense of elegance, her serenity, and her beauty all corresponded to his image of Fumiko. But what would happen if a woman who corresponded this closely to his image of Fumiko turned out to be someone else?

In the darkness at the Château Chantal he had intuitively understood everything about Fumiko, and a deep passion for her continued to burn within him. But now as he quietly considered the matter, it seemed to him that there were a number of things about this woman that were not quite right. Could this really be the woman with whom he was so desperately in love?

The fact that Yuko was so unresponsive was surely because she was afraid someone might be watching them. Those two men three tables away could very well be policemen.

Even though he claimed to have been her husband's friend while he was studying in Paris, she did not ask any questions about their relationship, and gradually he became unhappy and dissatisfied with the encounter. The woman's attitude of indifference seemed to envelope them like a palpable fog. Daigo finally decided that this stalemate had to be broken and said, "Your husband's area of study was quite different from mine, and I am four years older than he was, so there was a certain barrier between us at first, but then we made a trip to Barbizon that really brought us together." As Daigo spoke these words, he looked Yuko directly in the eye.

"I remember it well. It was in the middle of October. The weather in Paris was unseasonable, and that night a storm struck. There was a lot of thunder and lightning, and suddenly the lights went out. We must have spent an hour together in the darkened salon talking about all sorts of things. There in the darkness we revealed to each other our deepest feelings and thoughts, and we seemed to have reached an extraordinary feeling of intimacy."

In the midst of this declaration, Daigo seemed lost in a reverie of the past. Deep in his ears he could still hear the sounds of the storm outside the Château Chantal. He recalled even the elegant fragrance of Fumiko's breath.

"Didn't you make a trip to Paris on your own last fall?" he asked, but Yuko did not answer his question.

The next time he gazed into her large eyes, Daigo noticed a look of anxiety he had not seen there before. He saw that she was looking in the direction of his elbow. He realized that he had placed there, before Yuko came to the table, a copy of *Studies in Nutrition*. Yuko looked up and their eyes locked. She frowned slightly and her lip trembled. Daigo had a distinct feeling that she was either appealing to him for something or was seeking something. He experienced a flood of admiration for her.

"The books and things your husband left with me are in my room. Shall we go there, and I can give them to you?" He stood up with a slight smile on his face. He was certain that in a few moments in the darkness both their spirits would be set free.

Daigo's room was at the very end of the first-floor corridor and opened onto the garden. He hurried toward the room quickly and joyfully. He could hear the sound of Yuko's traditional Japanese sandals behind him. Taking out his room key, he opened the door, flicked on the light, and beckoned Yuko into the room.

"Please come in. As you can see it is a rather old hotel, so the room isn't much, but please make yourself at home." In fact, the room had a much homier feel about it than those in the big modern hotels. The sliding glass doors of the room opened out on the garden, but the view was hidden by the heavy velvet curtains that covered the windows. Beyond the glass doors was a veranda and beyond that the rather unkempt garden. This garden was different from the garden that fronted the restaurant in that here there were no guests walking in it, and it was only dimly lit by a few old-fashioned garden lights. Daigo was delighted at his good fortune.

The bedspreads and the mantel of the fireplace all matched the color of the curtains, with their olive-brown shades, and also the inviting sofa that dominated the room. It created a mood that was not entirely alien to that of the Château Chantal.

Yuko stopped in the doorway and vacillated, then in a low voice said, "Excuse me," and entered the room.

She sat lightly on the sofa that Daigo indicated with a wave of his hand. He returned to the door, closed it, and threw the metal bolt that secured the door. Yuko's gaze darted around the room uneasily. Her eyes came to rest on the two or three volumes that were piled on the table, and she quickly noticed that they were all books in Daigo's own field.

"What sort of thing was it that my husband left with you?"

Daigo did not answer, but paused and looked about the darkened room. "No one can see or hear us here. There is no one here but we two. We are free now to bring back memories and to talk. Don't you think it is safe for us to do that now? I expect I will never forget the words you left me with there in the Château Chantal. You said, 'Our meeting tonight has been a rare and fateful opportunity. I have a feeling we may never have the good fortune to have another such meeting on a night like this, in a salon like this. It would be wonderful, of course, if we met again someday in Paris, perhaps, or Tokyo. But even if that happens, I doubt if any subsequent meeting will have the magic of this encounter here tonight. . . . The sharing we have had here this evening is not something we have to talk about, but it will be a wonderful thing if it helps us face our individual futures.' '' The question that lingered in Daigo's mind was why should they not be able to tell about this shared experience with each other? ''You spoke of the courage and purity of our experience, but haven't we already demonstrated our purity and courage to each other by now? When I think of what this slender body of yours has accomplished, I am deeply moved.''

Yuko remained silent. Daigo heard his voice as though the words were being spoken by someone else, saying, ''We each made a promise to carry out our part of the plan, and I expect that you were really surprised to find that I was also able to clear up the food poisoning scandal.''

There was silence for a moment, then she suddenly seemed to gasp in surprise and said, ''Of course, you must be the one who left a copy of that magazine on my doorstep.''

''Of course I am the one. On that day I watched you for a time from a distance and then left. I remembered the words you said to me in France. But I could not be satisfied with that. I had a feeling that we might have to wait ten or twenty years before we got together again. Like Monsieur Chantal in the novel. I thought that both our souls would be released, would find freedom as a result of the agony we had endured.''

The memory of the rapture and the passion of that evening in France was suddenly recalled to Daigo, and more than anything, he wanted to experience it again. ''I want to repeat that experience with you. I want to have you sitting on my lap just as you were that night in France. After that, I don't care how long it takes, I am prepared to remain silent.''

He took two or three strides backward and, reaching the door, switched off the lights. The room was plunged into darkness. A faint light penetrated the room, but it was not enough to distinguish who or what was there. All they could see of each other was silhouettes. Once again the two of them were surrounded in darkness and silence. Daigo silently approached the sofa, seated himself next to Yuko, and grasped her shoulders from behind. When he had done this before, on that night in France, she had turned about and seated herself on his lap. She had turned her head, and in the darkness sought his lips.

Now, however, as he grasped Yuko's shoulders, she seemed to freeze and her body trembled spasmodically.

"Fumiko, it's me, Daigo. Do you remember that night?" But with a violent shove, Yuko pushed herself away from him. In a flash she clutched her purse to her breast and fled away from him toward the door.

"Hey! Wait a minute. Fumiko, we can be together again tonight."

But Yuko continued to flee from him, moaning softly to herself. He lunged at her, but she somehow avoided his grasp, opened the door, and fled the room.

For a moment Daigo lay stunned on the floor where he had fallen, his body bathed in cold sweat. It was the clammy unpleasantness of that sweat that brought him back to reality. It was a reality he did not want to return to. Instinctively he wanted to avoid reality, but the chill of fear and sweat brought him back despite himself.

At that moment he heard a knock at the door. A few seconds passed, then another knock. It was definitely not Yuko. The strength and determination of the knocking told its own story and sent a new chill of fear sweeping through him. Daigo felt sure the author of these knocks was one of the two middle-aged men who had looked them over from time to time in the restaurant earlier.

Suddenly Daigo leaped to his feet.

# 13

# The Nexus

"THE WOMAN APPEARED LIKE A PHANTOM ON THE EVE-ning of December third and on the afternoon of December fourth; those two occasions. No, we cannot really say she was a phantom, phantoms don't bump into people in the powder room of resort hotels and drop their purses all over the floor."

Odawara Inspector Sasaki and Detective Eda looked expectantly at Inspector Furukawa of Fukuoka. His eyes glittered behind the heavy black frames of his glasses. "The problem is the picture postcard. The woman she bumped into and who helped her gather up the things that had spilled from her purse recalled that among the things they gathered up was a picture postcard. It showed a snowcapped mountain, presumably Mount Fuji, and a lake in the foreground with an excursion boat on it. After questioning the lady on the subject many times, she finally admitted to believing that the picture was either of Hakone or of Fuji Five Lakes.''

"If the picture on the postcard was Mount Fuji, a lake, and an excursion boat, then the setting was surely Hakone," said Sasaki gravely as he nodded and stroked his double chin, as was his habit.

"Yes, my colleagues and I are natives of Kyushu, and most of us have never had a chance to visit Hakone, but fortunately the woman who made the identification was a Tokyo woman. And by the way, we have launched a full-scale investigation to see if there is any known connection between Yoshimi and Hakone or Fuji Five Lakes, but so far we have turned up nothing. It seems that not only was Yoshimi an influential figure in his university, he was also a behind-the-scenes mover in local political matters, so he was in a position to have earned many enemies as well as friends. At the same time, it turns out that he suffered from asthma and did not like cold places. At least that is what we heard from his close friends and relatives. That's not much in the way of evidence, but it's all we have at this point.''

Sasaki had listened to the whole account, nodding his head from time to time, but Eda continued to stare with sullen skepticism at Furukawa as he spoke.

"Nevertheless, as you said at the beginning, there is still the matter of a motive. Sure, there may be a strong possibility that this mystery woman poisoned Yoshimi, but that is only because you cannot think of any other suspects. And if we talk about specific leads on this woman, unfortunately, all we have to go on is the picture postcard some woman is said to have seen.''

"That may be so, but when we look to Hakone and Fuji Five Lakes as the origin of the murder, what evidence does that give us to go on?''

"Yes. Although that has been rather obscure from the

beginning, we now believe it was a contract murder. There is a strong possibility that our mystery woman committed the poisoning murder, but we have not been able to find such a woman among the victim's friends and acquaintances, so all we can do is suppose that she killed him as a proxy for someone else. That was a possibility, and in fact, it had occurred to me even before we turned our attention to the murder in Hakone, but at this point we cannot prove anything. This is what makes us think that it might be a murder by proxy.''

Inspector Furukawa continued speaking calmly, but the way he moved his head made the lenses of his spectacles reflect the fading sunlight, turning them opaque. At the same time, his features appeared to be creased with passion and intensity. The officers were meeting in a conference room of the Odawara police precinct, and early summer sunlight bathed the room.

''The killer appears to have been some sort of magician,'' said Furukawa with a bitter smile.

''I think you are exaggerating, but perhaps we ought to attribute some sort of unorthodox behavior to the killer; certainly there is nothing to prevent our investigation from developing in such a direction if it seems plausible. In fact, that is why I came here today. I want to find out if there is anything in your investigation that will confirm or deny anything I have found in mine. If you don't come up with anything that will help me, then we will have to go back through our unsolved cases and see if there is anything there that will give us a lead on Yoshimi's death. If we don't find anything there, then we will have to search the police records of the entire country to see if such a murder had been committed elsewhere, and if not, we will have to wait for one to happen.'' Inspector Furukawa broke off his monologue and took a sip of the tea that had been placed on the table in front of him.

Inspector Sasaki had small eyes in his round, fleshy face, and now they were squinted so narrow he almost appeared to be asleep, but he was watching Eda carefully. Eda knew the inspector wanted his opinion but was not going to ask for it. Eda began his statement by blurting, "We've had the woman under surveillance since the eighteenth." It was typical of Eda when he was under strain to speak and act with great intensity, but he tended to be more relaxed when he was questioning someone about a case.

Furukawa put down his teacup and looked over at Eda, who continued his statement. "We anticipated that someone would try to make contact with the woman. We knew that she had a motive for killing Midori Nagahara, but her own alibi is secure."

"In other words, this led you to suspect that she hired someone else to kill Midori for her?"

"Well, not exactly. My personal opinion is that the man's behavior does not lead us to that conclusion."

Eda hunched his shoulders in an irritated manner; Furukawa remained silent, waiting for him to continue. "That is why we put surveillance on her home in Kita Kamakura. Two days ago, during the holiday, my men followed her as she left home dressed in an especially nice traditional kimono and went to Tokyo."

Yuko Kume had taken the Yokosuka Line to Shinagawa station and from there took a taxi to the Sincere Hotel in Azabu. It was just 6:00 in the evening when she went into the French restaurant in that old-fashioned hotel. "There was a thin, intellectual-looking man, about forty, waiting for her at a table facing the garden. That was really about all my men saw as they hung around the entrance to the restaurant and the hotel lobby."

The man had ordered food and wine, and the couple spent just under an hour eating. The man seemed to be saying something to Yuko, but she kept her eyes on the table and seemed subdued. From the look of things it appeared that the man did not know her all that well. Then just before 7:00 the man accompanied the woman to his first-floor room.

"They had been in his room for only a few minutes when the woman came rushing out in a very agitated state. One of my men followed the woman, and the other knocked on the man's door."

"Naturally our men did not want to be rough with either suspect," said Sasaki to Furukawa. "It was just that my men wanted to find out everything they could about this man who was meeting secretly with Yuko."

"Of course," said Furukawa, nodding his head. It was not clear what connection any of this had with Furukawa's case, and so far Eda was not giving any explanation, but Furukawa had a hunch something was coming and listened carefully.

"Yuko seemed distraught. She immediately left the hotel and flagged a taxi. Although she was nearly incoherent, my man overheard enough to know that she was going home. He decided they could talk to her later and went back to help his partner, but they failed to turn up anything."

"You mean the man got away?"

"Yes, but only after my one detective had knocked several times on the door." Here for the first time Eda smiled, revealing a gap between his two large front teeth.

"You say your man knocked twice?"

"The room is on the first floor and looks out over the garden. It is one of those older hotels, and all the rooms have terraces, so it is quite easy to go in and out from the garden. As I say, at first my man tried knocking, but when there was no response, he tried the door and found it locked. It suddenly occurred to him that he could enter from the garden, but when he went around to the other side, he found the sliding door to the garden half open and the room empty.''

Furukawa and Eda sat in silence for a time looking at one another.

After a moment Furukawa asked, ''I don't suppose you turned up anything that had been left in the room?''

''Apparently he just scooped up everything he saw in a great hurry, dumped it into his briefcase, and took off through the garden. But this fellow is not a phantom or a superman; he did leave two things behind.''

As he spoke, Eda habitually stroked the line of his jaw. His eyes glittered, and he seemed pleased with what he was saying. ''The first item my men found in the room was a pair of glasses—thick, horn-rimmed glasses that had been left on a shelf in the bathroom. They were not sunglasses, and the lenses were of ordinary glass, so the mostly likely explanation is that our suspect does not ordinarily wear glasses, but was using these as a simple form of disguise.''

''That's very interesting.''

''The other thing they found was a scrap of an airline ticket voucher. It was floating in the toilet. Apparently the suspect tore up some old ticket and tried to flush the pieces down the toilet, but this one scrap floated back.''

''Could you identify the ticket at all?''

''We could barely make out the letters 'Fuku.' That is why we wanted to bring you into this, because we suppose the ticket was from Fukuoka.''

Again the two men's gaze met, and this time Furukawa felt some sense of comradeship with the obstinate detective.

''What did this man put down on his hotel registration card?''

''He used the name Akira Otomo and gave a Kyoto address. We checked out the address, of course, and no one by that name lives there, but at least we have a sample of his handwriting.''

From January 10 through 13 a man about forty years old had stayed at the Fumotokan inn at Hakone and had questioned one of the maids in detail about the daughter of the people who owned the Emerald View. On the evening of the eleventh he had heard Midori Nagahara play the piano, and the following evening he had asked many questions about Midori in a talk with Sadao Umezaki. Now Inspector Sasaki explained that the present suspect's handwriting matched that of the man who had visited Hakone.

''We also have some other leads on this man who called himself Ikegami when he was in Hakone. When Midori played the piano on the evening of the eleventh, it was as a special favor for her music teacher, who happened to be staying at the hotel at that time. They were accompanied by their niece, Fumiko Naruse, who is twenty-eight. A man telephoned her room at about nine and asked her to meet him in the nightclub downstairs. The man told her he had been on the same tour group with her to Europe last autumn.''

When the police interviewed Fumiko, she told them she had talked to the man for maybe thirty or forty minutes and at the time had believed his story, but after she got back to her room and thought about it, something seemed strange about his manner, something that was distinctly unpleasant.

''She said he told her that his name was Ikegami and that he was staying at a nearby inn called the Fumotokan.''

''When he was talking to her in the nightclub, did he ask about Midori?'' asked Furukawa.

''All he asked was whether Fumiko was a close friend of Midori, and when she said no, he let the matter drop. Mostly he asked about Fumiko herself.''

''I see.''

"As far as Yuko Kume is concerned, we sent a veteran detective to talk to her again the other evening at her home in Kita Kamakura," continued Sasaki after he had lit a cigarette. "At first she was silent as a clam, but after some urging by our detective, she burst into tears, and finally he was able to get the story from her. Three days ago, on the evening of March eighteenth, she had received a telephone call from a stranger who identified himself as Otomo."

The man had said he had been a good friend of her husband's when he was studying in Paris and that her husband had left some books and personal effects in his care. He had spoken to her very politely and said he would like to be able to return the things to her. He had sounded like a casual, middle-aged man, and she believed his story. She promised to meet him at 6:00 on the evening of the twenty-first at the restaurant of the Sincere Hotel.

She felt that the conversation during the meal was rather random and inconsequential, and she did not pay much attention to what he was saying. She was rather surprised when he suddenly stood up even before dessert had been eaten and said he would give her her husband's things.

"As soon as they got to his room, however, he turned out the lights and tried to assault her. She was in tears when she explained that she had suddenly hit him with her elbow and fled the room. The whole thing was a nightmare for her."

"So it turns out that she really knew nothing at all about this man."

"Yes. The detective who talked to her was convinced she is not lying about this. We have confirmation of the phone call on the evening of the eighteenth, because the woman at the main house took the call and transferred it to Yuko's detached house. It is my impression that this Yuko is a rather naive young lady to let herself be lured into a total stranger's hotel room just because he said he had some things that had belonged to her late husband.''

Inspector Sasaki stubbed out his cigarette, and his round, stubby fingers opened a drawer in his desk. He took out a single magazine and placed in front of Furukawa. It was the April issue of *Studies in Nutrition*. ''According to Yuko, on the afternoon of March fifth she was straightening up the house and at some point this magazine appeared on her doorstep. She had never seen it before and did not know where it had come from. Later, when this fellow Otomo called and made a date at the restaurant, since they did not know each other by sight, he said he would have some of his academic books on the table, so she would be able to recognize him. When she got to the restaurant, he had another issue of this same magazine on the table, and later when she went to his room, he confessed that he had left this magazine on her doorstep earlier. Yuko does not seem to know what the significance of the magazine is, but she asked us to keep it.''

Furukawa looked at the cover of the magazine, which was illustrated with a photograph of a large, clean-looking factory of some sort. This issue seemed to be a special one devoted to problems of children's nutrition. He reached into the pocket of his suit and drew out an envelope containing a photograph and laid it on the desk beside the magazine.

''I wonder if this is the man who fled from the hotel in Azabu. I wonder if we can prove that he is somehow involved in all this.''

What sort of agreement had these two reached, when had they done it, where, what had they said to one another? In committing this crime—no, it was still only a matter of speculation that they were guilty—but Eda was intrigued by the suspicions he had. The idea of murder by proxy was a fascinating one, and one he was somewhat familiar with through his reading of foreign novels. There were a million possible ways these two could have made their compact, it would all depend on the nature and character of the people involved. Nevertheless, one thing was certain, and that is that for two people to make such an agreement they would have to trust each other completely. Would the average person have that much confidence in someone else? From the time they mutually agreed to commit murder until they completed their plans, even if they were united by a deep sense of mutual trust, they must both have felt a certain amount of foreboding and misgiving. It was this sort of interest in human motivation that inspired Eda's intense involvement in the case.

The only conclusion to be reached was that Kohei Daigo and the mystery woman must have reached a specific agreement at some time in the past.

Today Eda and the other detectives decided to go over everything again from the very beginning. Now he had come to Hakone and was walking down the deserted street to the large old mansion of the Nagahara family. It would be some time yet at this high elevation before the cherry blossoms would be out, but the sky was covered with white clouds and the air was fresh on his skin. In the gardens of the houses along the road he could see masses of three-colored violets in bloom. Hakone was entering its very pleasant spring season, but this particular area, perhaps because it was surrounded by forests, maintained something of a melancholy atmosphere.

From the time he first appeared in Hakone on January 10 until he disappeared from the hotel room in Azabu, the evidence was was becoming more and more clear that the man they were seeking was Kohei Daigo, professor of nutrition at J university in Fukuoka. Everyone who had had any contact with the suspect—the maid at the Fumotokan,

Fumiko Naruse, Tadao Umezaki, Yuko Kume, and the two detectives that had followed Yuko—all were shown the photograph and all said he resembled the man in question. The suspect, of course, had always worn sunglasses or the heavy, horn-rimmed glasses, no doubt as a form of disguise, but the age and other physical features were all the same. He had received a telephone call from Furukawa who had returned to Fukuoka to check on Daigo's alibi. According to Furukawa, Daigo did not have an alibi for any of the times the suspect was known to have been in Hakone or Tokyo. On the night of March 8, when Midori had been murdered, he had told his colleagues at the university the previous day that he was going to Osaka to have an aged aunt put in the hospital. He had been away for two days on the eighth and ninth. Furukawa felt the fastest way to get the aunt's address so that they could verify that Daigo had gone to Osaka would be to ask Daigo's wife where the old woman lived, but in the end he decided not to do that. If he made inquiries of Daigo's wife, she would tell him about it right away, and there was always a danger that Daigo might call his aunt in Osaka before the police could get there and ask her to confirm his alibi.

Instead they sent a detective to the rural part of Kyushu where Daigo's brother lived and asked for the aunt's address on some pretext that did not involve Daigo. Having that information, they visited the old lady's home in the Tennoji district of Osaka. She was as old as Daigo had told his colleagues in the laboratory, but she was certainly not ill.

Akane dropped her jaw and looked intently at the photograph of Kohei Daigo. She frowned slightly and bit her lip. Eda was watching her closely with his deeply hooded eyes. He was ready to observe her slightest response. The impression Eda got was that her expression was that of one who is seeing a friend after a very long time, someone who had changed a great deal.

At last the girl looked up and shook her head. "No, I'm afraid this isn't the man. But you have to realize that I had stopped the car down there in the driveway and I was seeing him from there and it was quite dark up there on the hillside among the trees, but I am quite sure the man I saw was not of this type."

Among all the people who had seen the man who had been making inquiries about Midori and Yuko, Akane was the first and only one who said definitely that this was not the man.

"Mother gave birth to my older sister, but she is not my real mother." Eda had been escorted into the living room, and Akane was now answering in a low, soft voice the questions he put to her. The same housekeeper who had been present on his previous visit served them coffee and withdrew. The whole house was shrouded in silence. Akane explained that her father was at the hotel attending to his business affairs and that her mother had been so devastated by the murder that she had been taken to a local hospital where she was recuperating. The Nagahara home was built in the style of an old-fashioned English country home. The windows were quite small, and the wallpaper in the living room was in a classic pattern which gave the room a dark and somewhat gloomy atmosphere.

On the night of Midori's death there had been a gas fire burning in the fireplace, but now that was replaced by a potted purple orchid.

"I was brought into this family when I was two years old. It was after my real mother died. I was never told anything about that and I was too young to remember, but when I was eighteen, a friend of mine needed a blood transfusion, but when I tried to donate blood, I found that my blood type was different from that of my parents. When I asked my father about it, he told me the truth about my mother. That was the first I had heard of it.''

In other words, Akane was her father's illegitimate child.

''At the time, of course, I was shocked to learn such a thing, but as it turned out, there was no change in my relationship with my parents or my sister. When I think about it objectively, they were all very good about it and continued to love me, and I still felt that I was a part of the family.''

A slight smile lighted Akane's Western-looking features as she said this, but her voice seemed calm and controlled. Yet the very words she spoke seemed to attest to the repressed feelings she had. The question was, could these feelings be brought into the open?

''Please excuse me for having to ask you questions of such a very personal nature. I don't mean to pry.'' Eda quickly changed the subject. It was possible that Akane, who had been raised by a stepmother and under the shadow of an older sister, may have felt some very deep hatred for that sister. Now that he considered the fact, although the two women had been born of different mothers, there were certain similarities in their features. He doubted Akane would admit it if he asked if there were any hard feelings between her and her sister. Both of them seemed to be somewhat foreign-looking in their features, though Akane was a larger woman than Midori and her features were more distinct. As far as their overall build was concerned, Eda had only seen Midori's body after she was dead, but she seemed to have a sort of proud arrogance about her. There was something about Akane that made her seem to be more calm and generous than her sister had been.

''There are a few questions I need to ask you just for background purposes. On last December third and fourth, were you here at home?''

"Let's see, December third and fourth. Well I really don't know when you ask me suddenly like this. Why are those days important?" Akane returned Eda's gaze steadily as she asked.

"A certain incident occurred in Fukuoka on those two days, and we have reason to believe that there may be some connection between that incident and Midori's death. We are asking everyone involved in Midori's case where they were on those two days."

Eda did not feel there was any problem in revealing this much of the matter. If Akane had nothing to do with the two murders then there would be nothing wrong in revealing what they knew, but if Akane was the mystery woman they were looking for, to have a detective on the case mention the dates December 3 and 4 would let her know how much progress they had made.

"I suppose I was at home that day. I had an exhibit in Tokyo in November, but nothing special was happening in December. Perhaps if I think about it for a while something will come to mind." As Akane replied, she tilted her head to one side and reached for her coffee cup. It seemed that this was the first time she had avoided Eda's gaze.

"Yes, well if you think of anything, please let us know. Now I would like to review a few points just for the record. As I understand it, on the night Midori was murdered, she left the house at about six twenty-five to go to the Emerald View, where she was going to play the piano. At that time your mother, suffering from a cold, was upstairs in her room, and the housekeeper had gone home at six o'clock. You were reading in the living room, and Midori stopped in to say goodbye before leaving. Is that right?"

"Yes. I believe that is the way it was."

"And after Midori went out the front door, you were here in the living room the whole time reading?"

"Ah yes. When you talked to me just after her death, I

am afraid I was in a state of shock. There is something I left out. Just after my sister left the house, I suppose about six-thirty, I got a telephone call from Tokyo. It was from a woman on the editorial staff of a magazine for which I sometimes do illustrations. We talked about a job I am doing for them; we probably talked for about twenty minutes. I remember that no sooner had I hung up than I got a phone call from the Emerald View asking about Midori, who had not shown up to play the piano. After that, of course, everything was chaotic and the hotel sent some people here to look for her."

"Tell me about that phone call from Tokyo, was it something you had scheduled and were expecting?"

"Perhaps so, I don't remember clearly."

"I see."

Eda felt a deep sense of satisfaction that Akane had an indisputable alibi for the time Midori was murdered. The fact that Midori had been at home until twenty past six was proved by more than just Akane's testimony. The desk manager at the Emerald View also testified to this. On the evening in question Midori was scheduled to play the piano at a dinner party for a local politician, but her father was concerned that she had a habit of losing track of the time, so he had asked the desk manager to call the house and remind her of the party. He had called at twenty past six. Midori had taken the call herself and had informed the manager that she was just then leaving the house.

Thus there was proof that Midori had been alive at least until about 6:22 or so. Consequently, Akane, who had been on the telephone to Tokyo from 6:30 until about 6:50 and who had then right away received a call from the hotel, could not possibly have had the time to go to the garage, murder her sister, drive the car to the field on the slope below the house, and return. A car from the hotel with people looking for Midori had arrived at the Nagahara home at about 7:00, and at that time Akane was on the doorstep awaiting their arrival.

It would be necessary, of course, to verify that the editorial offices of the magazine in Tokyo had indeed made the phone call to Akane, but Eda was pretty sure it would turn out as Akane had said.

The important point was that Akane had only a vague alibi for the time when Yoshimi was killed but a solid alibi for the time when Midori was murdered. Now if he could only prove that she was involved in a conspiracy with Daigo.

Akane had been the one to give them the lead about the fact that there was a man on the road behind the house as Midori went to her lesson on the evening of March 4. Later, of course, she had denied that the man was Daigo, so it was possible that she was setting out red herrings.

Eda stood up from his chair, saying it was time he left, but as he did so he gave Akane a thoughtful look.

She said, "You showed me a photograph a few minutes ago. It was not a person I have ever seen around here, but I wonder, is he a suspect in my sister's murder?"

"Yes he is, for the time being at least."

"Where is he from, who is he?"

"I'm sorry, I'm not free to divulge that information at the present time."

"Oh really?" Akane's eyes seemed to go blank, and she looked toward the window where the sunlight was streaming in. "I wonder who he is? I am fascinated by the man, but of course if he is the one who killed my sister, I will hate him forever."

# 14

# At the Water's Edge

WHY HAD THEY BEEN FOLLOWED? THIS WAS THE QUEStion that preyed on Kohei Daigo's mind in the tumultuous days following the announcement of the new test results on the Popico cookies. Why had they been under police surveillance? Of course he could not really be sure that it was the police who had knocked after the woman had fled the room. And yet at the time he had felt instinctively that it was the police. He had scooped up the books from the table and crammed them into his overnight bag, grabbed his coat from the closet, and fled away through the hotel garden.

He had cut through the adjoining garden in front of the restaurant, ducked into the hotel lobby, and out the front door. There, fortunately, a guest was just getting out of a taxi, so he got in and directed the driver to take him to Tokyo Station. He had intended to go to Haneda Airport and get a flight directly to Fukuoka, but fearing that the police might be watching the airport, he took the bullet train to Osaka instead. There he spent the night in the station hotel and the next morning flew back to Fukuoka.

For a time he had thought of visiting his elderly aunt in Tennoji and telling her that if the police came around asking questions he would appreciate it if she would tell them that he had come to visit her on March 8. But he was physically and emotionally exhausted and put aside any thoughts regarding the murder he had committed. Besides, he had no way of knowing whether or not his venerable old aunt might start asking questions.

So he was filled with inner turmoil when he returned gratefully to his job at the university.

Since the previous spring, children had started coming down with cancer caused by a type of mold in the flour that was used to make the Popico cookies, and once this fact was established by his report and the responsibility for the matter was laid squarely on the shoulders of Minami Foods, the case had become a celebrated one throughout the entire country. Naturally the media and the public all celebrated his achievement. The response had been far more overwhelming than he had expected, and even within the university the sentiment in favor of appointing him to succeed Yoshimi was strong.

The telephone in his laboratory was ringing off the hook, and he was besieged with requests for interviews, speeches, and articles. When the university adjourned for spring break, a steady stream of visitors followed him to his home.

Despite all the attention, however, he felt hollow inside. He himself was aware of it; he had not been at all responsive either to his lab assistant, Yamada, or to his wife, Shihoko. He felt as though his nerves were shot. He began to wonder how he must appear to others. Surely they must think he was looking and acting strangely.

It was ironic. Just six months ago, before his trip to

Paris, he had been vainly self-confident, and perhaps that
was what had led to his attack of pessimism. He could not
shake off the feeling that he was on the edge of the preci-
pice of disaster. He felt he did not have much time left.
Now that he thought back on how things had turned out,
he felt that he and Fumiko had planned and carried out a
large and terrifying scheme. The question that now haunted
him was what would it have all been worth if he was not
able to meet Fumiko again and quietly reconstruct the mood
of their evening in Barbizon?

He was worried that the detectives who had followed
them to the hotel in Azabu might still be following him,
or they might have Yuko under surveillance. Daigo was
pretty sure, however, that they had not followed him. He
dreaded the thought of another encounter with Inspector
Furukawa, with that evil, penetrating glitter in his eyes
behind the heavy rims of his glasses. No matter what se-
crets he had, he sometimes felt that Furukawa would find
them out.

One reason it was hard for him to accept the idea that
Yuko had been followed to the hotel was the simple fact
that he now knew that Yuko was not his Fumiko. He had
calmly come to this conclusion after returning to Fukuoka.
The Fumiko Samejima he remembered was a larger
woman, and she was definitely more of a modern-type
woman. More than anything else was the fact that if she
had been his Fumiko, she would have recognized the urgency of his message and would not have fled from him in
panic. And certainly if she were going to meet Daigo there
could have been no more danger in wearing French clothes
and perfume rather than a traditional kimono with her hair
put up in the old-fashioned style.

Yet now it seemed apparent to him that when he had
looked at Yuko's beautiful eyes, surely as lovely as Fumiko's, he had been deceived into believing that she was the

woman he sought. On that magic evening in Barbizon he had shared his deepest feelings with Fumiko, and now he felt it was time to review those feelings. At the time he had experienced the most perfect love for her. The question was, in his encounter with Yuko had he been conscious of the object of his love, or had he only experienced the feeling of love and applied it to the object indiscriminately?

The fact remained that on that enchanted night at the Château Chatral he had shared his deepest feelings with that woman. And even though he had not seen what she looked like, he felt that they had understood each other and had become a part of each other. At the time he had experienced a feeling of peaceful ecstasy unlike anything else he had experienced in the world. Perhaps he was just kidding himself, but no! He could not accept that. He was not mistaken about that special evening when they had had eternity in their grasp. Was there anything else the world had to offer that he could believe in so completely as that? Indeed, the only thing he had to believe in was the faith she had given him. It was essential that he have a chance to meet her once again. Soon.

Suppose the Odawara police had pursued Yuko rather than him, then there was still some time left before they got on his trail. Now, while the police were still trying to learn the identity of the mystery woman, he would have to hurry and make contact with Fumiko and let her know how much progress the police had made. The Fukuoka police had already made a connection between the woman at the wedding reception and the Hakone, Fuji Five Lakes area. If he could manage to elude the police long enough to have one more meeting with Fumiko, then he would be able to endure a long separation. Surely the best thing would be for Fumiko to go away to some distant place where the Japanese police authorities would not be able to get their hands on her.

Daigo felt confident that he would be able to stay out of the clutches of the police as long as he knew that Fumiko was somewhere safe. Even if they arrested him for skipping out on his hotel bill, he was sure that no matter how hard they questioned him, he would not utter a word about Midori's death or about Fumiko's existence. Under those circumstances the police would have no choice but to release him.

Still, he had some time remaining, and if he used it wisely, he could use it well.

As he banished all thought of Yuko from his mind, her image was replaced by thoughts of Akane. She was the woman who most perfectly corresponded to the image of Fumiko that he had in his mind. He had only seen Akane on one occasion. On the evening of March 4, as he had approached Midori on the road above their house, Akane had appeared on the driveway below. There was still a good deal of light in the road, and Akane had leaned out of the car window to wave, so even though she had been some distance away, Daigo had had a clear view of her. She had appeared to be a lively woman with tawny, golden skin.

Daigo's recollection of Fumiko was that she had been a more slightly built woman, but he also remembered her courage and strength of will, and these corresponded to his impression of Akane. No matter what vulnerability Fumiko may have had within her, outwardly she presented a firm and forceful image.

Then there was the matter of the voice. When he had telephoned Midori from Fukuoka, Akane had answered. She had a husky, low-pitched voice. At Barbizon as well, Fumiko had had a low voice, although she explained it by saying that she was coming down with a cold and had a sore throat.

But the question was why would Akane want to have

her sister murdered? The only thing he could imagine was that perhaps Akane had also been in love with Michiya Kume. Perhaps that was it.

He was still not entirely certain that Akane was the Fumiko he was looking for. He began to wonder if there was some quick method by which he could learn whether or not she had been to Paris the previous autumn. He had to do it now before the danger became too great.

He could not afford to fail again; he had to make certain he had the right person this time.

April Fool's Day had passed, and on April 2 Daigo dialed Akane's number. Fortunately it was spring break and his wife had taken the children to the country to visit their grandparents.

The telephone rang four times before a young woman's voice answered saying, "Hello." Surely it was Akane.

Just to make certain he asked, "Is this Akane Nagahara?"

"Yes, it is."

Daigo took a deep breath and began speaking slowly, enunciating each word carefully. He did not give his own name, but merely said, "I am the man who met Fumiko Samejima at the Château Chantal in Barbizon. If this statement does not mean anything to you, it means that I have gotten the wrong number and you are welcome to hang up. But if you are Fumiko, I would appreciate it if you would listen to what I have to say and give simple responses to my questions."

At that point he stopped talking for a moment and waited for her reaction. One second passed, then another, and Akane still did not hang up on him. On the contrary, he was aware of a certain amount of tension, as though her breathing had gotten tighter, as if she was waiting for him to go on. He did. "You and I do not have very much time left. The police here have made the connection between the woman who was seen at the wedding reception and the Hakone, Fuji Five Lakes region. It is only a matter of time before they are in contact with the police there. I think it would be a good idea for you to go away someplace where they cannot get their hands on you, and you should do it as quickly as possible.''

The woman made no response to this, so Daigo hurried on. ''Before you go, however, I want to have a chance to see you again. I don't care when or where or how the meeting is arranged, I will leave that all up to you. But we are both in great danger, so make certain that wherever the meeting is you are not followed. Will you meet me?''

After a moment of silence, Akane's pleasant voice replied, ''On the slope below the Emerald View Hotel and about a quarter of a mile north along the lakeshore there is a small cottage with a red roof. You can get to it quite easily by branching off the private road that leads to the hotel. It is surrounded by forest and is the only building in the area, so you cannot miss it.''

''Right, the cottage with the red roof.''

''Yes. Originally it was a boathouse, but I have recently remodeled it and have been using it for a studio. No one ever comes near the place.''

''I understand. When?''

''How about tomorrow evening at ten?''

''Good, I'll be there. Make sure you are not followed.''

Akane replied in a cheerful, even mocking tone, ''Shall I tell you something as well? The police have a photograph of you and are showing it around when they question people.''

Akane Nagahara.

Inspector Furukawa turned the name over and over in his mind. And in his mind he could see the four facial photographs of the woman that Inspector Sasaki of Odawara had sent him. All of these photographs had been taken outdoors, apparently secretly with a telephoto lens, since none of them was a straight-on view of the woman. There was some sort of hazy background of trees, and all the photos were either profiles or angle shots, but by considering all four photographs together, he felt he could get a pretty good idea of what she looked like. He was also told that she was five feet two inches tall and twenty-five years old. He also had fingerprints of her right thumb and index finger as well as the information that her blood was type AB. His men who were assigned to the case were about equally divided on whether or not this information really added anything to their investigation.

They had shown the photographs to a number of people who had seen the woman who had been talking to Professor Yoshimi at the wedding reception on the night before his murder, and all of them had responded by saying she resembled the suspect, but they could not be sure it was the same woman. At the same time Furukawa realized that the only person who could really give them a positive identification was Kiyoko Sakaguchi, the woman who had collided with the suspect in the powder room, but she too had been uncertain whether or not this was really the woman she had bumped into.

According to the officer who had been dispatched to Tokyo to interview her, "At first she had been surprised when she saw the photos and said this was definitely the person she had bumped into, but when she looked at some of the other photos, she became increasingly uncertain. She had seen the suspect at close range, and the more she looked at the photographs, the more she felt there was just something about them that was not quite right."

She had said that there was a similarity, but that the woman she had bumped into had been wearing sunglasses, and in the end she could not positively identify the suspect.

The fingerprints and the blood type both turned out to be inconclusive as far as this case was concerned. They had taken all the fingerprints they could find from the living room where Yoshimi had been killed. They had discarded all those that clearly had nothing to do with the murder, and from among the ones that were left over, there were none that corresponded to Akane's prints.

By the same token, they had collected some hairs and some thread that had fallen on the carpet, but when they checked the hair for blood type, it was not AB. And yet in a sense all this was still inconclusive, since a killer who would take away with her the coffee cup she had used would not likely be careless enough to leave fingerprints behind, and if hairs were found on the floor, they could have come from anyone. In any case, it seemed likely that the woman who committed the murder had only spent a very short time in the living room. It seemed that the only way to indicate that Akane might be the murderer would be to show somehow that Akane and Daigo had gotten together at some time before the murders.

Inspector Furukawa was walking up the slope of the street, and the damp, warm wind came up off the sea to overtake him. Both sides of the street were lined with small tract houses that had been newly built, and the policeman felt vaguely irritated anytime he came to a building site where the house was not yet completed. As he walked he counted two doors past the small beauty parlor that was his landmark to the street where Daigo lived. Although it was evening, the beauty shop had just opened, making it easy for Furukawa to remember.

The question in Furukawa's mind was when and where had the two suspects gotten together and made their agreement? Detective Eda of the Odawara precinct had made it clear that this was the most interesting question in the whole case. At first he had listened to the younger officer's words simply out of politeness and because the man seemed to have so much difficulty in expressing himself, but now Furukawa was in full sympathy with what the man had said. And yet the fact remained that no matter how much they investigated Kohei Daigo's background, they could find no concrete evidence that he had been to Hakone.

All they had learned was that he had graduated from a rural college in Kyushu and that he had been a research assistant at the university and later had been called to J university as an assistant professor. As far as they could tell, he had never lived anywhere other than Kyushu. Although his wife had said they had taken a drive through Hakone while on their honeymoon, there was nothing more than that. At the same time, there was also nothing that suggested a link between Akane Nagahara and Fukuoka. This made it very difficult to support the theory that Daigo and Akane had conspired to commit murder by proxy.

Inspector Furukawa pulled his hand from deep in the pocket of his overcoat and pushed the buzzer above the name "Daigo."

A soft feminine voice responded to his call, and when Furukawa announced his name, he heard the gate lock release. Daigo's wife and two daughters had spent the time from March 29 to April 2 at the children's grandparent's home in the country. They had returned last night and were apparently at home today.

Daigo had left the house about 2:00 that afternoon in his own car. He had been carrying no luggage and was wearing a nice, dark blue, full length overcoat. Furukawa did not yet know Daigo's destination because the men who were tailing him had not yet reported. Furukawa had set out for Daigo's house just as soon as he had heard that Daigo had left.

"Please come in," said Shihoko with a smile on her round, heavily freckled face. The policeman noticed that

when she smiled there were crinkles at the corners of her
eyes and along the side of her nose. Furukawa had visited
the house four or five times since Yoshimi's murder, and
the fact that he had not been overly tough on those occasions owed much to Shihoko's charming smile. Today,
however, her smile quickly vanished, and she seemed uneasy, as though nervous about something.

"I'm sorry to keep bothering you like this, but I wonder
if your husband is in?"

"Why no, I'm afraid he just went out."

"Oh, really. I came by thinking he would be puttering
around the house on a Sunday afternoon."

"He was here until just a few minutes ago." The entry
hall where they stood was filled with fragrance of the blos-
soming sweet pea on a shelf on the wall. From further back
in the house came the voices of the two daughters.

"Pardon me for asking, but where did your husband
go?"

"He had to leave suddenly for Osaka. He has an elderly
aunt there who has been hospitalized since March. We got
a call saying she had taken a turn for the worse."

Shihoko did not know exactly when the phone call had
come, and although her expression betrayed no uncertainty, her voice seemed troubled. Perhaps it was just this
family crisis that made her feel uneasy. Furukawa decided
to increase the pressure. When the detective watching the
house reported that Daigo had left by car without any luggage, Furukawa had supposed he would be going somewhere in the city, but of course that was not necessarily
the case.

"I expect he will be spending the night in Osaka, then."

"He may. He just said he would call once he got there
and let me know how things are. He seemed quite upset
when he left the house." Shihoko went on to say that she

had absolutely no idea of what hotel he might be staying at in Osaka.

"I see. That's too bad, but I guess there is nothing we can do about it."

"What do you mean?"

"Well, we think we have found our mystery woman, the one who is the chief suspect in the murder of Professor Yoshimi. At last we seem to be just on the point of breaking this case wide open."

He spoke excitedly. Shihoko nodded, and with a slight frown of distaste asked, "Which woman is this?"

"Well, I wanted to discuss the matter directly with your husband and ask him to help us out a bit. It seems that some time ago this woman worked in Professor Yoshimi's laboratory. We just want to make a firm identification as soon as possible so that we can wrap this case up, but I guess if your husband is not here, there's nothing we can do about it."

Furukawa shrugged as though there was nothing to be done in the matter and took a cigarette from his pocket. Shihoko seemed uncertain whether or not she should invite him into the house.

"In any case, I am sure your husband has been very busy recently." Furukawa did not light the cigarette, but simply held it in his hand as he spoke casually. "I expect his stock has really gone up ever since his analysis in the Popico scandal came out. Of course I have certainly applauded his efforts in that matter."

"We appreciate your support."

"It seems your husband had his own opinion in the matter all along. According to what I read in the papers, your husband had been given a sample to analyze from the very beginning. And later when Yoshimi tried to block him, your husband knew what was right, and he never gave up until the truth came out."

"Yes." Shihoko pressed her cheek with the tip of her finger and looked perplexed.

"Oh, I believe your husband has been a man of great wisdom and understanding in this matter. It is clear that behind his scholarly ways and aristocratic manners, he is a man of iron integrity. Even when he was under the thumb of Professor Yoshimi, he was determined that the truth should be made public. And even when Yoshimi suddenly turned up dead, your husband never wavered."

"Well, it's nice of you to say so."

By the time Furukawa had finished singing Daigo's praises, Shihoko seemed much more relaxed. He pulled out his lighter and lit the cigarette.

"How about you, Mrs. Daigo, I suppose you knew all along that your husband would triumph in the end."

Once again Shihoko lowered her gaze, but Furukawa was quite sure that his praise had struck home. Presently she responded in her typically innocent manner. "Ever since last autumn when he went to Paris to attend a conference, my husband has seemed a bit changed. I don't know if it has anything to do with the business about Minami Foods or not."

"You say he seems a bit changed. In what way is he different from before?"

"I'm not sure I know quite how to explain it, but ever since he got back from Paris he has seemed very exuberant. I guess that's the best way to explain it. Sometimes he seems overly stimulated, and at other times he seems preoccupied. At one time I wondered if he might have taken up with another woman." Shihoko had been chatting along like a young girl, and suddenly she looked down and her face reddened slightly.

Daigo realized that the wind was rising. He was making his way along the shore of the lake, which was choked

with underbrush. He could hear the wind in the trees overhead and noticed that the blowing of the wind was now
continuous. In the sky he could see that the clouds were
moving swiftly. The overcast made the sky a milky white,
and there were no stars or moon. The surface of the lake
was a wall of darkness. The only way he knew the lake
was there was by the sound of the waves lapping on the
shore near his feet.

Once he had strayed too close to the shore and had
stepped into the water, filling his left shoe. That foot now
squelched along, unpleasantly cold, and that coldness soon
chilled his entire body. Nevertheless, thanks to the presence of a low pressure system the night was quite warm
and damp. Surely the coldness he felt was caused as much
by tension as anything else.

He had followed Akane's instructions and had no difficulty in finding the road to the boathouse. A private road
split off from the highway that followed the lakeshore,
passed the Emerald View with its surrounding Himalayan
cedars, and passed into the forest. The dirt road went
steeply downward and soon reached the lake. The boathouse should be about a quarter mile north, but the road
was gone. He had no choice but to try to make his way
through the darkness between the forest and the edge of
the water.

Perhaps there had been a road along here at one time,
but ever since Akane had taken over the hotel's boathouse
for a studio, no one ever came this way, and it was now
once again overgrown with grass and brush.

Daigo was quite satisfied that she had been intelligent
enough to suggest the boathouse for their rendezvous. It
was in such an out-of-the-way place that there was surely
no chance that any casual strollers would come this way.
And on top of that, the weather was cooperating nicely;
certainly no one would be out tonight.

At first when Akane had suggested Sunday evening as the time for their meeting, Daigo had thought it dangerous, but then, remembering her usual caution, he had decided not to protest. It was the last Sunday of the spring vacation, and he had feared that the hotel would be filled with people. But with all the guests, surely everyone would be too busy to notice what Akane was doing.

Daigo had made the familiar trip from Fukuoka to Hakone in five hours as usual, and he was confident that he had shaken off anyone who had tried to follow him. He had told his wife that he had to go to Osaka on account of his elderly aunt, and at the airport had actually bought a ticket to Osaka. Perhaps it was just his imagination, but he had the impression that a middle-aged man in a small car was following him as he took the Highway 3 bypass to the airport, and at the airport that man was joined by another middle-aged man and they seemed to be keeping an eye on Daigo.

When the flight to Osaka was announced, Daigo went up to the second-floor concourse for check-in. From the corner of his eye he saw the two men he thought were following him make for the counter to get tickets for the Osaka flight. Once they were occupied with purchasing tickets, he slipped through a service door and hurried down a deserted corridor to the other concourse where they loaded planes for Tokyo. He quickly picked up a ticket he had ordered earlier and boarded the crowded jumbo jet. He had done similar maneuvers at both the airport and the train station in Tokyo, and this time instead of taking the train all the way to Odawara, he got off at Atami and got a rental car to take him to Hakone. By the time he arrived at his destination, he was confident no one was following him.

It was 8:40 when he reached Hakone. He spent the next hour in a hotel restaurant. By the time he took the private road past the Emerald View he was extremely vigilant. He suppressed an urge to run and forced himself to walk as though he were out for an evening stroll. Several cars passed him as he walked along the road.

Daigo experienced a small shudder that passed through his body. This time the unpleasant feeling was not brought on by fear or cold. This time it was because dimly in the trees before him he could see the outline of a small square cottage with a faint light in the windows. Akane had described the place as a boathouse with a red roof. At this time of night he could not, of course, tell what color the roof was. In order to reassure himself Daigo thought back to what Akane had said. She had said it was the only cottage in the area and he need not worry about making a mistake. In fact it seemed to him that the faint orange light coming from the windows was a sign of some sort.

He tried to think what it might mean, but his mind was filled with the thought that there, inside the cottage, was Fumiko, his Fumiko. Daigo could restrain himself no longer; he began to run. Once he stumbled over a fallen log and went sprawling, and several times he stepped into the water.

The cottage was built on posts, with its floor above the level of the water. Boats were stored in the area beneath the floor. Now he could see that the wooden door was closed. He climbed the stairs and stood, trembling, on the porch in front of the door. Just as a precaution, he paused to look around. The trees behind the cottage were moving like black shadows, and the clouds were racing past overhead. His eyes were used to the dark now, and he could see that the surface of the lake was rising and falling in gentle surges against the pilings just beneath his feet.

He could hear nothing but the sound of the wind and waves. For Daigo this was the sound of melancholy loneliness. It was much like that stormy night at the Château Chantal. Another violent shudder went through his body like a spasm. Afterwards he continued to tremble, unable to stop the shaking. All human beings when faced with extreme situations of fear or surprise, joy or sadness, have the same physical reaction.

With a trembling hand, Daigo knocked on the door. He knocked once, then again. At last he heard a response from within saying, "Come in." The quiet, low-pitched voice seemed to well up from among the many natural sounds around him; it seemed very close to his ear. He opened the door.

The inside of the cottage was dimly lit by an orange-shaded floor lamp at the back of the room. Daigo stepped inside and closed the door, sliding the heavy wooden bolt home. A miscellaneous variety of furniture had been used to furnish the cottage. The table and chairs were rustic-looking. There was a small stone statue on the table, and some tall thing that he assumed was an easel. One by one his eyes roamed over each object in the room, searching for the figure of Akane. On one side of the room opposite the windows was a mantelpiece or a shelf. Facing the fireplace was a sofa set. Daigo could make out a shadowy figure sitting at the far end of the sofa. Perhaps the only reason he even noticed the vague outline of the silhouette was because it moved slightly. All he could see was the upper half of Akane's profile. Though she sat rigidly still and tried not to move or breathe, Daigo, by staring intently, could discern the faint rise and fall of her breast. Akane's long hair flowed down over her shoulders. Her dress was made of some loose, filmy material—probably silk or crepe.

"Fumiko," called Daigo in a faint whisper. He called her name once again and went toward her. As he did so, she reached out one hand and extinguished the floor lamp. A dim light reflected from the clouds made it barely possible to see. Daigo moved forward without hesitation.

Akane resumed her seat on the sofa. She sat with her back to him, but he nevertheless had the feeling that she was waiting to receive him.

As though in a trance, Daigo put his hands on her shoulders. Beneath the fabric of her blouse he could feel the soft but resilient flesh. As he brought his face close to the nape of her neck, he could smell the fragrance of her perfume. It was only then that he noticed that she was trembling slightly. In his inmost heart he felt a pang of pleasure so sharp it was painful.

"Fumiko! At last we've come together again."

She began to breathe heavily, then said, "Yes, Professor Daigo, at last we are together again."

There! She had spoken his name clearly. Her voice was husky but soft, and in it he seemed to hear overtones of both pleasure and melancholy.

"Why do you sound so mournful? We've both been though a lot, and now we are together again. Indeed, that night we were together before, we parted without ever seeing each other. You said it would be better if we never saw each other again and left the salon, leaving me there alone. We each expressed our intent, and we each had unshakable faith that we could carry out the other's role. You left me with complete freedom of choice. Doesn't the fact that we were so perfectly able to understand each other prove that our destinies are linked?"

After a brief pause, Akane murmured, "That dark salon." She seemed almost transfixed by the power of her emotions. Daigo felt she must be truly in love with him. "It's true. From the very beginning, our relationship has been cloaked in darkness like this."

"No, it was darker even than this in that salon at the Château Chantal. After all, there was that storm and the power failure that seemed to have darkened the whole village. And yet I am most thankful for that unexpected encounter. It would have been very hard to tell another person my inmost thoughts except in that perfect darkness. The ability to know that your own fate is shared by someone you have never seen before is perhaps something mankind has not known since the distant past when people lived most of their lives in darkness.''

Daigo talked without giving much thought to his words, while at the same time his hands were caressing Akane's body.

She had turned toward him now and surrendered herself to his hands. She was breathing heavily. "I, too, have been waiting. I was confident that the day would come when I could reveal myself to you. After all, you had enough confidence in me to share your deepest secret with me.''

"Yes, but you were the first one to take direct action. You spoke before of purity of desire. It was your forthrightness that inspired me to take action. But you did not play fairly with me. All I had to go on was the name of Midori Nagahara, and the Emerald View Hotel.'' Once again, deep in his mind, Daigo could hear the voice of Fumiko saying, "The sharing we have had here this evening is not something we have to talk about, but it will be a wonderful thing if it helps us face our individual futures.'' Now, however, rather than speak in words of the experiences they had been through, it seemed that everything was in a void. No doubt Fumiko also felt the same way. Ever since that night they had each had a very real other self. They had thought the same thoughts at the same time, and they were able to read those thoughts instantly.

No, it did not matter what pointless words they used, they would flow through each other's ears like music.

"From the very beginning, you knew not only Professor Yoshimi's name but my name and position as well, but I wonder if you know how much difficulty I have had in searching you out.'' As Daigo murmured these words, he unzipped Akane's dress. "On the other hand, however, you did send me some messages. I followed your instructions exactly at the time of the Yoshimi incident. Then I discovered the picture postcard of the hotel among the New Year's cards, and I realized that the time had come for me to make my move. Still, I had my doubts."

He was nuzzling his face in the cleft between her full, rich breasts. There too he could smell a strong scent of perfume. Just as on that earlier night, her fingers stroked the nape of his neck, like a mother caressing a child.

"It would be best if you went away to some distant place—the sooner the better. You should go to some place where the Japanese police cannot get you."

"I understand. Even though you are a university professor, you will have to be careful too. As I told you earlier on the telephone, the police have a photograph of you."

"I'll be all right. As long as I can know that you are in a safe place, I will be able to get through this all right. It will be tough for a while, and we will just have to endure it. But eventually the time will come, somewhere in this world, when we two can be together again like this. The promises we make will last forever."

Daigo's lips were moving softly across her shoulder toward the base of her neck. Akane was sitting on his knees with her back to him. He ran his chin along her shoulder. Their lips found each other, and in that moment, their two bodies became as one.

Once again Daigo became conscious of the sound of the wind beating against the windows, reviving sad memories of the French wind rattling the windows of the Château Chantal.

Even after their breathing came back to normal, his fingers continued to fondle her breasts. The small hard nipples were imbedded in the marshmallow softness of her breasts.

They were like buds that had not reached their fullest development, and this bespoke the charming freshness of her body.

Daigo brushed back her hair and nibbled gently on her ear. Soon he noticed that no matter how much he probed the soft folds of her earlobes, he could find no trace of their ever having been pierced. He had forgotten about that detail, and now as he sat with Akane on his lap, the awful truth suddenly occurred to him. That night at Barbizon when he had kissed Fumiko's ears, he had noticed the tiny holes where they had been pierced.

For a moment Daigo sat utterly still, frozen with shock. Akane quietly rearranged her clothing and resumed her seat on the sofa. Perhaps the overcast had increased, for the faint light being reflected into the room seemed a bit brighter. Daigo gazed intently at the darkness, trying to make out the deeply chiseled features of Akane's profile. She appeared mysterious and elegant to him. And yet he felt a deep sense of bitter disappointment, accompanied by a terrible feeling of fatigue. Oddly, he did not feel the rush of anger and vigilance he had expected. He was not certain he would recover a second time from the disappointment of having failed to find his Fumiko.

He forced himself to speak, but his voice was strained. "Akane, you must explain to me what this charade is all about. You must tell me everything you know. Why did you come here tonight pretending to be Fumiko Samejima? Where is the real Fumiko?"

Daigo sensed some slight movement on her part, and her breathing became faster, but she answered in an elegant, straightforward manner. "I came here tonight because I wanted to learn the truth. I wanted to find out the true relationship between you and Fumiko Samejima."

"But how? How could you possibly know that Fumiko and I even had a relationship."

"Ever since my sister's death I have spent a great deal of time thinking about her activities, and I think I have some idea about what she may have done."

"But you knew my name; you called me by name. When I telephoned yesterday, I intentionally made a point of not saying my name. Did Fumiko tell you about our relationship?"

"No. She never said anything about it. If she had told me, I would not have had to resort to this sort of adventure. The fact is, Professor Daigo, I learned your name from Detective Eda."

"Even so, you are obviously very close to Fumiko. Tell me, please, what is going on? Where is she now? What name does she use? For a while you did a brilliant job of tricking me. You got me to divulge my secret, so now I have the right to ask you to tell me what you know."

For a few moments Akane sat in silence, then she nodded briefly twice and began to speak softly, but she did not answer Daigo's questions right away. "Two and a half years ago, at the time Michiya Kume died mysteriously, my sister came under intense police scrutiny. You see, she had been Kume's lover, and the suspicion was that she had murdered him out of jealousy. Such a thing was entirely possible, given the time and method of his death. It was calculated that Kume died at around six on the evening of October twenty-eighth as a result of gas inhalation at his apartment in Yotsuya. Apparently he had spent the whole day in his study working after his wife went out in the morning. He was working feverishly to complete a translation and had been up all night the previous night. My sister went to visit him around four or five o'clock that afternoon. She entered the apartment and found him asleep in the study. In a fit of jealousy she decided to kill him. She put out the fire in the gas heater, opened the gas valve, and left. By the time Yuko arrived home at seven he was already dead. The autopsy showed no sign of his having taken sleeping pills or anything like that. Naturally, my sister did not have a solid alibi for that afternoon."

Daigo remained silent and listened to Akane's story.

"We also have to take into consideration the fact that a murder of this sort would be very much her style. She loved Kume with all her heart and soul. Indeed, it was because she loved him so completely that she could not ignore Yuko's devotion to her husband; she was not willing to continue as the third party in a triangular love affair. Being in love, she was determined to possess her lover's body and heart completely. When she was not able to have that, she killed her lover with her own hands. She was the sort of woman who was cold enough to be able to do that."

In the back of his mind Daigo recalled Fumiko saying, "She is a woman who must not be allowed to go on living. There is a coldness about her that is intolerable. She is proud, and because of that pride she killed a person two years ago."

"You . . . you don't mean that . . ." Daigo's voice was a hollow whisper, and he was not able to complete the awful question.

Akane continued, "The fact is, at that time, I too shared the same suspicions with the police, that perhaps she really did murder Kume, but there was no proof. Yet as time passed, during the next two years, I came to see the truth. Although my sister survived the police investigation, she seemed to have collapsed inside."

A note of infinite melancholy seemed to creep into the tone of Akane's low voice as she continued. "It is true that my sister had a proud, cold spirit, but there was also another side to her nature. As a person she was very discerning and had the ability to look unflinchingly at the truth. There is no doubt in my mind today that she murdered Kume with her own hands. Ever since that time, I do not believe she ever tried to make herself think otherwise, and in her heart she was always conscious of her guilt. I have lived in the same house with her for the past two years, and even though we were only half sisters, the anguish and the conflict she was going through were evident to me.''

Akane paused in her narrative and began to weep quietly.

"Do you mean that . . .'' the words sprang from Daigo's lips only to die in a moan of grief. At last he was able to speak. "Do you really mean that Midori Nagahara was Fumiko Samejima? The Fumiko who detested Midori and wanted to see her dead was none other than Midori herself?''

"When you telephoned yesterday and mentioned the name 'Fumiko Samejima,' some of the vague suspicions I already had were strengthened. You see, Fumiko Samejima is a pen name my sister once used when she published a volume of poetry.''

"Did Midori make a trip to Europe alone last October?''

"Yes. I knew something must have happened to her while she was on that trip. She was different when she came back. The most obvious change was the mere fact that she stopped using the perfume she had always used in the past. But the first real inkling I had of what was going on came when I noticed that she could not read through the newspaper article reporting the murder of Professor Yoshimi. I suppose that when you mentioned Yoshimi's name to Midori, you also explained to her that he was the one responsible for the outbreak of cancer among children.''

"Of course I told her about that. She was clearly as angry about it as I was, and she shared my hatred for Yoshimi. I believe that was the main link that united our hearts.''

"Yes, I can see how that would be so.'' Akane was weeping again. "Last summer, that would be three months before Midori made her trip to Europe, a beautiful little girl who was taking piano lessons from her was suddenly struck down by cancer. She suffered terribly and finally died. Even though my sister was not a member of the girl's family, she was greatly saddened by the child's death.''

"Ahhh.'' The moan escaped from deep in Daigo's throat. He put his hands over his ears and fell forward. But even with his ears covered, he could hear in his mind the sound of Fumiko's voice. The affection, the dignity, the silken skin and elegant fragrance, ah, what a woman she had been, and to think, Daigo had strangled her with his own hands! Daigo, with his head down on his knees, continued to moan. His consciousness was shredded.

The first time he had seen Midori at the Emerald View, Daigo had been overwhelmed with a feeling of fear and a sense that their destinies were linked. And again that fateful night in the cold garage Midori had not put up much resistance. Daigo himself had been puzzled by that after he had killed her. At that time he had again wondered what sort of destiny linked him with her. Without realizing it, the killer had become the killed. Without his understanding anything about it! Now that he stopped to think about it, it seemed clear that she had planned all of this from that very first night.

What was it Fumiko had said that night? "Maybe the woman put some sort of curse on me, but I swear to you that my heart will know no peace until she is dead.''

When Daigo had asked if she had loved the man who had been killed, she did not answer, but simply nodded her head. Why had it not occurred to him at the time that a person so filled with hatred for the murderer and with a desire for revenge would hardly ask someone else to commit the murder for her. If a person wants true revenge, he or she will make sure that the person on whom they are getting revenge knows what is happening and experiences a full measure of agony. Many times Daigo had recalled the word "courage" that Fumiko had used and had mulled over its meanings. Actually, the answer he was searching for had been right there in front of him the whole time: Fumiko's courage was nothing less than the decision to invoke her own death sentence.

Fumiko had casually selected Daigo to be her executioner. Apparently she had killed Yoshimi, the object of Daigo's hatred, as a way of compensating him for what he was about to do unwittingly. First she had devised a solid alibi for Daigo, and then she had committed the murder. Also on that night in Barbizon she had informed him of the days and times that would create an alibi for herself, and of course, these were precisely those days and hours when Yuko Kume would be at work. Even though Midori would be murdered, she insured that no suspicion would fall on Yuko, and perhaps this was intended as some small token of apology to her.

As an additional kindness, she had done all she could to make things easier for Daigo. She must have guessed that later Daigo would try to find her, and she had fixed it so that even though he failed to locate her, he would still be able to believe that Fumiko existed somewhere. She seemed to have anticipated everything.

Without realizing what he was doing, Daigo leaped to his feet and rushed toward the door.

"Wait! Professor Daigo, please wait!" Akane grabbed him by the arm, and only then did he realize that he had gotten to his feet. "Please, wait. Can't we recreate that original scene again from the very beginning?"

"From the beginning?"

"Yes. Tonight. Now. There is no one here but the two of us. It will be an experience we can share. Don't you see? This is what I have been pursuing too. An unwavering love, to have a tie with someone who can intoxicate my very soul. I want to fully savor the experience my sister had; this is what inspired me to risk the danger of meeting alone with you, a murderer. Think about it. What do we mean when we speak of love? To what extent is it an emotion based on reason? There have been many cases where one falls in love with a person one knows nothing about. Nothing is more mysterious than to meet another whom you've never known before in complete darkness and to love. At such a time one must use one's intuition to understand and share those inmost thoughts and feelings that cannot be spoken to one's lover. Surely this is the most wonderful sort of love.''

Daigo made no reply to this, and Akane continued. ''But perhaps all of that is really just an illusion. It is clear, however, that you loved Fumiko who was Midori, and you did not hesitate to kill Midori who was really your Fumiko. On the night of the murder you probably felt you loved Fumiko, though there was no reason for you to do so. And on that same night, you probably felt you hated Midori, although there was no reason for that either. You ought not to have strangled an unresisting victim whom you did not hate.''

Once again a memory began to tingle in Daigo's mind, and the fear within him was like a violent storm that lashed him both physically and emotionally.

''Love and hatred and all the urges that drive people are nothing more than illusions. I had not understood that before. Indeed, precisely because I had not understood it before, I came to have a faint hope that I might have a chance to do it over again.''

''Do it over again? What do you mean?'' he asked.

''Well, when you stop to think about it, human life is as insubstantial as the foam on water. In that condition, if we feel the urge to grasp something eternal, the only thing we can turn to is something we believe in. I came to the realization that I had the capacity to believe in things. You see, Professor Daigo, we can share this experience here tonight, and through the bond that is formed between us we will both be able to go on searching for pure love.''

Daigo thought numbly to himself that she was right—the only thing that would keep him going would be to have something to continue to believe in. Unconscious of what he was doing, he gently began to stroke Akane's hair. ''Surely I can believe in you.''

He gently squeezed her shoulders and turned to walk toward the door. He slipped the bolt and opened the massive wooden door to find that the mist and rain were thicker than ever and that the wind was howling. The sky was whiter than it had been earlier, and the clouds were moving faster. Thunder rumbled in the distance. The trees of the forest strained and groaned. The lake was whipping itself into a lather.

# Postscript

On Monday morning, April 4, Detective Kazuo Eda of the Odawara police district telephoned Inspector Furukawa in Fukuoka. The points he made were as follows: (1) In October of the previous year, Kohei Daigo had been in Paris attending a meeting. There was a strong suspicion that at that time he had met with an unidentified woman and planned the strangulation murder of Midori Nagahara. (2) There had been a telephone call from Kyoko Sakaguchi in Tokyo which had turned up some new leads concerning the mystery woman. The previous day Mrs. Sakaguchi had been shown a photograph of Akane Nagahara. She was asked to verify that this was the woman she had bumped into in the ladies room at the hotel, but she was unable to give a definite answer. Later, however, she did suddenly think of something. When they were picking up the things from the woman's purse that had spilled on the carpet,

246

Mrs. Sakaguchi had gotten a close look at the mystery woman's profile. She had noticed that the woman had pierced ears and that she was wearing a small pair of gold earrings.

When Mrs. Sakaguchi was shown a close-up shot of Akane in profile, she felt that it was not quite like the woman she had bumped into, but could not put her finger on what was different. Now, however, she was able to say for sure. Akane's ears were not pierced, so she could not be the mystery woman. The mystery woman they sought had pierced ears.

As a result of this communication Detective Eda once again checked the information they had on record concerning Midori Nagahara, and he made a startling discovery. No one of Midori's acquaintances except herself had been abroad between recently. Midori, it turned out, had traveled alone to Western Europe and had been in Paris in the middle of October. It also turned out that Midori had pierced ears.

Eda sent by express mail to Fukuoka a set of Midori's fingerprints taken from her room, and a recent photograph. He also added a note saying that Midori's blood type was universal O.

Inspector Furukawa went through the fingerprints taken from Yoshimi's living room but which had still not been identified, and among them he found ones that were identical to Midori's. Also, among the hairs that had been found on the floor where Yoshimi's body had fallen, they found some that definitely had come from someone with type O blood.

When Midori Nagahara's photograph was shown to Kiyoko Sakaguchi and others who had seen the mystery woman at the party, they gave a positive identification.

All these developments led to the conclusion both in Fukuoka and Odawara that the killings of Yoshimi and

Midori were the result of a plot by Kohei Daigo and Midori Nagahara. The theory was that they had met in Paris and plotted the murders. As a result of that plan, Midori had poisoned Yoshimi on December 4. It was supposed that Daigo had agreed to somehow repay Midori for the murder of Yoshimi, but the details of that were not yet clear. On the basis of Midori's nature and position, it was supposed that Daigo had agreed to murder someone whose identity Midori would make known to him. It seemed likely that instead of carrying out the second murder according to the plan, Daigo had treacherously killed Midori, his fellow plotter, instead, to insure that she never revealed their plot.

On the evening of April 6 the Shinagawa Prefectural Police issued an all-points bulletin on Kohei Daigo, who was wanted as an important witness in the murder of Midori Nagahara. On that same afternoon, the faculty of the medical school of J university in Fukuoka met and set May 10 as the day when they would vote to chose a successor to Professor Yoshimi in the Department of Hygiene. It was almost inevitable that Daigo would be chosen to fill Yoshimi's position. By now the role he had played in the Minami Foods scandal was widely known. As a consequence, Daigo had received much recognition and support in the popular media, and even from those who had formerly been on Yoshimi's side. Also, Daigo's main competitor for the position, the professor at the private university in Kagoshima, had withdrawn his name from consideration pleading poor health as the reason. The lab assistant Yamada, however, maintained the same attitude as he had before, that he was on the right side, and in that spirit he was awaiting Daigo's return to the university.

Kohei Daigo, however, did not return to Fukuoka after his secret meeting with Akane at Hakone on April 3. On the evening of April 6, when the all-points bulletin was first issued, he was loitering in a corner of the international

concourse of the Tokyo airport. The plane he was scheduled to take to Paris via the polar route was to leave in an
hour and a half. He had a vacant expression on his face
which radically changed his appearance as he stood and
watched the waves of people move through the concourse.
His eyes were glassy, and the only thing that occupied his
consciousness was the thought of the darkness at the Château Chantal and the sound of the storm raging outside the
windows.

He needed once more to let his body sink into one of
the armchairs in the salon and to confirm with his five
senses the presence of that illusion that had visited him
once before. And yet instinctively he had a feeling that he
would never reach that destination again. This feeling was
not just the result of his natural pessimism; rather, it was
because he knew that we can never embrace illusions in
our arms.

## About the Author

The bestselling mystery writer in Japan, Shizuko Natsuki has written over eighty novels, short stories and serials, forty of which have been made into Japanese television movies. Several of her short stories have been published in *Ellery Queen's Mystery Magazine*. Her first mystery to be translated into English was *Murder at Mount Fuji*. Ms. Natsuki lives in Nagoya City, Japan.

# RUTH RENDELL

"Undoubtedly one of the best writers of English mysteries and chiller-killer plots!"
—*Los Angeles Times*

**The new first lady of mysteries, in the grand tradition of Agatha Christie.**